THE PRIME OF MISS DOLLY GREENE

In the heart of southwest London, just a short stroll from the Thames, lies an enclosed and overgrown bike path and a single row of cottages. Foremost among Tinderbox Lane's hotchpotch of loyal residents is professional Tarot reader Dolly Greene. When, one stiflingly hot summer's day, Dolly reads the cards for the hedonistic Nikki, her usually professional patter is interrupted by a sudden vision — a flash of Nikki's face, covered in blood and bruises. A few days later, when the body of a battered woman is washed up by Chiswick Bridge, Dolly is haunted by the belief that Nikki's time may have come . . . but can she be sure? How far is Dolly prepared to go to act on her intuition?

THE PRIME OF MS DOLLY GREENE

THE TAROT DETECTIVE

E. V. HARTE

ISIS

LARGE
PRINT

First published in Great Britain 2017
by
Constable
an imprint of Little, Brown Book Group

First Isis Edition
published 2018
by arrangement with
Little, Brown Book Group
An Hachette UK Company

A catalogue record for this book is available
from the British Library.

ISBN 978–1–78541–583–8 (hb)
ISBN 978–1–78541–589–0 (pb)

Published by
F. A. Thorpe (Publishing)
Anstey, Leicestershire

Set by Words & Graphics Ltd.
Anstey, Leicestershire
Printed and bound in Great Britain by
T. J. International Ltd., Padstow, Cornwall

This book is printed on acid-free paper

For Imogen

CHAPTER
ONE

"OH MY GOD, I'm going to die."

"Well I should think so, Nikki. We all have to die one day."

"*What?* Am I dying? Is that what you're saying?"

"I'm saying," clarified Ms Dolly Greene, "that you mustn't be alarmed." People always panicked when the Death card showed. They'd seen the Bond movies, and they thought — except thinking didn't really come into it. "Don't be alarmed, Nikki. There's nothing ... absolutely nothing to worry about. It can look a bit ominous, can't it?"

"*Ominous?*" The client didn't know what it meant. "What's the skeleton —" she jabbed a chipped, turquoise nail at the offending card. "There's a *skeleton*! Am I going to die, Dolly? Is that why I came here? Something drew me here, and it wasn't Maurice Bousquet, I'll tell you that, *dirty old bugger*, excuse my French. But there's no point me coming here just so you can say I'm dying. No way. I'm not paying for that."

Dolly glanced up at the woman. She looked half dead already, poor thing, face all flabby with terror. "You're not going to die," she said. "OK?"

It was a hot afternoon, airless as hell, and the woman — Nikki — had arrived already jittery. Dolly had ushered her into the little study — a large broom cupboard, really, more than a study. But she couldn't use the kitchen for consultations while her daughter was living at home; the little house didn't have a separate sitting room, and she certainly wasn't taking clients into the bedroom. The broom cupboard was the only space left.

Dolly had fussed about, trying to put the woman at ease, waving incense over the cards, muttering private words that may — or may not — have meant anything, while Nikki fidgeted and sweated, and fanned herself, and complained. She'd had to park the car miles off, she said: if it hadn't been for the heat, she would have been better off walking.

Well, of course she would.

Dolly Greene lived halfway down a bike path, in a teeny-tiny mews house, in the depths of the depths of outer southwest London; a part of London between two other parts, surrounded by ex-council houses, mostly: a corner of London so like and so unlike any other that it didn't really have a name. You couldn't get a car down Tinderbox Lane. Tesco and the other supermarkets wouldn't deliver. Dolly's clients needed to be sent lengthy directions, on top of the directions she (or her daughter) had put up on the website. Even then, the pathway was ludicrously hard to find and quite often, no matter how carefully Dolly tried to steer the clients in, they reached a point where, like Tesco, they simply gave up and turned home again.

But Nikki would have known about that. She'd been down Tinderbox Lane to visit Maurice Bousquet, who lived next door. Nikki would have known exactly what she was letting herself in for, at least as far as the parking was concerned.

Nobody visits a Tarot reader down a bike track in the depths of the depths of outer southwest London unless they're feeling pretty damned troubled about something, whether they know it or not. And Dolly was always conscious of that. She sympathised with her clients. Too much, sometimes. In the early days, she'd had to learn how to shake it off, because once the inhibitions dissolved and the punters started talking, and the cards began to do their work — people would tell her everything. *Everything*. And she felt for them. Of course she did. It was exhausting. But it was her life, and mostly she loved it.

Dolly made a living from her Tarot cards because, frankly, she had to squeeze a living out of something, and at the time of the divorce, given her peculiar gift, and her interest in other people's lives, it was the obvious choice. But the cards were more to Dolly than simply the tools of her trade. She depended on them to help her see things more clearly. In fact she would ruminate with them several times a day. And although sometimes, she couldn't deny, they ruminated back in unfathomable gibberish, generally that wasn't so. Generally, Dolly's cards knew the answers before she did. The trick, of course, was in learning how to decipher them . . .

★   ★   ★

There was an embroidered hanging at the broom cupboard window, blocking whatever small, greasy breeze might have seeped in. Dolly would have pulled it back, but the half darkness was useful. It was calming, and it helped her to concentrate. Nikki, her client, was still staring, goggle-eyed, at the Death card. Dolly leaned across the small table and patted her hand.

"It's the smoking, isn't it?" Nikki said. "Is it the smoking, Dolly?"

Dolly shook her head. "The Death card tends to represent the end of something which has served its purpose, and the dawn of something new . . . it's a very . . ." she was turning more cards now, flipping and twisting them like a Las Vegas croupier. The clients expected it. They needed it. When people came to see her they expected various things: to be reassured, above all, that they weren't being fooled — and so she employed all sorts of charlatan's tricks to help them believe it: murmurs and gazes, wrist flicks and silent nods. Dolly could have read the cards over baked beans and toast, if she'd needed to, with the telly blasting. But the punters didn't like that, and neither did she. They liked a show. For £40 who wouldn't? ". . . The Death card," Dolly continued, "can actually be a very *hopeful* card, Nikki. Out with the old, in with the new. That sort of thing. Let's have a look, shall we?"

The Tinderbox Tarot Lady (aka Ms Dolly Greene) frowned and hunched over the table, show on hold, just for a moment, while she actually looked at the cards. She had placed them in a loop of ten around her, in a personalised variation of the Celtic cross. It was her

4

opening spread: her overview. After that there were other, more traditional spreads. But to Dolly, this was the big one: the one that threw the widest light. And here it was:

The King of Cups, the Knight of Cups (reversed), the Emperor (reversed) . . . and Death . . .

Death, indeed.

CHAPTER
TWO

The great advantage of living along a bike track was the silence. The little room — the broom cupboard — was quiet and soothing in its half darkness. She and Nikki sat opposite one another, a small table draped in shimmering cloth between them. On a shelf at Dolly's shoulder, there smouldered from the incense burner a resin of myrrh and some dried mugwort, which offered a strong, sweet, pleasant smell, and which seemed to induce in Dolly a dreaminess she found conducive during her readings. Whether it was habit, ritual, mere showmanship — Dolly didn't know and hardly bothered to wonder any more. In any case, the incense, the candlelight, the silence, the dark walls, the closeness of the room — they combined to set a tone, and it helped. *Every Little Helps*, as they say at Tesco, which didn't deliver down Tinderbox Lane.

". . . Lots of men in your life, Nikki . . ." muttered Dolly.

"Don't I know it."

Dolly was silent. *Too many men*.

"Better than none, though, right?" Nikki said brightly.

Dolly had none. No men in her life. But for now, that wasn't the issue.

"Lots of men in your life. You need to streamline, darling. That's what the cards are saying."

"Hm."

Too many men and every one of them causing her strife. Added to which, she was — well, honestly, it looked very much as if she was pregnant. Dolly wondered if the woman realised it yet. It might help to explain why she looked so ill. "You're having a few problems with someone in authority, are you?"

"Who isn't?"

". . . Well that's right," chuckled Dolly, not looking up. ". . . Who isn't? Problems with: is it your husband, or your boss? There's a powerful man making your life difficult. Actually a couple of men . . . but I think it's your boss, is it?"

"I haven't got a boss, Dolly."

"No? . . . We all have a boss, Nikki, one way or another." Dolly repositioned herself, untroubled. "A landlord, or a partner . . . Even Rupert Murdoch has shareholders."

"You what?"

"Someone with power over us. Someone we have to appease . . ."

"Appease, what? What are you talking about? I don't even understand what you're saying. Talk in English, will you? I'm not paying you to talk in bloody Greek."

Dolly bit the inside of her cheeks. When people got angry it made her smile: from nerves, mostly. "Keep your hair on," Dolly said. "I'm just saying, you've got a man who's paying the bills for you. Calling the shots, yes? And maybe — you have a job on your hands, keeping him happy. Am I right?"

Nikki shuffled in her seat, and the seat creaked. She was a big woman, aged anything between twenty-eight and fifty: big boned, voluptuous: all cleavage and hair and turquoise nails and cheap gold bangles. The seat, £5.99 from IKEA, was too small for her. (Too small for anyone but a child, Dolly often thought. *You get what you pay for.*) It was only a matter of time before the wretched thing collapsed.

"Keeping him happy?" repeated Nikki. "Trust me, Dolly, I think I know how to keep a bloke *happy.*" It sounded smutty, as intended. But it sounded hollow, too. Unconvinced and unconvincing. Slightly pathetic. Dolly refrained from patting her hand again. "It's him who can't keep *me* happy, if you must know. Only pays the bills when he feels like it. When he wants to have sex with me, Dolly. And how am I supposed to rely on that?

He's a bully. He doesn't care about you — and he's *making you miserable . . . But not so miserable it stops you from playing around* — "A few men in your life, Nikki."

"Yeah. Yes, you said that. Frankly."

"I know I did. You need to streamline."

"Yes, well," she laughed. "Easy to say, Dolly. How am I going to do that? Especially now, with the Death hanging over me."

Dolly glanced again at the Death card. The usual, soothing patter was ready and waiting, at the tip of her tongue — it should have been simple. In the right context, the card could signify nothing more than a spring clean: an approaching kitchen clear-out ... But today, the card didn't sit quietly, hinting of loose-handled saucepans, it *shimmered* — was that too strong? Death insisted on her attention. It dominated the spread. It loomed, dark and heavy. Dammit —

The last time it shimmered like this, the client had left her consulting room aware that somebody young and close to her was in danger: her grandson had been knifed to death at a bus stop in Hackney two days later.

... And the time before that, was before she'd turned professional. Dolly had been reading the cards for herself. She'd been alone in the house, at a loose end, and she laid ten cards on top of the marital duvet. The Death card had shimmered. She'd put the deck away, annoyed: but in her mind's eye, the Death card shimmered on.

Philip had come home that evening and told her their marriage was over. (End of marriage. Death Number One.) The young husband of a female colleague had suffered a rare heart attack in the bath. (Death Number Two.) Philip told Dolly that he "needed to be with her": not *Dolly*, of course, but *Madeleine*, his bereaved colleague and lover of sixteen months.

That was over seven years ago. Dolly had only started to read the cards back then. Even so, she should have known — if not about the heart attack, then at least about the heat of Philip's love for Madeleine. Or lust. Or whatever the hell it was. Madeleine and Philip

9

had a new, young family now. Philip inhabited a world of nappy wipes and playdates and Tupperware snack boxes, all of which Dolly had long since left behind. Madeleine had curdled with motherhood, the way some women do, and Philip was no doubt wondering why he'd gone to all the bother. Dolly still missed him a little. She suspected that he missed her.

Never mind.

Dolly had never been an ambitious woman. She didn't much care for possessions and as time rolled by grew increasingly indifferent to all the usual measures of success. Add to that an unsettling — almost Touretteish — frankness, and a somewhat disruptive and unreliable sixth sense — both of which grew more marked with each passing year, it was unsurprising, perhaps, that in her early middle age she found herself where she did: here, on Tinderbox Lane, with a shortage of clients, a shortage of funds, a shortage of husband, and a woman on the point of tears in front of her, on a chair on the point of collapse.

Never mind. And she didn't mind. Not really. She had her daughter, and her cards, and her tiny, pretty house. She didn't want much more than that.

"Do you have children, Nikki?"

"Only the one, Dolly. But he's a big lad now. Well, he's a spindly little sod. But he's thirteen. Or fifteen. If you know what I mean . . . One's enough for me, Dolly! It's enough of a job looking after myself." The woman gave a little laugh. "Trying to find a man who can keep up with me. If you know what I mean."

"Well, but . . ."

"Plus — I think I must be infertile, to be honest with you. It's not like I haven't taken chances . . . After Toby I never seemed to fall pregnant. Not with his dad or anyone else, really . . . Maybe it's because I'm so large. That's what I used to think. I'm a big woman, Dolly."

"Hardly," said Dolly.

Nikki laughed again. "Too Big for a Baby! . . . Sounds like one of those TV shows, doesn't it?"

"You're not big, Nikki," Dolly said. "*I* was big, mind. When I had my daughter. Still haven't lost all the weight, twenty-odd years on!"

"You skinny thing!" Nikki chuckled.

Dolly wasn't skinny, she was normal. *Buxom* . . . Whereas Nikki was definitely *voluptuous* . . . Dolly glanced up from the cards, acknowledging Nikki's friendly lie, and the silliness of it all: fat, thin, *buxom*, skinny — who cared, as long as the chairs didn't collapse beneath them? Dolly and Nikki chortled, in league together for the moment: individually shaped women against a Uniform World. It was nice.

Dolly said carefully: "So if you did find you were pregnant, say, would that be . . . a happy surprise? Or . . ."

"Chance'd be a fine thing, Dolly."

". . . You've got the King of Cups, Knight of Cups — You've got the Lovers, Nikki . . . Looks to me like you — How do I put it politely? You've been at it hammer and tongs . . . and not . . ." she chuckled, "dare I say it, Nikki? Maybe not exclusively with the errr . . . the same chap?"

"Very clever," Nikki said. But she sounded more irritated than impressed. Slightly nervous.

"Not me, my love. It's the cards . . ."

Nikki said nothing.

". . . The chap you're shacked up with," Dolly continued.

"I'm not shacked up with anyone," she snapped. "Except my Toby. And he's not there most of the time. So far as I can tell . . ."

"The chap who pays your bills, then."

"*Some* of my bills. When he feels like it."

"All right. The chap with all the money: the boss, so to speak . . . he's a dark fellow is he? Dark hair, dark skin?"

"That's right. Toby's dad. Thinks he owns me and he doesn't . . . But we don't live together. Christ no."

Dolly nodded, frowning at the cards. *She was missing something.* What?

"What's it saying, Dolly?"

". . . Like I said, you and your boyfriend. Boyfriends. You need to streamline . . ."

"What do you mean, 'boyfriends . . .'?" There was a short silence. "OH!" she burst out, full of sudden, inexplicable rage, making Dolly jump. "What's that filthy sod been telling you?"

"What? Who?"

"He may be 'dark', as you put it, but so are a lot of people. Frankly. And no *thank you*, Maurice Bousquet is *not and never has been* — he is *not* my boyfriend and he never *was* my 'boyfriend'. *Dirty old bugger.* What's he been saying?"

Actually Maurice Bousquet hadn't said anything. At all. He'd never even mentioned Nikki's name. Dolly suppressed a giggle. "I never said anything about Maurice, Nikki. You did."

But Nikki wasn't listening. "He's *sixty-one years old*, Dolly," she said. "*Sixty-one!* I swear, I don't know what I was thinking."

"Well," Dolly said soothingly, ". . . the fancy takes us, doesn't it, Nikki? From time to time. Sometimes thinking doesn't really come into it."

Nikki smiled. She leaned forward. The chair creaked. "I'll tell you what, though," she said. Dolly caught a whiff of her deodorant, her perfume, her sweat. "Old he may be, but he's *not all bad*." She winked. ". . . If you know what I mean, Dolly. *Knows what he's doing . . .* Which is more than can be said for most of them."

Dolly gave a half-hearted smile. It was more information than she wanted. Perhaps. Maybe not.

She'd known Maurice for a long time now. They shared a garden fence, which they chatted over when the weather was fine; and the wall between their houses was flimsy enough, she could generally hear him shuffling about next door. He could be surly sometimes but he wasn't unattractive. Still slim and reasonably fit — from what Dolly saw, there was a surprisingly steady supply of women passing through his house (although none seemed to stick around for long). Maurice could be good company. He was funny, in his surly way: flirtatious, egocentric, occasionally warm and, judging by the tantalising scent of Caribbean stews that sometimes seeped across the garden fence into Dolly's

13

kitchen, he could cook, too. Sometimes, though he was a good ten or fifteen years older, and really only interested in himself, she wondered what it might be like to be one of the women who flitted through the cottage next door.

But she didn't think it often, and not for long. He complained too much. And in any case, Nikki was right, he was *old*.

Nikki giggled, an idea suddenly occurring to her. "I'll bet he's had a go getting into your knickers, has he?"

Dolly didn't respond and the question hung in the air, briefly. Nikki, after all, had come to Tinderbox Lane to find out about herself, not about Dolly. Her gaze returned to the cards, and after a silence she said: "By the way — I presume you sign some kind of a — whatever it is doctors sign. Or priests or whatever. Solicitors and that . . . Anything we say in here, it's confidential isn't it?"

"Of course," said Dolly.

"I'm serious. Christ alive — Not that I've even said anything, right? I'm just saying . . . as far as all that goes, nothing happened. Nothing. And if you said different, I'd say it was a lie. Yeah? You understand? I swear, I'd send someone round and I'd fucking —"

"Hey! No need for that . . . Anyway, it's not me you need to be frightened of, darling . . ." Dolly indicated the Knight of Cups. "It's that sleazeball. Your young man. He's the one you need to watch . . . Is he violent, Nikki?"

"No."

14

"Well," said Dolly. *Liar.* "You be careful of him. Especially now."

"What do you mean, 'especially now'? What are you trying to say? Are you holding back on me? I didn't pay you £40 *not* to be told things."

"If you carry on yelling at me —"

"Apologies," Nikki said, leaning back, holding up both hands. The chair creaked. "You just got me riled up, talking about my fella like that . . . He's not my fella anyway. If you know what I mean." (Dolly didn't.) She leaned forward again, the chair creaked again, and the small room sweltered in her sugary scent. "But he takes care of me, you know?" Slowly, politely, carefully, Dolly nodded. There was something about the woman that was out of kilter. Something alarming — and Dolly didn't alarm easily. She stole a look at her watch.

"I've got another ten minutes yet."

"Of course you have. Do you want to ask a question? I can do a spread for a specific question, if you like."

"I just want to know if he's going to marry me, Dolly."

"You mean — the young man?" Dolly indicated the Knight of Cups.

"Who else would I mean?"

It was a good question. There were so many.

"Sometimes I think he hates my guts. I mean — when he wants it, he's all over me. Aren't they ever? . . . Or he used to be, Dolly. To be honest with you. He won't touch me now . . . Never. Not since —"

Dolly looked up from the cards. Still polite. And what she saw only lasted for a second. It was the

15

woman's face, a bleeding gash above her right eye, a bleeding swollen lip, the imprint of a knuckle on a waxen cheek, and a flap of seeping skin where his ring hit the bone: and the woman, dead-eyed; and a tiny heart somewhere inside that mountain of hot, voluptuous flesh ... *BOOM* ... which stopped beating.

Not yet, though.

Dolly said, "You need to be careful," and regretted it at once. "I mean to say — of course we all do. But it looks to me as if you might be ..." She couldn't say, "pregnant". It was Tarot-reading taboo. Etiquette forbade. Never tell a punter they're pregnant or dying. Aside from anything else, the cards could be wrong. Dolly didn't think so, not this time. Nevertheless. She nodded to herself, eyes back on the cards. "I'm just saying, if the young man has a temper on him ..."

"He doesn't."

BOOM. Dolly jumped.

But it was only the front door banging. Her daughter Pippa, back from college. *Thank goodness.*

Dolly didn't often feel like this. Perhaps it was the closeness of the weather, the sickly sweet mix of the client's sexuality, her cheap perfume and ineffective deodorant ... But today, she could hardly wait to bring the session to an end.

CHAPTER
THREE

Twenty-two-year-old Pippa was at the breakfast bar eating last night's cold pasta when Dolly ushered her client through to the door.

"That your daughter?" Nikki asked, looking at Pippa. "Still living at home, is she?"

"Seems to be!" Dolly said, sort of laughing — because thereby hung a tale. There was only one bedroom in the mews house on Tinderbox Lane — and it was Dolly's. Since Pippa had broken up with her boyfriend, and since she point-blank refused to stay at her father's house up in Ealing — despite having a whole room to herself (with a bathroom en suite) — the two of them were sharing it: and not just the room, but the bed. Dolly, at the grand old age of forty-five or so, was too damn broke to provide her only daughter with a bed. Worse than that, in some ways, she was too damn broke to have a bed of her own.

"Just for a month or two," Pippa said, licking her fork with (Dolly thought) an uncalled-for exposure of pasta-spattered tongue. "I'm staying 'til I get myself sorted." She grinned at her mother. "That's right, isn't it, Mum? Bit of a squash though."

The woman nodded. "Like my Toby. He's a useless sod. Can't see him ever leaving, frankly. I wish to God he would. Well — except he's always with his dad, these days." She shrugged. "You can't win, can you? Well, thanks again, Dolly."

"Keep in touch!" said Dolly. "And take care of yourself."

Nikki hesitated at the door before stepping out into the shimmering afternoon heat. "I never thought I'd say it," she said, "but roll on winter! Don't you think so?"

"We'll miss it when it's gone," replied Dolly. She followed Nikki out on to the lane, unwilling yet, though she wasn't sure why, to see the woman slip out of sight. "You remember where you left the car?"

"Ye-eee-s," the woman chuckled. "Bloody miles away."

"Well. Take care now — take care of yourself, Nikki," Dolly said again.

Nikki didn't reply. It was too hot. She swayed on away up the pathway, into the sultry afternoon, all boisterous curves and jangling jewellery. *She's only a punter*, Dolly told herself. *Not even a very nice one* . . . And yet Dolly found herself shouting after her, one more time: "*You be careful, Nikki.*"

Nikki raised a lazy arm and kept on walking.

And then, through the deadening heat, the sound of an Abba song echoed along the lane behind her: . . . "Gimme Gimme Gimme (A Man After Midnight)".

Dolly might have smiled — what ringtone could have suited her better? But as Nikki delved deep into her bag and pulled out the phone, there mustered something softly around her: a dirty, black-rimmed, red-brown cloud of light . . . Dolly shivered, and turned back into the house.

"Bloody hell," observed Pippa, needlessly. "What a slapper!"

Dolly frowned, primly. "Not really, Pips. I imagine a lot of men find her very attractive."

"Attractive? She looked like a prostitute, Mum! A professional prostitute . . . who also happened to have sat on a bicycle pump."

"I thought she looked very sexy."

"No, you didn't."

"Well. It doesn't matter what I thought really, does it? There's no need to be mean, Pips."

"*I'm not. I'm just saying . . .*"

"Well, don't." And then Dolly felt bad. She loved her daughter. But sometimes she just wished she could send Pippa to some kind of finishing school. Pippa was beautiful and funny and quick and warm — but she could be uncouth. There was no need for her to snigger about Nikki. What was Nikki to her, after all? And there was no need for her to *lick her fork like that, either.* "Darling, if you're going to eat that pasta, why don't you put it on a plate? How was your day?"

Pippa shrugged. "Derek West was his usual annoying self."

"Professor West? The one you call Professor Dirty?"

"Professor Filthy. Yes. He asked me to stay behind because he wanted to 'discuss my essay'. Like hell."

Mmm, said Dolly. Her mind was still on Nikki.

"He was quite helpful in the end, though. Plus he said my essay was good. Plus he didn't make a grab, so no complaints really . . . How about you? How many nut-jobs have you had in the broom cupboard today? Was that the last?"

"That was the last, yes. Maurice Bousquet recommended her. Weirdly. I must remember to thank him."

"Maurice next-door?"

"She was one of his lady friends . . ."

"Don't say lady friends, Mum. It's gross . . . Do you think he pays them?"

"The lady friends? I doubt it. He's as tight as a . . . Mind you — I don't think it was exactly a love match. She kept calling him a dirty old bugger . . . She told me," Dolly chuckled, "you'll love this, Pippa. She told me he was great in the sack."

It took a moment for Pippa to absorb. "That's disgusting."

Dolly said, slightly disconcerted: "It's not that disgusting . . ."

"It's *disgusting*. He's ancient. Plus she — I don't want to be rude, Mum — but she's fat."

"What? So what? Are you saying only women who look like Elle Macpherson should be allowed to have sex?"

"Elle who?"

Dolly sighed. "Never mind. I probably shouldn't have mentioned it. It's confidential."

A silence fell. Pippa was annoyed because her mother had wrong-footed her on the feminist front, which wasn't meant to happen. She felt stupid; also, actually, as if she hadn't been terribly nice. After a while she asked her mother if business was picking up since they'd launched the website. Pippa's boyfriend (now ex) had been meant to help with directing traffic towards it. He was doing a diploma in Social and Digital Media Marketing and Communications, so it was very much his area. The problem was, he and Pippa weren't seeing each other any more . . . and so now the three-month-old website, so lovingly and hopefully designed by mother and daughter, languished in the ether with a billion others, spectacularly ignored by everyone.

"How many nut-jobs [she always called Dolly's clients nut-jobs] have you got booked in for tomorrow?"

"Only one booked, so far. I mean, only one, *full stop*. People never book in on the day. And it's not like I get many walk-ins . . ." Dolly hesitated. Her finances were not in great shape: never had been, and probably never would be. On a good week, she might see twelve clients; on an average week, she might see nine. It was not a great living, but she only needed to get the word out. If she could count on seeing just eleven or twelve clients every week she might not be rich, but she'd be safe. As it was, the little mews house on Tinderbox Lane was only ever a phone call away from a spot in the estate agent's window. "I thought maybe you could put a little poster up at the college for me, Pippa. Could you do that?"

"Of course!" Pippa said.

Pippa was studying for a Masters in Environmental Strategy Tools at the same college as her ex. "I can put posters all over the place, Mum. In the student bar and stuff. We could design one tonight if you like. I'm not going out."

"Oh!" Dolly was grateful, of course . . . It was just that earlier Pippa had said she *was* going out.

"What shall we have for supper?" asked Pippa.

Pippa took a lot of exercise — running and yoga and netball for the college. She could eat whatever she liked. Dolly, on the other hand, was *buxom*. This afternoon, after seeing the shape of Nikki, and fearing for her IKEA chairs, Dolly had made what she was pretty sure had been a decision to skip supper tonight.

"I thought you had netball practice?"

"Cancelled."

"Oh! OK. Well then. I'll go to the shop. What do you fancy?" Dolly had been planning to watch a documentary about stone circles over a cup of decaff tea enhanced by artificial sweeteners. Clearly, eating actual food and designing posters with her daughter would be more fun. And they needn't go crazy over dinner. They could have some sort of salad, maybe — a goats' cheese salad . . . a warm goats' cheese salad with croutons . . . with*out* croutons. Dolly loved food. She was a good cook. Sod the decaffeinated tea.

CHAPTER
FOUR

The nearest shop to sell fruit and veg not covered in a thick layer of petrol fumes was a good twenty-minute walk away: a dreary trek, since Dolly didn't own a car, along a busy road. Dolly left Pippa bent over an iPad, and set out into the heat.

She was heading homeward again, sticky and tired and resenting the weight of her groceries, when a gleaming, tank-like vehicle pulled up beside her. It was her new neighbour, Mr — Mr . . .? Pippa called him "Heart Attack Hubby", because of his red face; or sometimes she called him, "Mr Frosty-Fuck", *because his surname rhymed with* — Bloody hell, what was his name? Dolly prepared her face for politeness and waited for the name to come.

"I knew it was you!" he said. He sounded, as always, vaguely accusatory.

Poor man, thought Dolly. In that short moment, in that short sentence, he exuded everything that was least appealing in the opposite sex: chippiness, aggression, entitlement . . . He was a small, hot, angry man, forever teetering on the edge of some kind of ludicrous and pointless explosion, whose name continued to escape her. Even so. Manners must.

"Mr *Buck*!" Dolly smiled triumphantly. "How nice to see you."

"*Fraser*, if you please, my dear! Fraser Buck, at your service!"

"Nice to see you, Fraser," she said again. It *would* be nice too, as soon as the lift home was forthcoming. She wasn't sure if he'd offered it yet, so she waited politely.

"Actually I've been wanting a word," he said.

"Oh yes?"

He slid the car into neutral and rested his wrist on the steering wheel. He was wearing a pink striped shirt and cufflinks. *Never trust a man who wears cufflinks.* (Dolly made a mental note to pass that wisdom on to her daughter.) His cufflinks shone in the sunlight. They had diamonds — crystals? — something glittery on them. Goodness, they were ugly. Never mind. He said: "Have you got a mo?"

"Of course! What's up?"

"Rosie's ever so upset . . . She's beside herself."

"Oh? I'm sorry to hear it." Dolly wasn't certain if Rosie was the wife, aka Mrs Frosty-Fuck, or one of the two small daughters. The Bucks had only moved into Tinderbox Lane a few weeks ago and had so far kept themselves to themselves.

"Rosie's a bit — well, I say 'a bit', actually *very*. She is VERY concerned . . . exceedingly concerned about our mutual quote-unquote, 'neighbour'."

"Maurice?"

"I must admit I haven't as yet caught his name. I mean the coloured gentleman who lives between the

24

two of us, at Number Three." A grin. "Who wanders up and down the lane muttering to himself."

"Maurice." Dolly felt her hackles rising. She and Maurice were not close. Nevertheless, when it came to a choice between Mr and Mrs Tank-Driving, cufflink-wearing Frosty-Fuck and her old neighbour of the past seven years, there was no question where her loyalty lay. "What about him?"

"Rosie says he's a bit — and please, Donna, don't get me wrong. There is not a racist bone in my body."

"I'm sure."

"Rosie herself is a passionate anti-racialist, and she can get actually quite irate if she thinks people are behaving racist around her . . ."

"Right you are." Dolly put her shopping on the ground.

"Having said that, I myself *do*, in this day and age . . . that is to say, I am conscious that people from different cultural communities can and do . . . how can I say this nicely?"

"I don't know. I can hardly hear what you're saying anyway," Dolly replied. "Are you headed back to Tinderbox? Can I get in?"

"What I'm trying to say," he said: "Rosie says he's been acting inappropriate round herself and the girls. *Looking at them* . . . in a way that Rosie felt was highly . . . inappropriate." The hand above the steering wheel clenched into a red-skinned fist. "I love my girls, Donna. I love them to bits. And if that 'man' so much as . . ."

25

"*Maurice?! To the little girls?*" Dolly was torn between laughter and outrage. Outrage won through. "Really, what a vile thing to say, Mr Buck! And honestly, what perfect . . . *poppycock!* He's been living next to me and my daughter for the past seven years and, believe me, my daughter — not to mention her friends — wouldn't *hesitate* — They can spot a pervert from two hundred miles away: like most children can, these days. Trained like sniffer dogs, Mr Buck . . . Maurice may well have given your wife the eye. I'd be surprised if he hadn't, frankly . . . But that's completely different. Obviously."

Heart Attack Hubby shook his head, disconcerted by the forcefulness of Dolly's tone, even if the words had passed in a blur. What, exactly, had his wife actually said anyway? He couldn't remember. He'd been so angry, he hadn't listened.

"Seriously," Dolly said. "It's a vile accusation. And dangerous, in this day and age. *What did your wife actually say?*"

A double-decker bus thundered by, followed immediately by another one. They drowned his voice completely, but she watched his angry mouth moving, felt the violence in his ugly, clenched fist . . . *Heat exacerbates everything*, she reminded herself. But even so . . . the man was a lunatic.

She interrupted him: "I'm sorry. I can't really hear what you're saying. But believe me, Fraser, you've got the wrong end of the stick. You're worrying unnecessarily. Maurice can have a funny way of saying things sometimes. He tends to have a little joke up his sleeve most of the time, and he isn't always inclined to share it . . . but really —" At last, Dolly laughed. Maurice Bousquet was a mystery all right, but there was nothing mysterious about his sex life. She could hear it, often enough, in all its inglorious detail, echoing through the bedroom wall. "Your daughters are safe."

"But you can't *know* that," he persevered. "How can you?"

"I'd be prepared to bet my house on it."

"Rosie says you've got a daughter. Is that correct? Has she ever mentioned anything?"

"I just said."

"Hm?"

"I just told you. No. Absolutely not. Nothing. And nor have any of her friends."

Fraser Buck gave up. He'd been going to offer her a lift, but not now. She could make her own way home. She looked like she smelled of joss sticks, anyway. He moved his wrist from the steering wheel to gear stick. Flashed his little teeth.

"All right," he said. "Well — thanks for your time, Donna. Sorry to bother you."

"It's Dolly."

"And if you do have any thoughts, let me know . . . you can't be too careful, can you? So many evil bastards out there . . ." The front passenger window was rising slowly as he spoke. "We'll have to get you round for a cuppa one of these days, yeah?" He grinned, gave her a thumbs-up through the glass, and pulled away.

CHAPTER
FIVE

By the time Dolly and her groceries returned to Tinderbox Lane, her head a confusion of hostile thoughts about the new neighbours, and impractical ideas for posters, an hour had been and gone; and so was Pippa.

Pippa left a little note on the kitchen table:

*MUM: CHECK YOUR MOBILE — I
SENT YOU A TEXT!!! Xxxx*

And on the mobile, a text:

Not sure where u got to Mum?? Nicoles having one of her meltdowns :(gone round to cheer her up :) Well do poster tomorrow I swear!! Xxxx <3 <3 :) <3

Dolly sighed. Too bad. On the bright side, her stone circle documentary wasn't started yet, so she could still watch it. And the goats' cheese salad — dammit — she would have it anyway. Just maybe not with so many croutons.

Pippa hadn't emptied the bin. The remains of her cold pasta were dribbling out from beneath the lid.

Dolly dealt with it at once, before she sat down. It wasn't, she reminded herself, as if Pippa intended to be a slob. It was just that she *simply didn't see the mess*. Dolly wished she was still young and carefree enough to leave cold pasta dribbling out of kitchen bins without feeling compelled — nay, *possessed* — by the need to clean it away . . .

And that, she reflected, in a nutshell, was the heartbeat of middle age: a conviction that somehow all the fear and pain and uncertainty of life could be washed away with a spritz of disinfectant and a germ-free breakfast bar: a bin without cold pasta dribbling out.

She wiped the cold pasta smears off the swing-top pedal lid with the appropriate cleaning product, pulled out the bin bag, since it was almost full, and lugged it out into the warm evening air.

And there was Maurice Bousquet, in the middle of the very same chore.

"Ha!" she said. "Great minds think alike." She was pleased to see him. She'd been infuriated by the insinuations of Mr and Mrs Frosty, and she wanted, privately, to assert her loyalty to him. Also, she wanted to learn more about Nikki. "*Amazing* this weather, isn't it? Almost eight o'clock and still so warm . . ."

"*Beautiful*! Ha ha ha," Maurice laughed. Maurice often laughed when there was nothing obvious to laugh about. Ha ha ha. The same three beats, every time. On first hearing they sounded rich and deep and warm and heartfelt. On first hearing, his laugh made him a lot of friends. Until the friends discovered that it wasn't really much of a laugh after all, and more of a nervous tic, a wary and slightly hostile bark, disguising what was, actually, an unusually surly outlook. Dolly was quite surprised to hear him say anything so positive, least of all about the English weather. "Makes me feel homesick, Dolly," he added, "all this sweaty-sweaty heat. Feels like home, ha ha ha . . ."

"Got any plans to visit?" She always asked him the question, but he never seemed to have any plans. Or he was never very straightforward about them in any case. So far as she could make out, he'd not been "home" for forty-odd years or more. She wasn't certain he'd been "home" at all, not in the fifty-eight years since he'd left it. So he couldn't, in all honestly, have been *that* homesick. Could he? No matter how much he hated to spend money. What was money for, after all, if not to visit home after fifty-odd years of feeling homesick?

"Heavens, *no*," Maurice said. "Tell me, Dolly — how am I going to pay for a long-distance flight like that?"

They were standing at the end of their little gardens, bin bags sagging at their feet. And it was such a lovely evening. Dolly heard herself saying: "Are you interested in stone circles, Maurice?"

"Stone what?"

"Stone circles. There's a documentary on the telly. I thought . . ." She felt shy, suddenly. "I thought you might like to come in and watch it with me. Are you busy?"

This was a major development. Maurice and Dolly had been exchanging pleasantries around the dustbins for seven years now — since the divorce, when Dolly first bought the house. Why, she wondered (and so did Maurice), was she pushing the boundaries tonight? Was it —

She blushed.

Oh, holy cow.

In the beat before Maurice responded, Nikki's words bounced between her eyeballs . . . *Old he may be, but he's not all bad.*

Gross! Or not. Or something. *Lonely she may be.* A bit sex starved, she most definitely was . . . She didn't want to have sex with Maurice. She did *not* want to have sex with a man who'd had sex with sex-crazed Nikki. *Ugh.* The thought of it helped her to pull herself together.

"Stone circles," she said, "Probably aren't your thing. They're sort of ancient, mystical —"

"I know what stone circles are," he said, "What do you think?" He tapped his forehead. "This brown skin prevents any general knowledge penetrating?"

"What? Oh, *no.* For goodness' sake —"

"Ha ha ha. Well I don't want to watch a programme about stone circles. No thank you. But I have some chicken curry on my stove — too much for me. Why don't you come and help me eat it, hmm?" He smiled, or not quite. But he looked at her with a light in his eyes, as if he knew the joke, and he had read her mind —

Dirty old bugger.

And he wasn't unattractive.

Dolly laughed: "Maurice, do you know how long I've been wanting to try your chicken curry? The smell of it's been wafting over our garden fence, making my mouth water these past seven years . . ."

"Ha ha ha . . ."

"And now, on the hottest night of the century — which I should think it is, you know —"

"Sure feels like it . . ."

"You ask me if I want to eat your hot *chicken curry.*"

"Well do you?"

"Well — I don't see why not," said Dolly. And then she laughed again. "I mean — *why not?* I can read your cards if you like. Would you like that?"

"Oh my goodness! Ha ha ha. I don't think so. Will it cost me?"

Dolly assured him not. She wanted to mention Nikki, to thank Maurice for recommending her, but something stopped her. Instead she picked up the bin bag at her knees, heaved it into their communal tub — and told him she'd be with him in a few minutes.

Dolly returned to the cottage. She fetched out the cards and checked her reflection.

. . . Oh dear, never mind . . .

She put on some lipstick and sprayed some scent and headed outward. Then realised she'd left the cards on the breakfast bar and headed back.

Ten minutes later she was knocking on Maurice's door, through which, until now, she had never been invited. On this occasion, in combination with the heat, her perfume, and a painful sense of her own foolishness, the smell of the spicy curry made her feel a little sick.

CHAPTER
SIX

"Ah!" he said. "There you are! — Well come on then! Door's open. Come on in!"

Maurice's ground floor was a symmetrical image of her own. It comprised a single room, hardly fourteen foot wide, with a skinny staircase to the right; a small window at the back with a small kitchen sink beneath it, and in front of that, a small kitchen table (Dolly had a breakfast bar). Dolly had managed to squeeze a two-seater sofa into the front half of the room, and in her house there was even space to arrange a kitchen chair in front of it, for when visitors came. That was because she had hung the TV above the breakfast bar, thereby freeing up one corner. Maurice had only one armchair in the front half of the room, and one old telly; partly because the telly, being so old, was the size of a large cupboard and occupied a lot of the space, and partly because he was selfish and didn't much care if his visitors had a place to sit.

Dolly's study/broom cupboard stuck out at the end of the house, and opened on to a small back garden. A similar space backed off the same wall in Maurice's house, but Maurice, or perhaps his predecessor, appeared to have removed the partitioning door. He used the space as a passageway to the garden; a place to put the fuse box and an ancient-looking boiler, and a mountain of junk he couldn't bring himself to throw away.

The room was bare and uncared for. If it hadn't been for the photograph of beach and Piton Mountains above the empty grate, and the smell of curry, it would have been a most depressing place. It still was, really. His ancient easy chair looked as if it had melded to the shape of his bony backside over the years; ditto the grubby crochet cushion, half fused into the upholstery behind it.

"It's quite like mine," Dolly said, looking around her, trying to find something positive. ". . . You've got the stairs . . ." She gave up. "I bought a bottle of wine — well, most of a bottle. Do you want some?"

"Place needs a lick of paint," he said. "And a new boiler."

He was wearing a comedy apron, with a cartoon, bikini-clad woman's body on the front. Dolly wasn't sure where to look.

"It does need a lick of paint," she nodded.

"Don't you go agreeing so fast!"

"Well. It *does*," she said. "Where do you keep your glasses?"

"I'll do it up when I win the lottery, Dolly . . ."

"Of course you will."

"I'll win it one day!"

"I wouldn't be too sure about that."

"Just you wait," he said. "Ha ha ha." He did the same numbers every week and had done for years. Ever since years and lottery numbers were invented.

"Well then, you're an idiot," Dolly said.

"Ha ha ha. We'll see!"

Maurice didn't want to drink wine. He had his cold beer. So Dolly polished off the bottle herself. Half bottle. Two thirds. Too much, in any case.

As they ate the curry Maurice, who liked to talk, treated Dolly to the sob-story of his life. She'd heard it often enough but, with the excellent curry, there came an extended version. First, there was a perfect childhood . . . a Caribbean idyll . . . Christian values and sunshine, mangoes and honest faces, and an endless supply of fresh fish. And then came *England* and the drab, unkind English . . . and race riots . . . and Enoch Powell . . . And then (in this, the extended version) a period of appalling drudgery in the post room at the *Daily Mirror*; a period spent saving for a sunny retirement back home, only for the dream to be smashed apart when the *Mirror*'s owner, Robert Maxwell, plundered everything: Maurice's pension, Maurice's savings —

"But hang on," Dolly interrupted, "you can only have been about twenty when Robert Maxwell died."

"I was twenty-four years old, Dolly. Ha ha ha."

"Well — you can't have been thinking that seriously about a pension, at the age of twenty-four."

"Let me tell *you*, Dolly Greene," he cried triumphantly, "only a *white, middle-class WOMAN* who has never tasted hardship would assume any such thing!"

"Well but —"

He leaned forward, across the delicious curry, and looked earnestly into her eyes. "Believe me, Dolly," . . . it was such a rich, deep voice . . . "I have been thinking about my retirement pension since the day I left St Lucia." He swigged on his beer bottle — and grinned.

"Maurice, you were three years old."

They laughed. It was a preposterous statement. He knew it, and he didn't care. And so he continued with his sorry tale, while Dolly nodded sympathetically and slurped back the rest of the wine.

"But you're not working now, Maurice. And you own your own house. So what's keeping you here? I mean, since you hate it so much? Why don't you sell up and go home?"

"Ha!" he said. Highly satisfied. Another trap, obligingly stumbled into. "But I don't own this house, Dolly! It's housing trust . . ."

"Housing trust? Really?"

"I mean it belongs to my wife. More or less. Last I heard. I don't have two beans to rub together since my wife walked off with everything."

"Her and Robert Maxwell."

"Not to *mention* Robert Maxwell. Ha ha ha. God rest his wicked soul." Maurice winked at her. Dolly laughed. He was funny. And he had a wonderful laugh and a deep, rich, warm voice. And he wasn't in bad shape. And my goodness, he cooked delicious curry. "In any case," he said, "I've got no kids. No family. I'd have no one to go home *with*, Dolly." And then he leaned towards her again, *dirty old bugger*, "Unless *you* want to come? Hm?"

Dolly necked the glass.

"Ha. Ha. Ha. How about *you* sell *your* house, Dolly, and you and I could sail off into the sunset together. We could leave tomorrow! How about that?"

Bloody hell, she must be pissed. She needed to collect herself.

"Nice idea, Maurice," she said. "Very nice. Can I think about it?"

He looked startled.

And then Dolly winked.

"HA!" he roared, waving a finger at her, quite relieved. "For a moment there . . ."

"Scared you, did I?" She smiled, but she was a little hurt. What would have been so dreadful about retiring to St Lucia on Dolly's savings, after all? *She* was the one who ought to be frightened.

"I'm not being funny," he said. "You're an attractive woman, Dolly. No mistake . . ."

"Very nice of you," said Dolly.

He waved it aside. "You don't need me telling you that . . ." (She did though.) "I'm just a bit jumpy, Dolly. That's the truth. I had the new woman round here yesterday. Rosie next-door . . . the mum. Except she didn't bring her *kids* along, ha ha ha. Certainly not! She was all covered in perfume, *oh my goodness*. Carrying a bloody great chocolate cake . . ." He cackled. "She had one thing on her mind, Dolly. And I'll tell you what it was . . ."

"Please don't," said Dolly.

"The inside of my underpants!"

"Oh, come on."

"Ha ha ha — She never had a black man before, Dolly. That's what. She wanted to know if it was true what they say ha ha ha."

"Ha ha."

"I'm damn serious! I was *insulted*. She was treating me like a *sex object*, man."

Dolly chortled.

"I had to ask her to leave, Dolly. I had to kick her out of my front room!"

"*No!*"

"I swear to God, and she was so damn *angry*. She's got mental problems, I tell you that Dolly. I thought she was going to kill me . . ."

Hell hath no fury . . . reflected Dolly. It explained a lot — assuming, that is, that Maurice was telling the truth, which he generally wasn't. Dolly changed the subject. "By the way — thank you so much for sending your friend Nikki my way. That was very kind of you."

His smile vanished. "What's that?"

"I didn't realise you even knew what I did for a living. I mean, not *really*. So when Nikki called —"

"Nikki? Nikki who?"

"*Nikki*." Oh dear. "Your friend. The lady. Voluptuous. Very sexy . . . Long dark hair. She spoke very fondly of you." Well, not really. "That is . . ."

He screwed up his eyes, cocked his head to one side. "*Nikki*, you say?"

"She came to see me today. I read her cards. She said you recommended me, and I was very grateful. In any case I got the impression you knew each other quite well — she'd been to Tinderbox Lane before —

Maurice . . ." But he wasn't budging and suddenly Dolly was embarrassed. "Oh come on, Maurice. You know who I mean. You told her to come and see me, and I read her cards . . ."

He shook his head.

Dolly gave up. "Well. Never mind. Forget it. I just wanted to thank you for putting the business my way . . . It's been very quiet ever since — Well, ever since *ever* really. Ever since I started. So I'm always grateful for extra work. I was going to read your cards, to say thanks. But it seems like I don't have anything to thank you for. Except the curry."

"Nikki . . . Nikki . . ." he said, tapping the table, seeming to think. "I don't know any Nikki."

"Well, maybe you know her by another name." Dolly wished she'd never brought it up.

"Maybe I do," he said. It seemed to settle the question. "You want to read my Tarot cards now, do you, Dolly? Ha ha ha. Not sure I like that idea. You're not going to tell me I'm about to die?"

Dolly felt exhausted, suddenly. Tired of Maurice's nonsense. She shook her head. "I don't think so, no," she said. "Or not tonight. Maybe another night. I think I'll head home."

"What? All of a sudden?"

"But thank you," she added quickly. He sounded hurt. "Thanks for a lovely evening . . . Maybe I can read your cards next week? If you like? I'm sure they won't say anything bad. You look like you're in pretty good shape!"

"You bet I am," he smirked. It was faintly lascivious. It was unnecessary.

"Well," said Dolly, "good night!" She stood up and knocked over her chair; not surprisingly, perhaps, in such a small space, and after all the wine. Even so. Her exit wasn't quite the glide she would have wanted. She could feel his eyes on her arse, and it irritated her.

As she opened his front door and stepped out into the cool summer night (he stayed seated), she spied her darling Pippa walking up the path towards home. "Darling!" she cried. "You're back. Thank God! I was worried . . ."

Pippa stared at her, nonplussed. "You what?"

CHAPTER
SEVEN

There was a lot of teasing the morning after. And the evening after that. Pippa stayed at home to do the poster, as promised, and she wouldn't let it drop.

Dolly and Maurice sitting in a tree
KAY-I-ESS-ESS-I-ENN-GEE

"For goodness' sake, Pippa, don't be such a baby. I was having dinner with my neighbour. What's wrong about that?"

"Nothing."

"Well then."

"It was you who said he was so fantastic in the sack," she said.

"Oh, you're too revolting! I never said any such thing. I felt sorry for him, that's all. And I wanted to thank him for sending me Nikki . . . Anyway he claimed he had no idea who she was, so the whole thing was a bit of a washout . . . Good curry though."

They finished the poster and printed off five or six copies for Pippa to distribute, and Dolly updated Pippa on the various accusations flying between households on Tinderbox Lane. Pippa was delighted. "Looks like

Mr and Mrs Frosty-Fuck are going to rock our little community to its core," she giggled. "Do you think Tinderbox Lane classifies as a 'community'?"

"I don't really think you should call them Frosty-Fuck," Dolly said mildly.

"— But I'm definitely on Maurice's side. Aren't you? The Mrs looks like she's been gagging for a Frosty for years."

"*Well* . . ."

"— All that goody-two-shoes cake-baking. Plus that fucking *weird* smile she has melded on her face —"

"Since when did you get such a good look at her?"

"She asks me to babysit almost every time I walk past the door."

"*Does she?*"

"And as for Mr Frosty-Fuck —"

". . . Pips . . ."

"He's obviously got a secret bum-boy tucked away somewhere. Or a dominatrix. Or a dog. *Something weird*, anyway. Because *Mrs* Frosty definitely isn't doing it for him. His closet's got to be chock-a-block with —"

Dolly's mobile rang.

"HELLO!" cried Dolly gratefully. *HELLO* to whoever it was.

But it wasn't anyone.

". . . Hello? . . ."

Nothing.

". . . Who is that?"

Someone was sobbing.

"Hello? . . . *Hello?*"

*And that was when Dolly first saw it — the body.
And she saw it as clear as day: bloated with river water,
a rat's tail of black hair slicked to its back, strangulation
marks on the neck.*

"*Nikki!* Nikki? Is that you? What happened? Who is
it?"

"You haven't told him anything, have you?" said the
voice.

"No. Nikki?"

*And she could see the blowflies circling. But that was
impossible. Nikki wasn't dead.*

Dolly flicked them away — the blowflies only she
could see. She flicked at midair while her daughter
stared at her, open mouthed. "Nikki, what's happened?
What's happening?"

"Nothing."

"Nothing? Where are you? Why are you calling me?
Has he hurt you?"

The woman was panting now; wheezing and panting
as if she couldn't breathe. She wouldn't stop.

"Sweetheart . . . *Nikki.* Calm down. Are you down
by the river? No, of course you're not. Are you at
home?"

Nikki said: "I'm coming over." And then the line
went dead.

Dolly stayed waiting for her long after Pippa went to
bed. But Nikki never showed up.

CHAPTER
EIGHT

The weather broke. Rain everywhere. Very quickly, the long, hot summer was a long, hot distant dream, and so — to be brutal — were Dolly's concerns regarding Nikki. Dolly had tried her mobile several times after the fateful call, but never got an answer and — after that — life moved on. The vision of the water-bloated body didn't return to haunt her, and there was no mention of it washing up anywhere in the news. The memory faded. Nikki had been a one-off client, and Dolly had enough problems of her own. Financial, mostly. Astonishingly, there had actually been a drop in inquiries since Pippa put the posters round college.

And then one day Pippa came home with the Filthy Professor in tow. Professor Filthy had spied one of the posters and, in his words, found it "hilarious". He said to Pippa, "Your mummy sounds like quite a character! Do you think — *forgive me for laughing* — but do you think she would read MY cards?!"

Pippa said no. (Or so she claimed.)

But Professor Filthy insisted. He took down the telephone number and the website address while Pippa was standing right there beside him and in the end it seemed silly to hold out. Especially as it was pissing with rain outside, and it turned out he actually only lived two or three streets away from Tinderbox Lane, and he had offered to drive her all the way home — on the off chance of an appointment. And especially as — and maybe this was weird, Pippa wasn't certain — she knew the professor was divorced, and she knew Dolly was lonely. And she thought — that if her mother was willing to imagine ancient Maurice next-door in the sack without barfing, then her standards were pretty low. Professor Filthy . . . might not be as disgusting as Pippa thought he was. Added to which, her mother was broke. Professor Filthy wanted to book a session in the broom cupboard. And no matter what way you looked at it — that was £40 in the bank.

So — to cut a long story short: one rainy afternoon a week or ten days after the dinner with Maurice, Dolly met the Professor. Who only lived two or three streets away.

Dolly was on the phone. Pippa came in, soaked from the five-minute walk along the bike path, with Professor Filthy padding in right behind her, and it was obvious to Dolly from the tension in her daughter's face that — whoever the man might be — Pippa was torn between dismay and hopeless laughter.

"This is Professor West, Mum. He's my professor. Turns out he only lives a couple of streets away."

"Ah," said Dolly. "Professor West. Yes. Pippa's mentioned you . . . Actually you look quite familiar. I think I must have seen you around and about."

"He spotted me putting up more posters and he absolutely insisted . . ."

Professor "West" stood between them, grinning, his wet clothes steaming, making the room feel damp and, inasmuch as it was possible, even smaller than it usually did. He was over six foot and their little mews house wasn't built to fit him.

"It's what I love about this bit of London," he said. "So village-y. We probably know *hundreds* of people in common — I mean faces of people. Obviously. People in the shops . . . Yours looks familiar . . . So, you're a 'Tarot reader' are you? Isn't that remarkable."

He had a bossy, jutting jaw and thick glasses, and his jeans were too short. And even Dolly, who didn't care much about fashion, noted how his trouser waistband reached halfway to his nipples. He looked like a paedophile priest, circa 1983. Every woman's dream then.

"Yes, I am a Tarot reader," agreed Dolly. She looked from Pippa to the professor. The professor looked from Pippa to Dolly.

"Well?" he chortled, rubbing his palms together. Very clean fingernails. "I'm ready when you are. I hope you're not going to tell me I'm about to die!"

Funny one. She'd never heard that before.

"Professor West's wife has just left him, Mum. Unfortunately . . . So I thought . . ."

Dolly glared at her daughter. Did Pippa really believe her mother was this desperate? And did she really think her mother was so vague she wouldn't have worked out that Professor "West" was the same Professor Filthy West who'd been attempting to get off with her daughter for the last eighteen months? She waited for

Pippa to finish the sentence. She was damned if she was going to help her.

"I thought . . ." said Pippa. What *had* she thought?

"I've heard a thing or two about these so-called 'Tarot' cards," said Filthy, oblivious to the tension flying this way and that. "Possibly a bit sinister."

"Not really," said Dolly. She thought she heard footsteps on the bike path. She glanced through the window, but Filthy's large, damp body had caused the glass to steam up. Whoever it was, walked on by. No one was coming to her rescue, then. "I charge £55," she added.

"How odd. I recall it says £25 on the poster."

"That's the student rate," Pippa said. "Sorry. Didn't I make it clear?"

Filthy had noted the temperature at last. He sensed that the mood wasn't quite right: that he must be doing something wrong, but he couldn't tell what. He ploughed on: "I tell you what, girls, how about you read my cards for the student rate, Dolly — is it really your name, or is it a sort of stage name?"

"It's my real name. And no — I'm sorry. I'd love to give you a discount, but I can't . . ." She tried to think of a reason why. "I simply can't."

"Let me finish! How about a £30 reading and then I take both you ladies out to dinner! How about that?"

CHAPTER
NINE

She gave him a reading for £55. Good. They needed the money. His cards weren't terribly exciting, which wasn't surprising because, in many ways, neither was he. He was lonely — but you hardly needed the Tarot to tell you that. He was fearful . . . He was lazy and depressed. In any case — she helped him to feel better about his life: while allowing him to snigger about the absurdity of having his cards read at all . . . And in the end she felt sorry for him, because whether or not a man claims to think the Tarot is absurd, the process of getting his own cards read will always bring out his vulnerability . . . And so it was that two hours later, she and the professor were sharing a table at the Taj Mahal, eating vegetable bhajis. Pippa, of course, had long since slithered off.

"It's very difficult, isn't it, in this day and age . . . forming ordinary, healthy relationships with members of the opposite sex. Have you tried any of these website thingies?" he asked her, crunching loudly on a poppadum, and not leaving any for Dolly. He'd already told her about his marriage breakdown. (She'd nodded ruefully and swallowed the wine.) He'd already told her about the sort of perfect woman he was looking for.

Afterwards he looked at her sympathetically and said: "I suppose with ladies your age it's more a sort of *whoever-you-can-get* scenario. Is it?" And the funny thing is, he meant it kindly. He was really trying to imagine himself in her shoes. "Whereas *men* . . . Someone like myself . . . Just by the fact of being *male*, we tend to have quite a choice. We can pick and choose a little bit."

"Are you sure?" Dolly asked. "You're not exactly Brad Pitt yourself."

He took it on the chin. Assuming, that is, that he heard it at all. He was like a runaway train. Jabber-jabber-jabber. (And they say women talk too much.) It was hard for Dolly to get a word in. She wasn't on his ideal-woman hit list, in any case. Too old, too poor, too plump, and too weird, what with the Tarot.

He said: "I had a date with one of these internet girls. Ladies, I should say. One of these ladies who put up pictures of themselves that really bear no relation . . ." he tailed off. ". . . Anyway she was pretty rough round the edges. To be frank with you . . . But she was amusing in one particular aspect. And I shall tell you for why."

Dolly asked herself: *Why am I still here?*

She said: "Derek, I hate to be rude. But I have an early start . . ."

Filthy held up a hand. "Let me quickly tell you this amusing anecdote. You'll find it highly amusing." He started laughing in advance. "I forget her name . . . What was it now? She lived around here. Well, they all do. That's the point of these agencies, isn't it. Convenience. She was a ginger thing. Through no fault of her own . . . But *slim*. You know. Perfectly . . ." He made a shape with his hands.

"Let's call her Judith," snapped Dolly.

He shut up for half a second, and a shadow of fear passed over his face. "How extraordinary," he said. "D'you know, that actually was —"

"Please, Derek. Tell the story. I want to go home."

". . . *Judith* . . . had a date with a PC Plod. If you per-lease . . . *Excuse* the alliteration. Well, I say he was a PC Plod. Actually he was an Inspector Plod. Recently divorced. Smart uniform. Excellent pension and so on . . . The Judiths of this world could hardly ask for more. One would have thought."

What a snob you are, thought Dolly. She kept it to herself. The sooner he told the story, the sooner it would be over, the sooner she could go home, the sooner — with luck — she could never lay eyes on him again (even if he did live only two streets away).

"Well, *Judith* thought she was on to something. Dinner was fine. PC Plod was quite personable. Albeit — you know — in his PC Ploddy way. But, you know . . ."

"I don't think I do know. No."

"Well —"

"Never mind. Carry on."

"He invited her back to his place for a 'drink'. So to speak. And you'll never guess what she found!"

Dolly said, "What?"

"Well, this so called 'Inspector Plod' didn't live in a house at all, did he? He did not. Did he live in a flat? Dolly, he did not. He lived in a . . . wait for it . . . he lived in a *caravan*. On Barnes Common."

It *was* rather curious, in truth. But then again, divorce could do terrible things to a person's finances. Dolly didn't react.

"No but wait for it," giggled Filthy. "It gets even worse! So he invites Judith in for the drink. Into his little caravan. Judith goes in, Dolly, *clop, clop, clop* with her little shoes. And what do you suppose is stretched out on the couch?"

"Well, I don't know."

"Go on, guess! I tell you what, Judith screamed so hard she screamed the monkeys off the trees. Or she would have done. If there'd been monkeys on Barnes Common . . . Only a bloody great *cobra*, Dolly! A giant cobra! Yes! A bloody great snake! And that," he said, snapping his fingers for the bill, "is what happens when you go internet dating. Thank you Judith of the ginger hair. For the valuable lesson. Because you just never can tell who's out there. Not from the pics. It's a dangerous business. Dolly. It really is."

He paid for the curry. He wanted to walk Dolly to her front door but she was adamant she could make it on her own, so he dropped her at the top of Tinderbox Lane. It was still raining as she climbed out of the car, and he sensed that the evening hadn't gone well.

"I'm sorry," he said, with the engine running, and Dolly with both feet already on the pavement. "I talk too much."

"Not at all," said Dolly.

"It seems such a shame. When we live so close. Sort of a waste . . . Would you be willing to see me again?"

". . . It's not really a matter of willing or unwilling, Derek . . . I just get the feeling we're probably not terribly compatible."

"But you must be lonely, Dolly?"

Not that lonely, she wanted to say. Instead, she shook her head. "Good luck and everything! And thank you for dinner. I shall keep a wary eye out for any snake-loving inspectors I meet!"

"You do that! And by the way, if you happen to change your mind . . ." Really, he was too pathetic. If Dolly didn't escape quickly, she'd wind up inviting him in out of pity. "Maybe we can meet up for a drink one day? Remember, I'm only round the corner!"

She didn't know much about cars, but she reckoned the professor's looked a bit low slung and flashy for a man of his age and appearance. As he accelerated round the corner she shuddered; a mix of relief and something not far off revulsion. Pippa *Greene* she muttered, striding into the semi darkness of Tinderbox Lane, *I am going to murder you!*

Obviously, she didn't mean it.

CHAPTER
TEN

Dolly would have hated the council to put in street lighting, but there were times, and this was one, when the tasteful abundance of shadow on Tinderbox Lane could be a little frightening.

There were just seven cottages on her short road. It was a cul-de-sac, topped by the ugly, noisy Station Road at one end, and by a small, drab patch of scrubland, leading to the back of a train station, at the other. At Number One Tinderbox Lane, furthest from the main road, there lived a single man, aged somewhere between late twenties and early forties, named Terry Whistle. He rarely stepped outside except at night, and when he did, he moved with the silence of a cat. He wouldn't have needed to worry about the lack of street lighting, due to the luminous, light-giving whiteness of his skin. Terry Whistle did something with computers, which involved having a beard and staying inside the house most of the time. Dolly and he rarely saw each other to speak. But she spied him often enough, slinking up and down the lane, always alone, always with his eyes fixed to the ground. And he cut such a thoroughly dismal figure, even Pippa couldn't bring herself to be cruel about him.

On Pippa and Dolly's other side, at Number Three Tinderbox Lane, there was Maurice Bousquet; and beyond him, at Numbers Four, Five and Six, were the new neighbours, the Bucks, aka Heart Attack Hubby and Mrs Frosty-Fuck. The three cottages, having been empty for years, had been knocked into a single residence over the spring, put on the market and snapped up at an exorbitant price, all in the space of a fortnight in the summer. The developer had removed the street numbers, and either he or the Bucks had given the property its name. At any rate someone, somewhere, had apparently opted to call it "Windy Ridge", and there was an italicised sign bearing that name, just above the new front door.

Number Seven Tinderbox Lane was the cottage closest to the main road. Its windows had been boarded up for as long as Dolly had lived there. Nobody seemed to know who owned it. However, according to Rosie Buck, who told Pippa, who told Dolly, the house had apparently recently been "purchased" by the same developer who *did such a super job* on Windy Ridge, so it would not be empty for long. Rosie seemed to think this was a cause for celebration, and it probably was. Empty houses tend to be a magnet for trouble.

It was only nine-thirty at night as Dolly made her way up the path: not late, but already dark. Dolly hadn't thought of Nikki for a while, but the image came to her just then: Nikki shuffling away down Tinderbox Lane, that dirty brown cloud of light surrounding her. Where was Nikki now? What had become of her? Why had she never turned up that night, or made any attempt, after that mad phone call, to make contact since? Dolly wondered if she should make one more attempt to find out. But of course she shouldn't. It was none of her business.

There was a slight breeze, causing the leaves to rustle. And there were heavy raindrops falling, which to a nervous ear could sound a little like footsteps. She trudged on, humming to herself softly, for courage.

Something moved.

Dolly stopped. "Nikki?"

A figure was coming towards her. Not Nikki, a man. Tall. Stocky. Too large to be Terry Whistle. He was coming directly towards her, and his eyes were shining and . . . *Holy Christ! Who or what — ?* Dolly had time to wonder quite how drunk she was, and then he stopped.

He was youngish — thirty maybe. Dressed in a suit. Skinny tie. Aftershave. Good looking. Dark. Unsmiling. Staring at her. He was blocking her path.

"Excuse me," she said. He didn't move.

"You must be Dolly," he said. It was a South London accent.

"Why?" she said.

A pause, and then his face cracked into a grin. Perfect white teeth. "'*Why?*'"

"I mean — yes. I am Dolly. Who are you?"

"You're the Tarot reader," he said. "Maybe you can read my cards one day. Would you do that?"

"Well — yes. Of course I could. Who are you?"

"Me?" he sounded surprised. "I'm Ade. Adrian Bousquet. Maurice's son. I've spotted you a bunch of times."

Ade was shaking her hand. A strong handshake. Smooth skin. A waft of aftershave. Chunky gold bracelet. Grey suit. Some sort of hybrid, Dolly thought: half stockbroker, half gangster. Whatever he was, it was sexy. And frightening. Maurice had definitely told her that he didn't have any children, but Dolly thought better of mentioning it. She said, "Well, it's good to meet you — at last. Your old man makes a very fine curry."

Ade gave a bark of laughter. *Ha Ha.* Like his dad. "I'll tell him you said so," he said. They were still shaking hands. *Why wouldn't he let her go?* "Next time, Dolly, promise you'll read my Tarot cards, yeah? And don't you go telling me I'm about to die!"

Dolly laughed. Like she'd never heard that one before. He released her. Dropped the hand and strode away without another word. She watched him disappearing, squeezing the light from her little pathway, and a chill passed through her.

She wasn't great with faces, it was true, but she was almost certain she had never seen his before. When, she wondered, had he spotted her "coming and going"? And why would Maurice have lied about the existence of his own son?

Perhaps it was because he felt guilty. Or perhaps he didn't believe he was the father. Perhaps all sorts of things. What was certain was that Ade's appearance on Dolly's warpath was a blessing for Pippa, who was sitting at home at Number Two Tinderbox Lane awaiting her mother's return with some trepidation. She'd asked several friends if she could stay at theirs

56

tonight, hoping to avoid her mother, at least until the following day. But, as luck would have it, nobody was picking up their phones and so, after an hour of guilty skulking at the yoga studio, she'd skulked back home again. When she heard the door key turn she hit the TV remote control OFF button, and leapt to her feet.

"*Mum!* Before you say anything . . . I. Am. So. Sorry. Nicole asked me to stay over at hers but I knew you'd be so pissed with me I just had to come home. Was it awful? I'm sorry I abandoned you, but you have to understand he's my *tutor*. It was just like the whole thing was so *sick* and I just — can I make you a cup of tea?"

Dolly said: "Did you know Maurice next-door had a son?" She sniffed. "What's that smell?"

"What smell?" She sniffed. ". . . Did he slobber all over you, Mum? I am *so sorry*. Or did he just bang on about me? I swear he's obsessed with me. It's so gross. He is so gross. You have to believe me, Mum. I am so so so sorry."

"I've just bumped into a young man who said he was Maurice Bousquet's son. But I didn't even know he *had* a son. Did you?"

So Pippa was not in the firing line, after all. "Maurice's son?" she said, happily. ". . . Actually that's quite weird."

"Well it is weird, isn't it?"

"Well no — that is — it's weird because I actually knocked on Maurice's door, about twenty minutes ago. I thought I heard a crash. Something being thrown at the wall or something — I was a bit worried."

"No!"

"And by the way — you left your mobile behind. Somebody rang you."

"But what about Maurice?"

"Check your mobile, Mum."

"Pippa! What about Maurice? Is he all right? Did you call the police?"

"No. I just said. In the end I just went round and knocked on his door."

"And he was all right, I presume?" said Dolly. "I mean you wouldn't be sitting here if he wasn't all right?"

"Yes, he was all right. He was fine. Well he said he was. He said his boiler was broken . . . But he only really opened the door half a centimetre." Pippa shrugged, uncertain Dolly would approve. "So I left him to it. I mean — he was fine, Mum. Talking and everything . . . I felt a bit of an idiot. So I left him alone."

"And did you see the man. The son. Did you see Ade? — Pippa, what is that smell? Can you smell it?"

"What smell? I can't smell anything. And no, of course I didn't see 'Ade'. Through a half-centimetre gap in the door. Do you want a cup of tea?"

Dolly did not want a cup of tea. What she wanted was to go round to Maurice's house and ask him what was going on.

"He's not going to tell you though, is he?" Pippa said. "You've been living next to him for seven years and he hasn't told you he has a son yet." Now that she realised the heat was well and truly off her, Pippa switched the television back on. The news was showing.

58

It was the local news. There was a police officer in a visibility jacket, talking about . . . "Ooh, look! That's by the boathouse, isn't it, Mum? Down by Kew . . . Simon's dad had an allotment down there. It's the —"

"Well — maybe he *wasn't* Maurice's son! Perhaps he was a . . . I don't know . . ."

"Maurice was going on about the broken boiler. Maybe he was the plumber?" Pippa said, but she was more interested on what was on the TV. ". . . Looks like there's a body, Mum . . . Down at Kew. They've got one of those little tents up. I wonder how many bodies they pull out of the Thames every year?"

"Hundreds I should think," said Dolly.

". . . Hope it's not Simon's dad."

Dolly glanced at the telly, not terribly interested. She didn't know Simon. Didn't know the allotments. "The 'Ade' I just met on the lane did *not* look like a plumber," she persisted.

"Really? What does a plumber look like?"

"Don't be a smartarse," Dolly said. "And by the way — we haven't talked about what happened tonight yet. Your ghastly professor."

"Come on, Mum. He wasn't that bad. Plus we got an extra £55 —"

"Don't you *ever* — *EVER* — do that to me again. You hear that? NEVER."

Pippa couldn't help it. When people got angry it made her giggle.

It was only a quarter to ten. Was it too late to knock on Maurice's door? Pippa said it was. She also warned

Dolly that, judging by his manner previously, she would be unlikely to get much of a reception. Nevertheless Dolly, having downed a couple of glasses with the professor, was emboldened by slight drunkenness. She explained to Pippa, as if it was the answer to everything, that she'd promised Maurice a card reading.

"I owe him," she declared, heading for the broom cupboard and fetching out the cards. "And I'm a woman who always repays her debts."

". . . Mum . . ." warned Pippa.

"It'll be fine. In any case, for heaven's sake, if that man wasn't Maurice's son then who the hell was he? I think I have a right to know. Don't you?"

"If Maurice doesn't want to tell you, then he won't."

"But the cards will!"

"Assuming he lets you read them."

Dolly winked at her. "He will."

But Pippa wasn't emboldened by slight drunkenness. Also, she had glimpsed Maurice's face through that half-centimetre gap, heard his voice. Something was amiss.

"Mum," she said, serious now. "It's not funny. Don't go . . ."

But Dolly was already gone.

CHAPTER
ELEVEN

"Maurice?" Dolly stood outside his door, almost, but-not-quite shouting. She had no specific plan in mind — she rarely did — only a lot of questions she wanted answering and a general feeling that now was as good a moment as any to get them. "Maurice! It's Dolly. You there? I just remembered I promised you a reading. And I've got my cards . . ."

As she uttered the words, she realised how they must have sounded to a man on his own, at this time of night. She gave a silent, electrified skip of horror and spun away. She was back in her own front garden by the time he pulled open his door.

"Hello, hello," he said. It sounded slightly creepy. "You want to read my cards, do you?"

"No. Sorry. I changed my mind."

"Ha ha ha." It didn't sound in the least bit merry. It sounded wretched. In fact everything about him seemed miserable: his voice, his shoulders, the silhouette of his body against the light. She would have continued her retreat, but he plucked at her over-tuned heartstrings.

"I would certainly like you to read my Tarot cards, Dolly," Maurice said. "I've never had it done before.

And there's a first time for everything. Isn't that right? Even if it's a whole lot of mumbo jumbo, and I'm not saying it is, Dolly. I can't pay you though."

"I already told you it was free," she said. "You think I'd come knocking at your door, and then *charge* you for a reading? Business isn't that bad. Yet."

"Well then, I would love a reading," he said. "And you're right. You did promise me. So. Have you had dinner?"

"Of course I have."

"All right then. Are you coming in?"

She hesitated. "By the way, I met your son, Ade. He seemed like a nice chap . . ."

"He's not my son. Are you coming in or aren't you?"

There were several reasons why she accepted. And really, though she might flatter herself, sympathy for a lonely old neighbour was not the foremost.

"Ha ha ha," he said, as she stepped through his doorway. "Curiosity killed the cat."

She said: "Are you going to offer me some coffee?"

He fetched her rum and Coke, which she could have done without, but he wouldn't take no for an answer. He kept it stashed away in the back, by the boiler.

"You've put the door back in," she said, watching him ferreting away.

"It was always there, Dolly. Just hidden by all the junk."

He sat down, gave her the rum and Coke, clinked glasses with her. "Happy reading," he said. He sounded slightly creepy again. He obviously thought he was going to get lucky.

Dolly said: "Just to be clear, Maurice, I am here to read your cards, because I am curious, and I want to find out who that man was on the lane, who seemed to know everything about me. Who said he was your son. I'm curious. Also about your friend, Nikki —"

"I don't know any Nikki. I told you already."

"She called me a while back sounding terribly upset . . ."

"How's your drink, Dolly? Do you want ice? I have ice . . ."

Dolly shook her head. "I'm not staying long, Maurice. Forty-five minutes . . . I'm just here to read your cards." She looked at him, smirking back at her, sitting at his little table with his thighs splayed. He wasn't hearing. He still thought he was in with a chance. Before she sat down, and without hurting his feelings or his pride, she needed to be certain that he understood. "*Do you understand?*"

"Absolutely I understand. Of course I understand. You think because I am a black man . . ."

"Oh for goodness' sake. I'm just making it clear that, despite the time of night — don't — *do not* — get any ideas. I'm going home in forty-five minutes. Pippa's waiting."

"Ha ha ha."

"Ha ha. Yes, indeed . . ." She settled opposite him and placed the tools of her trade on the table. She kept the cards in a wooden box, with the mugwort resin, and when she unfastened the lid, its sweet smell wafted into the room. She cast around for a saucer, and found one by the sink, which due to the kitchen's dimensions, she could reach without standing up. She crumbled some resin on to the saucer and set it to smoulder. Maurice watched in silence. She could feel his nervousness; a gravity settling between them. Good.

"All right then. Maurice," she said, breaking the silence. "Shall we read your cards? Find out your secrets? Are you ready?"

"Ha ha ha. Dolly, I don't have any secrets!"

She chuckled. "We all have secrets, Maurice."

Solemnly, he chose his cards, and then laid them, face down, in a small pile in front of him, just as she had instructed.

"You can ask me questions, if you like," she said. "I can try to answer them. But I generally like to do a sort of overview at first, just to get us started. Is that all right with you?" Her hands were resting on the cards he'd pulled out, not yet turning them over.

He shrugged. "You do it how you do it," he said. "Maybe I'll ask some questions later."

Dolly looked at Maurice's cards and — which must have been irritating for him — began to chuckle.

"Ooh my goodness, Maurice . . . Well, well, well —"

"*What is it?*" he snapped. "What can you see there that's amusing you so much, Dolly? It's rather insulting . . ."

Dolly apologised. She generally made it a rule not to drink alcohol when she was reading, particularly for this reason. It made her tactless.

"You wouldn't be laughing, I suppose, if it said I was going to die."

Actually the Death card had turned up. He must have noticed. And it seemed to be suggesting that, yes, death was in the air — something around him was dying. Possibly even him. But he was correct in assuming that the Death card was not the source of her laughter. In fact, looking more closely at his spread, she wondered quite what was. There wasn't much to laugh at, after all: a meanness with possessions, which seemed to stultify everything else; a miserable habit of self-denial driven by . . . *what?* She wasn't sure yet; untrustworthiness in matters of the heart (that loomed large). He was dishonest . . . He didn't like himself . . . He didn't appear to love anyone or anything . . . except . . . money.

"Money, money, money," she muttered.

"What's that?" he sounded sharp.

"Gosh, Maurice," she said, her eyes on the cards, "you need to be kinder on yourself . . . you're walking wounded."

"Ha! Well, Dolly, who isn't, at this stage in the game?"

"What stage is that, Maurice?"

"Ohhh. Ha ha ha. I feel old, Dolly."

"You're not that old." Dolly felt she'd been defending Maurice's age a lot lately. "I don't think so. There's a female in your life, Maurice. She's posing a bit of a threat to your wellbeing. Is that right?"

"If there's any woman posing a threat to my wellbeing at this moment in time, Dolly Greene, I'd say

65

it was you. Ha ha ha. I think I'm going to regret inviting you in . . ."

She ignored that. "Or maybe *you* are posing a threat to the wellbeing of *this woman*? Might there be anything in that? Is there a woman in your life, Maurice, who maybe you're not looking out for as much, perhaps, as you should?"

"No."

Dolly thought, once again, of Nikki. "OK," she said. "Well maybe this particular lady is *worrying* you for some reason? No?"

"No."

Dolly took a deep breath. He was hiding something — and not just from Dolly, from everyone.

"You're very secretive," she said.

"Ha ha ha . . . Is that you or is it the cards talking?"

"Both," she said. "You know, Maurice, if we work together we can get so much more out of this."

"You want me to tell you the answers, Dolly? I thought you knew the answers! I thought that was the point!"

She pressed on. It didn't much matter anyway because whatever toxic dynamic there was between Maurice and this unhappy woman — she was hardly the dominating note in his spread. Money, money, money . . . And that was why Dolly had laughed when she first turned over the cards. Maurice made such a song and a dance about his poverty — as if he were the only poor man in London; the only one who understood what poverty meant. But his cards said something quite different —

"So? What else can you see?

"Money," she said. "That's what I see. It's everywhere, Maurice! Literally."

"Ha ha ha. Chance'd be a fine thing, Dolly."

"Down the back of the sofa, in the cracks in the walls — it's like . . ." she laughed . . . "It's like this entire house is lined with gold! Walls of gold, Maurice! . . . Looks to me like you've come into a fortune."

"Ha!"

"Or you soon will, if you haven't already . . . Or if not *you*, Maurice, someone in your family maybe? That gentleman I met on the lane . . . who was or wasn't your son . . ." she chuckled. "He seemed like a rich man. Gold bracelets and posh aftershave and everything. Lovely! Perhaps he's making you a fortune? Is he?"

Maurice didn't reply but Dolly could feel his mood darkening. She might have stopped there, but she was curious. She thought she'd try to lighten the mood, tease him a bit, and then return to the question of Ade. Ade and the money. He was obviously loaded.

"Don't tell me you finally won the lottery, Maurice?"

Maurice ignored the question. "I told you, that man is not my son. Don't mention him again."

"*But why?*" asked Dolly. She looked up from the cards. "Why can't I mention him, Maurice? It's not very fair. You've obviously told him all about *me*. He wanted me to read his cards!"

"Oh did he indeed? I'll bet he did. And I suppose you read them, did you?"

"No — I told you —"

"Of course you did. That boy always gets what he wants."

Dolly pulled back. "No. I told you, he —"

Maurice leaned forward and, in a flash, brushed all the cards off the table. The saucer went flying, and the mugwort, too. It lay there on the lino, smouldering, slowly burning a black stain on to the Ace of Pentacles. "And I suppose you told him everything, did you? What did you tell him?"

"What?" Dolly was appalled. Her precious cards were scattered across the floor. "What did you do that for, you idiot? Look! You've burned a mark there. On my Ace of Pentacles."

"I don't give a damn about your Ace of Pentacles. Pick up your damn cards and get out of here. What did you tell him?"

Dolly stared at Maurice. She stood up. "I didn't tell him anything," she said. "How could I? I only met him for two minutes on the pathway." The cards were on the floor between them. She didn't want to get on her hands and knees in front of him; nor did she want to leave them there.

"Get out of my house. I don't like *witches* in my house," he said.

She said, "Not until you've picked up my cards."

She waited, very upright, trying not to shake or cry. Silently, Maurice bent down and gathered the cards, the box, the lump of mugwort resin. He handed them to her. "Now. Go, please."

His lower lip was trembling. He looked angry and ashamed. If she stuck around another second he would start to apologise and she would no doubt feel sorry for him again. She didn't want to give him that chance. She took her tools and left.

CHAPTER
TWELVE

She would have liked to slip home without having to explain events to Pippa, but that was impossible. The house was too small. All roads led to Rome, or at least to Pippa, sitting at the breakfast bar, watching telly. *Only one way through this*, Dolly decided, fumbling with the lock. Her head was throbbing. *I'll brazen it out*.

The bright lights of her own kitchen made her inexplicably, suddenly dizzy: added to which, Maurice's attack had left her feeling foolish. Pippa took one look at Dolly and leapt up from her breakfast stool. "Mum! What *happened*?" Dolly dropped the house keys, then the cards. Pippa caught her in her arms, just as Dolly's knees buckled.

They drank sugary tea together, and once Dolly was stronger they discussed — with growing, gossipy relish — the Great Mystery of Maurice and his Secret Son. "He can't stop lying," Dolly couldn't stop saying.

"I know."

"It's virtually impossible for him to start and finish a sentence without contradicting himself somewhere in the middle. I used to think it was funny. Now, I don't know . . . It's almost like we're living in a *horror movie,* Pippa."

"Not quite, Mum."

"No, but it could be. He's obviously hiding something."

Pippa said: "What did the cards tell you?"

Dolly didn't want to answer. She needed time to think about them. "Money, mostly," she muttered. "He's money-obsessed."

"Like, *stolen* money?"

She shrugged. "Just lots of it . . ."

"You think it's something criminal?"

Dolly shrugged. "All I know is he looks bloody miserable."

"The wages of sin are death."

"Hm?"

"It's on a poster by the bus stop. I never know what it means."

Time for bed. "Well," Dolly said, standing up. "I suppose we'll get to the bottom of it in the end, one way or another . . . Pippa, seriously, *what is that smell?*"

"*What* smell?"

"*That* smell . . ." Dolly sniffed. "Tarnish."

"*Tarnish?*"

"Metal. Tarnish. Decay. Can't you smell it? Have you never put your nose down the barrel of a gun?"

"— Have you?"

"Of course not. But I should think that's what it smells like. Mixed with . . . rotting animal . . . And it's coming from next door. And I'm telling you, Pippa, you're looking at me like you think I'm crazy but —"

"I am *not* . . ."

Around mid-morning the following day, Maurice came knocking at Dolly's door. He looked puffy, as if he had only just climbed out of bed. His eyes and his skin had taken on a yellowish glow, and the sugary, sour smell of rust, or decay, or tarnish — whatever it was — clung to him like a dirty fog.

There was a raised step at Dolly's threshold and he looked up at her with pleading, puppy-dog eyes. "Morning Dolly," he said.

"God, Maurice, you look dreadful! *What is that smell?*"

He shook his head. "I'm not feeling too good . . ."

"I can see that."

"I just wanted to say I'm sorry about yesterday . . . Ha Ha Ha . . . I was very rude."

"*Very*," she said. But she felt for him. "Do you want a cup of tea?"

"No."

"Do you want to talk?"

"No."

"Maurice — I'm worried about you. Are you all right?"

"I'm fine."

"I think you should see a doctor."

"I'm fine . . . They found a lady's body. Did you hear?"

"What's that?"

72

"Washed up in Kew. On the news this morning."

"Oh . . . Yes. Pippa was saying last night . . . Horrible. By the allotments. A woman, was it?"

"Murder, Dolly. Right on our doorstep."

"Is that what they're saying? Was she . . ." *Dolly saw it again: the water-bloated body, the marks on the neck, the coil of thick, dark hair.* "Maurice, do they know who she is?"

He shook his head sullenly, and changed the conversation. "I'm sorry you met Ade. He had no business, talking to you."

She had so many questions. But only one, the wrong one, blurted out: "MAURICE *WHAT IS THAT SMELL?*"

He stared at her.

"But you must be able to smell it! You reek of it!"

He stepped away from her, offended. "I only came to make peace, Dolly. After yesterday. Maybe another time."

"No — wait. Don't be cross, Maurice. *Can't you smell it?*"

"Sure thing, Dolly. Sure I can." Maurice turned away, fed up and unhappy.

"Maurice! I'm sorry. Come back! . . . I've got questions!"

He didn't even reply.

She closed her front door behind him, and the smell stopped.

She was shaking: shaking so much that her hand completely missed the switch when she tried to turn on the kettle. It wasn't the argument with Maurice that had upset her. Or, not directly . . . It was the body down by the river, with the rope marks round the neck, and the thick black hair and the staring eyes — she couldn't stop seeing it. Did Maurice already know who it was? Did they both already know it was Nikki?

The day stretched ahead. Dolly had no clients booked, which meant she had time to brood. She scoured the internet for information about the corpse, but there seemed to be few details available: an unidentified female body had been spotted by a jogger yesterday afternoon, at the river's edge . . . Marks on the flesh suggested violent assault, and possible murder . . . The woman had been dead for "some time". (*Some time*, indeed. What did that mean, exactly?) No one had been reported missing who fitted the woman's description. It could be "some time" (again) before any further information became available.

Dolly found herself calling Nikki's mobile. Not once, but many times throughout the day. Each time, as she waited for Nikki to pick up, and Nikki never did, she pictured the mobile abandoned by the river's edge, face down in the mud, its facetious ringtone disturbing no one but the crows.

CHAPTER
THIRTEEN

Dolly didn't feel she'd given Filthy the best of readings. However, he informed Pippa, who reported it to Dolly, her words had crystallised numerous issues in his life, and as a result he felt more confident than he had in years. He admitted to Pippa that he'd approached the experience, "with tongue firmly in cheek", but had come away a good deal calmer and wiser. Pippa told him that this was often the case, which was true.

On the Saturday morning, mother and daughter were lying in Dolly's bed, drinking coffee, discussing ways to boost Dolly's business. It was a mild autumn day and the bedroom window was open. Pippa, who considered herself practical and modern, especially where her mother was concerned, said: "What you don't realise, Mum, is that Tarot cards are — like, *having a moment* right now. This time a couple of years ago, I used to tell my friends you read Tarot cards for a living (and when I say 'for a living', we both know I use the expression loosely . . .)."

"It pays for that coffee you're about to spill on the duvet, my friend. And it pays for the heating and the council tax . . . And it pays for —"

"Yeah. But listen. This time last year, my friends weren't even sure what Tarot was. Whereas now? They all want to learn how to do it! Even Grandpa Filthy wants to learn. Or so he says. He says you should organise a course at the college, and I think he's right."

Dolly considered this. The idea of standing up in front of a group of strangers didn't naturally appeal.

"He fancies you, Mum. It's like I don't exist any more."

"Don't be gross, Pips."

"I'm not being gross. I'm just saying, he wants to help you. So why not? He says he'll put in a word with the faculty, and they'll provide a room for you. They won't charge rent or anything because it won't be official so you can probably do the whole thing cash in hand. I reckon we could get *at least* ten people to start — and then word'll spread. You only need to get fifteen people at five quid a go. It could be bringing in another hundred or so a week."

Not to be sniffed at.

"Plus, it gets you out of the house. You must be fed up, sitting in that broom cupboard all day."

Of course she was.

"So you're up for it?"

Dolly considered. Not that she needed to for long. "Bloody hell, Pips, of course I am! A hundred a week? Imagine what we could do with that! *Why not?*"

"Good for you!" Pippa beamed, and gave her mother a quick hug. "I knew you would! . . . Only slight thing . . . I told Filthy I reckoned you'd be up for it . . . and he sort of said he wanted to have dinner with you to discuss the 'curriculum'. Which *obviously* is crap. We all know what he wants and we all know he's not going to get it. But if he's really willing to help make this happen, it must be worth enduring one dreadful dinner — mustn't it?"

Dolly was saved from replying (and yes, of course it was worth it) by the sound of footsteps on the front path.

"Hello-oo?" came a voice. "Anyone in?"

"Mrs Frosty-Fuck!" Pippa whispered. "I swear, that woman hounds me! Tell her I'm not babysitting tonight. I've got a shift at the Bull's Head. OK? Tell her to leave me alone!"

Dolly, still in her woollen pyjamas, went downstairs to relay the message.

Rosie Buck would have died before she opened her front door in a pair of woollen pyjamas. With utmost tact, she pretended not to notice her neighbour's *faux pas*.

In fact Rosie Buck opened the door each and every morning, always looking exactly the same: the same expensive jeans, a half-size too small, the same expensive mid-heel, pointy ankle boots, the same fussy little sweaters from Whistles, the same never-a-bad-hair-day; and, beneath the yellow hair, despite all the money and creams and effort she put in to pretending it was anything other, the same unhappy, unpretty, desperately perky face.

She was carrying a paper plate with two large slices of Clingfilm-covered, pink-iced birthday cake. She pushed the plate towards Dolly. "Te-dar! . . . It was little India's birthday yesterday!"

Stop all the clocks.

"Seven years old already!" said Mrs Buck.

Cut off the telephone.

"I can hardly believe it, Dolly. Can you? Time just *spins* by!"

"I hardly can," Dolly agreed. "Tell her happy birthday from me." She took the cake. "Thank you for this."

"I was wondering if Pippa was around tonight to babysit. Is she in? She didn't reply to my text."

"Oh. I'm not sure. That is, I know she's working tonight." Dolly had a brainwave. "But *I* can babysit. If you like. I could do with the cash."

"*You?*" Rosie Buck grinned, and her mind raced. Fraser would say she ponged of joss sticks. Which was silly. Dolly didn't smell of joss sticks and nor did her house. She was actually a very attractive woman, in her own *madcap* way! Even so, Fraser wouldn't allow it. He'd taken a dislike to Dolly, after the conversation. Which meant he'd insist on Rosie booking someone from the agency. "Can I text you about it later?" She laughed: "We may not actually be going out after all, so can I get back to you? You'd have to promise me, none of your funny magicky business, all right! Not with the kiddies!"

"My funny magic business," replied Dolly, "costs extra."

More laughter. "Oh, I'm sure it does! I didn't mean to imply . . . In fact that reminds me — I've been meaning to ask you, Dolly — I'm hosting class coffee morning next term — aaargh . . . *my turn!* And I was thinking it might be a giggle if maybe you could pop round with your cards and read some of the mums' fortunes . . . I'd pay you, *obviously!*" She waggled a finger. "But only the happy news! OK? No telling any mums they're about to die! They'd never forgive me!"

"I would never tell them that," said Dolly. "Just let me know the date."

"The other thing I wanted to chat about," Rosie dropped her voice. "Fraser mentioned he had a little word with you a few weeks back, about . . ." she indicated Maurice's cottage. "A certain neighbour of ours . . ."

"That's right. I told your husband he had absolutely nothing to worry about, Rosie. Maurice is a lovely man. He's just got a bit of a funny manner sometimes."

"How long has he actually been living here?"

"On Tinderbox Lane?"

"In GB."

"Oh — well . . . Since before you were born, I should think."

"I only ask because, as Fraser says — with this Pakistani community grooming tragedy going on everywhere, or wherever, and nobody daring to come forward and actually *say* anything . . . It makes you think twice, doesn't it?"

"He's not Pakistani."

"I know that. I'm not stupid. And I'm not saying he's 'into' the kiddies. God no. I think Fraser may have run away with the impression . . ."

"That's certainly what he was implying," Dolly said.

"What? Golly, no. Gosh — *no*, Dolly. Absolutely not. How awful! No, I just think he may be a teeny bit *peculiar*. That's all I was saying. And I'm only wondering if, as an attractive woman, *you* ever had any issues with him. Of a . . ." Rosie's face reddened. "Of a sexual nature. I'm sorry to ask . . ." Dolly realised, to her shock, that Rosie was actually trying quite hard not to cry. She reached out, but Rosie glimpsed her approaching touch, and veered back, as if it would burn her. "*I think he's been looking at me through my bedroom window*," she said. It sounded desperate.

"At you? Or the girls? I don't understand."

"What? No! Not the girls. Christ, no. Me. I mean . . . *me*."

"Really? Are you sure?"

"*Yes. I am sure.* Of course I am sure."

She was lying. It was obvious. "You actually saw him?"

Rosie hesitated. "It was more like a — *movement in the shadows* . . . I was terrified, Dolly."

Dolly shook her head. "Well, it was probably a branch or something. Honestly, Rosie. I should forget about it. I've known him a while. And, yes, he's got his own way . . . But he's no peeping tom."

"I'm not saying —"

"As I said to your husband, it's not like he's got a shortage of women in his life. With the greatest respect — and I don't mean to be rude, you're gorgeous, and everything. But he's not going to waste his time lurking in the shadows of his own street trying to catch a glimpse of you in your bathrobe . . . not really . . . Not when he's got women coming and going in his own house." Dolly attempted to smile, to take some of the sting out of her words.

"That's not what I meant," Rosie muttered miserably.

"Then what —? I don't understand!" Dolly was growing impatient. "What did you mean?"

"It doesn't matter. I was being silly." Rosie stepped backwards out on to the lane. "Forget it. Forget I said anything. I'll let you know about the babysitting."

(She never did.)

CHAPTER
FOURTEEN

Dolly was sitting alone in her study a day or two later, drinking coffee and making plans. The smell of the tarnish came to her in bursts. Her irrational fears for Nikki she had tried her best to set aside, but the hum of Maurice's misery was harder to ignore: it was a sort of psychic tinnitus buzzing through the party wall, and try as she might, she couldn't drown it out.

She had a date with Filthy two nights hence, and in front of her, the beginnings of a schedule for an introductory course in Tarot, entitled "Tarot Talks". She was wondering how long she could spend discussing each card before people would begin to get bored (wondering how anyone could ever be bored) . . . when the psychic buzz from next door — *stopped*. Suddenly. And in its place, a male voice:

"GET OUT!"

— Followed by a heavy thud. Dolly's chair shook. She heard the coffee pot rattling on the breakfast bar in the kitchen.

"GET OUT OF THERE!"

Was it Maurice's voice? Whoever it was sounded so angry, she couldn't be sure.

And now they were fighting — she could hear it all: the vicious little catches of breath, the scuffing feet, the slaps and the punches and Maurice — was it Maurice? *"GET . . . OUT . . . OF . . . MY . . ."*

There was a horrible *crack*, and then the sound of a body — it sounded like a body — hitting the floor.

Dolly yelled out — and yet, somehow, in her horror, remained frozen to her seat. She could hear panting, frantic and animal. And then footsteps across Maurice's bare floorboards, and then a kick. And a groan of pain. And then, another kick.

She shouted again, and this time words came out: "I'M CALLING THE POLICE!" she yelled.

"Hear that?" It wasn't Maurice's voice.

Dolly's mobile phone was on the kitchen counter. She left her seat, squeezed past her desk, ran towards it — and tripped on the doorframe, stubbing her toe in the process. It took a moment — an eternity — to recover.

When she finally reached the front door and threw it open, she spied Fraser Buck hurrying up the lane away from her.

"Hey!" shouted Dolly. "Hey, Fraser!" It was a small and traffic-free lane, and he was only forty yards away. It was unfeasible that he couldn't have heard her, yet he didn't look up. He turned up his garden path and disappeared inside his house.

First things first. She needed to check on Maurice. She limped up the pathway towards Number Three, gathering pace as her toe came back to life. As she raised her fist to bang on his front door, it pulled open and Ade Bousquet stepped out. He nodded at her politely, and closed the door behind him.

"Dolly, the Tarot reader," he said. He smiled. "We meet again."

"Is he all right?" she said.

"Who? . . . Dad?"

"I heard a fight."

Ade looked confused. "A fight? I don't think so."

"I definitely did. Is he OK?"

"Dad?"

"*Yes*, Dad! I mean Maurice."

"Dad's not in."

"I heard a fight." She didn't move. They were squeezed together on the doorstep. Ade was a foot taller, and probably double her width. He looked down at her, smelling of aftershave, smiling as if amused.

"Oops," he said. "Think you've been communing with the funny fairies again, Dolly! I reckon you've been hearing voices. I was on my own in there. I *don't think* I've been fighting with myself ha ha ha . . ."

"No," she shook her head. She tried to reach for the door but, accidentally or not, he shifted his body — a minimal movement — and his vast chest blocked her. "Ade," she said. "I heard a fight. I need to talk to Maurice."

Ade considered this: "Well. Let's call him then, shall we?" he said. "Dad? Coo-eee? Dad?"

She hesitated. ". . . Maurice?"

Silence.

She shouted louder: "Maurice? Are you in there?"

"I told you, Dolly. No one's in. You've been hearing things."

Dolly began to panic. "No!" she said. But suddenly she wasn't entirely, completely, one hundred per cent sure. "Maurice? *Maurice!* Are you all right? Let me in!"

Ade laughed. She slipped a hand beneath his arm and tried again to reach the door.

"Door's locked," said Ade. As if she was stupid. "I was just going out. You want me to open it for you? You want to see for yourself?" He produced a key and unlocked the door. It swung open. And there before them was Maurice's room: silent, orderly, empty.

Again, Dolly called out Maurice's name. "Hello? Maurice?"

Nothing. He wasn't there.

Ade said, "OK?"

"Where is he? What have you done to him?"

Ade sighed. "I think you should go back to your own house now, Madam Tarot. Everything's OK. Except — *oooh! Hear that?*" He cupped a hand to his ear. "Yeah . . . It's Freddie the Unicorn. I think he's calling you."

She didn't move. "I don't understand."

"Go home," he said, enjoying the moment. "Go on, get going! You mad old bint."

She took one last look into the empty room, and then Ade closed the door.

She didn't mention the smell in there. There was no point. Nobody seemed to notice it but her, and she had already laid on enough of a crazy-woman show for one afternoon. Dolly did as he suggested. She turned around, and went home.

CHAPTER
FIFTEEN

Dolly's closest friend, Sandra, was a solicitor and also divorced. It was she who had first introduced Dolly to the Tarot, and she always claimed to have psychic abilities, although Dolly had never seen much evidence of them. At times like these, when Dolly frightened herself, "Psychic Sandy" (as Pippa called her) was always the first person Dolly called. The scene that had just played out on Maurice's doorstep was not the first in which she been left humiliated and confused by something she alone had seen or heard. And though usually such incidents led nowhere, helped no one, and signified nothing at all — there had been a small handful of occasions when they'd proved to be eerily prescient. The difficulty was in knowing how to distinguish the one from the other.

Alone in her own cottage, with the buzz of Maurice's disharmony quite silent now, Dolly was at a loss as to what to do. Should she call the police? She didn't want to. They might think she was mad. Should she wait until Ade had definitely left, and then try Maurice's house again? Or should she simply (her preferred option) return to making notes for her Tarot Talks, and pretend nothing had happened? She asked the cards.

Turned over the Emperor and the Hierophant: the cards of Authority, Order, Power and the Establishment. The very cards she didn't want.

She called Sandra.

Sandra said: "What are you calling *me* for? You know what to do. Knock on the poor man's door again, Dolly. And *call the police*. Pronto. I'll be round this evening, as soon as I've finished work. It sounds serious."

"I can't call the police!"

"Why not?"

Dolly said: "What if I imagined it all? They'll think I'm crazy."

"So what if they do?"

"He's probably not even in the house, Sandra. Anyway, I don't trust the police."

"When have you ever had anything to do with them?"

"I haven't — but —"

"For God's sake, Dolly!"

"What if Pippa has some weed hidden away somewhere? I bet she does . . . And what if they come with their sniffer dogs and find her weed — and then she gets a criminal record, and she'll be banned from every job she ever applies for — not to mention America — and all because I'm . . . Sandra, I'm almost certain it *was* real —"

"So *get a grip*! Maybe you *are* hearing voices. If you are, you probably need to listen to them. And if you're not hearing voices then maybe your neighbour is lying unconscious, bleeding to death on the other side of the wall. And you're standing there talking to me about Pippa's possible weed stash. I've got goose bumps, darling. The Universe is telling me —"

"I'm not asking the Universe, Sandra. I'm asking you."

"Get round there. Call the police. I'll call you back in an hour."

CHAPTER
SIXTEEN

Dolly took the advice. She returned to Maurice's house and banged on his door. Nothing. She peered through his front window. Nothing. She picked up a stick and threw it at the upstairs window. Nothing. It was shut tight. Finally, she called the police.

There was a lot she could have told them: about Death cards, and the smell of tarnish, and hearing voices, and bloated bodies in the river — and, above all, the disappearance of Nikki, whom she was increasingly convinced was at the heart of it all. But she kept all that to herself. She told the operator she thought she may have heard a fight in the house next door, and that she was worried for her elderly neighbour.

"He's sixty-one," she said, though it wasn't relevant. "So not *that* elderly. I think there's been a family feud. Or it might be something else. I've knocked on the door, and he's not answering." She gave her name and the address, warned them she lived on a bike path, and waited.

Dolly was no anarchist. On the other hand, maybe she was. Either way, she didn't like or trust the police, for all sorts of excellent reasons, none of which sprang to mind at that instant. When she glimpsed the two officers heading towards her, both smiling — not at her, but at something one of them had said, she felt a rush of warmth and gratitude.

Sergeant Raff Williams was a thickset gentleman, with a calm face and woolly, greying hair . . . Dolly may not have liked or trusted the police *per se* (for all sorts of excellent reasons, none of which immediately sprang to mind), but she liked and trusted the look of this one at once.

He smiled at her. "Dolly Greene? Are you the lady who made the call?"

"Absolutely I am. Thank you for getting here so quickly."

"You mentioned an elderly gentleman, possibly in need of medical help. Have you called an ambulance?"

". . . No —"

"Perhaps we should do that? Which is his house?"

"I'm at Number Two." Dolly indicated the cottage behind her. "This one is his." They were standing outside Maurice's garden gate. "But — wait. Don't call an ambulance yet. We don't even know if there's anything wrong. He may not even be in there."

The two men awaited clarification. Why would she have called the police, after all, if nothing was wrong?

"What I mean is — I think there *may be* something wrong. I want you to check. I heard the fight, but then his son — at least I think it's his son — came out of the house and denied any knowledge of anything. I looked through the window and there's no sign of any trouble." Dolly's gaze flicked from one man to the other, gauging their reaction. Neither seemed terribly concerned or impressed. "I'm sorry. I probably shouldn't have bothered you. I'm just worried . . . I've been trying to get hold of his — well, I don't know, his 'girlfriend', I suppose. She hasn't picked up the phone for a few weeks now — and there was that poor pregnant woman washed up down at Kew a few days ago, which made me think —" She stopped. "I'm sorry. I'm talking nonsense . . . I just think there's something wrong."

Sergeant Raff Williams shook his head. *Intelligent eyes*, Dolly reckoned. *The right sort of age* — This was not the moment. "Don't apologise, madam," he was saying. "It's a good thing you called us. I wish more people in this city had neighbours as thoughtful as you."

"Well — hardly," Dolly was embarrassed. "Actually he and I had a fight. He's been behaving quite oddly lately. It's one of the reasons I'm worried. And then there's this son who's suddenly turned up . . ."

The younger officer interrupted her. He nodded at Number Three. "This is the house, madam?"

"That's right . . . Do me a favour, though. Please don't call me madam."

The older one (the one she fancied), i.e. Sgt Raff Williams, winked at her and grinned: "Right you are, miss," he said. "I'll knock on his door, then. Check he's OK." He turned to his partner. "Do we have a name?"

The younger one (she didn't fancy) was already tapping into his handheld computer: "Mr Maurice Bousquet," he read. "Is that correct, madam — Mrs —?"

"Dolly Greene. That's correct," said Dolly. "And his son's called Ade. Adrian. But he's not in the house now. He's gone."

"Ade Bousquet?" the younger one said. He glanced at his colleague. "You thinking what I'm thinking, Raff?"

"Can you describe him?" asked Raff.

"Of course I can. But don't you think you ought to go and see if Maurice is OK first? It was a nasty fight."

The younger one said: "Miss, it's helpful if we can first ascertain what, to the best of your knowledge, may be waiting for us on the other side of the door."

"That'll be why she called us, Ollie," said Raff, smiling at Dolly again. "She doesn't know, does she. Are you coming, mate?"

They stepped into Maurice's small garden. Raff beat on the door, just as she had done a little earlier. "Mr Bousquet?" he shouted. "Are you in, sir?"

Dolly watched and waited.

"Mr Bousquet? Police here." Sergeant Williams peered through the front window and then put his mouth to the letterbox. "Mr Bousquet," he shouted. "We're here because your neighbour believes you may be hurt or in trouble. Are you all right in there? Are you able to come to the door?"

He waited a little longer and straightened up. "There doesn't appear to be anyone inside," he said to Dolly. "And you're correct — it's all neat and tidy. What time did you say you heard this fight?"

Dolly said: "About half an hour ago. Maybe a bit more. Oh, wait!" She pointed to the old, grey net curtain upstairs. "It twitched!" she cried. "He's up there! *Maurice? MAURICE!* Come out, will you? Are you all right?"

"Mr Bousquet? Police here. Can you come to the door please?"

"Is he obliged to?" Dolly whispered. "I mean, does he *have* to come to the door? If the police ask?"

"Of course not," Raff Williams replied. "But he doesn't know that, does he?"

"He might," Dolly said.

This time Ollie, the younger man, rapped on the door. "Come to the door please, Mr Bousquet. We need to check you're OK."

A long wait.

Dolly whispered: "Can I get you a cup of tea?"

"He's coming," said Ollie. "Wait there."

Dolly edged forward to see. As Maurice's door pulled open, she was standing quietly beside Raff Williams — at such an angle that she was the first to glimpse his face.

The stench of tarnish caught in her throat.

Maurice looked puffy and ill and angry and frightened, and on his face —

"*Oh my —*" she muttered.

And on Maurice's face: a gash above the right eye, a swollen lip, the imprint of a knuckle, and a flap of seeping skin where a ring had hit the cheekbone . . . And somewhere nearby, inside a mountain of voluptuous flesh . . . *BOOM* . . . a tiny heart had stopped beating. Dolly was never so sure of anything.

She staggered backwards and was caught in the strong arms of Sergeant Raphael Williams.

"I am asking you politely to get the hell off my property," Maurice said. "All of you." He glared at Dolly. "Get off my property, or I'll call the police. Ha ha ha."

That was all he said. "And then he closed the door.

So the fight had been real enough. And the wounds, of course, she had seen before, on Nikki's face, on that sweltering day in the summer. What did it mean? She simply didn't know. Sometimes, these things meant nothing at all: an interruption in normal service, nothing more than that: a moment for Dolly to hold on tight, while the ground shook beneath her. What did it mean? *She didn't know.* But after this, the question of Nikki's whereabouts could no longer be ignored, if only for Dolly's peace of mind.

Dolly stared at the closed door, her body shaking. Raff Williams took one of her hands.

"Are you all right, Mrs Greene?"

"Miss Greene," she said. "Actually *Ms* Greene. Dolly. I'm Dolly." She pulled her hand away, embarrassed. "There's a problem, officers . . . How can I explain this? You'll think I'm insane. I had a visitor, a client, just at the end of the summer — in that terribly hot spell, do you remember?"

"I remember," Raff nodded. "A few weeks back."

"It was unbearably hot, remember? I should think you were suffering, in those heavy vests. We were all suffering . . . I should explain I'm a Tarot card reader.

That's my job. People come to see me and I read their cards for them."

A pause. A tiny sigh from Ollie, the younger man. He looked at his partner. "Who's copping the paperwork on this then, Raff? Think we need to report it? I'm not sure there's anything to report."

"No, but you don't understand . . ." said Dolly. "There's so much to report." Another pause. Dolly knew how it sounded. She was conscious of the two men waiting, indulging her — but she had to ask: "The pregnant woman from the river who washed up at Kew the other day. Tell me, has she been identified yet?"

"Not that I am aware," Raff Williams said. "I wasn't aware she was pregnant. You know anything about her, Ollie?"

Ollie shrugged. "The floater down at Kew? No one knows much about her. Drunk, I presume. They usually are . . ."

"You're going to think I'm crazy. But I think she's connected . . ."

"Oh yes?" replied Raff, very politely. "How's that then?"

Just then the men's radios burst into life. Someone needed them, somewhere else.

Raff Williams smiled at her, not quite hiding his relief. He tucked away his notebook. "Any more problems, Dolly," he said, "don't hesitate to call us. All right?"

"All right. But what if —" Dolly asked.

Ollie, walking backwards, raised his hand and made the shape of a phone. "999," he mouthed.

"I know, but —"

"It's our manor," Raff said. "There aren't that many of us on this patch any more . . . Any problems, chances are it'll be us two again . . . But with luck, you won't be needing us, right?"

"No. Yes. Of course not . . ."

They were gone.

CHAPTER
SEVENTEEN

Pippa's reaction to her mother's otherworldly insights tended to be fairly consistent: she would never — quite — admit to believing in any of it, and she never allowed Dolly to read her cards. Pippa maintained this was because they gave Dolly the opportunity to ask too many nosey questions. But it was also (Dolly rightly suspected) because the truth of the cards sometimes disconcerted her. Not that it mattered much anyway: mother and daughter skirted around the issue, a mutually indulgent truce having been drawn between them long ago.

But this latest thing, this possible murder on their own doorstep, Dolly couldn't skirt around or keep to herself. When Pippa returned from college that evening, she told her about the image of Nikki by the riverside, and her conviction that Nikki was dead; and about the little heart that stopped beating, and about Maurice and Nikki both bearing the same facial wounds.

"All right," Pippa began patiently (it had been a long day and she was hungry), "so in the vision this afternoon, were you absolutely certain —"

"It wasn't a *vision*," snapped Dolly. "For goodness' sake. Don't be silly. I'm not Jesus."

Pippa snorted.

"Yes. Thank you. Very funny." Dolly felt stupid: out of sorts, and out of her depth: "I'm just saying . . ." And then she burst into tears.

This was highly unusual. Dolly rarely cried. So Pippa cancelled her plans and the two of them set out on an early evening trudge through the streets of Barnes, Mortlake, Sheen and possibly beyond, in search of a woman whose surname and address neither knew, and whom Dolly had convinced herself was already dead.

"What will we do if we find her?" Pippa asked, forty-five minutes later. They were walking past a block of flats on the Lonsdale Road, and — not entirely surprisingly — they'd not spotted her yet. "I think we need to formulate a plan, Mum. If we're going to pretend we're detectives. The detectives on TV always have plans."

"Of course they do. Because they're supposed to solve the whole bloody mystery in under an hour, *with the ad breaks* — and Pippa, without wishing to state the obvious, they're detectives. I am a Tarot reader and you — are a barmaid/student of environmental marketing. Of course we haven't got a plan. But no one else is doing anything, and if she's been murdered —"

"If she's been murdered," said Pippa. "I'm still not sure how it's any of our business."

"It's our business," said Dolly, "if Maurice is getting his face bashed in as a consequence of it."

"But he isn't . . . I thought that was a — not a vision, but a — you know, like a — well, a *vision*, Mum. Did you actually see the wounds on his face, or did you imagine them?"

"THAT'S THE WHOLE POINT, PIPPA," shouted Dolly. "I DON'T KNOW!"

It was one thing, tramping the streets in search of visions, to help her mother feel better. It was quite another, getting yelled at in the process. Without another word, Pippa turned back towards Tinderbox Lane.

"I'm sorry," said Dolly. "Pippa, I'm so sorry."

"Forget it."

Dolly followed her, apologising.

"Forget it, Mum. It doesn't matter. This is stupid. That's all. It's stupid, and it's a waste of time. If the woman has been murdered, and I'm sure she hasn't —"

"Someone has, Pippa!"

"— Then I'm sure the police will find out about it soon enough. *It's not our problem.* As you say, you're a Tarot reader, and I'm a student. And I've got a lot of work to do, and I'm hungry, and I want to go home. Are you coming?"

"Wait!" said Dolly.

Pippa stopped. She waited. But in the end, Dolly couldn't think of anything to add. Pippa was right. They were on a hiding to nothing, out here. What could they possibly achieve? She shrugged, deflated, and they continued homeward.

By the time they reached Tinderbox Lane they were more cheerful, looking forward to risotto for supper, and discussing which of them most resembled Sherlock Holmes. Or Simon Templar. Or the guy from *Hawaii Five-O*. Their cultural references didn't overlap much, but both were fighting their cases energetically enough that they didn't notice Ade Bousquet coming the other way. Pippa smacked right into him.

"I'm so sorry," Pippa said.

He ignored her. He smiled at Dolly over Pippa's head. It wasn't a nice smile.

"You feeling better, Mystic Meg?"

She was struggling to come up with a suitably tart response, and he was watching the struggle when, from inside his jacket pocket, a mobile began to ring to a song: *Gimme Gimme Gimme (A Man After Midnight)*.

He didn't move to answer it.

He looked at Pippa. Possibly even licked his lips. "That your daughter?"

Finally, he reached into his pocket, and cut off the sound. "She looks like you, Dolly."

"She looks like her dad," Dolly said. She was staring at his pocket: "Was that —"

"It was," he said. "My mobile. And I need to take that call. See you later, girls."

Pippa watched him leave, jaw a little slack: "Bloody hell Mum —"

"Stop dribbling, Pippa."

"What? I wasn't. But you never told me he was so gorgeo —"

"Don't you realise what's going on?"

". . . Well . . . that *was* Ade, I presume?"

"Yes! Of course that was Ade! And that was *Nikki's* phone! *Ade* has *Nikki's* phone. *Nikki's* gone missing. And Maurice — is fighting with Ade, and talking about dead bodies washing up in Kew. Don't you see, Pippa? Can't you see what's going on?"

Pippa sighed: "No, Miss Marple, I cannot. But I agree with you, he doesn't much look like a plumber. Let's go home and have dinner."

CHAPTER
EIGHTEEN

There was a time when Raff Williams's motor-home had been his pride and joy: the greatest extravagance of his life. He and his wife bought it, new, in 1995, for a princely £15,000. Shelley had inherited £9,000 from her mother, and Raff had saved £6,000 for a rainy day. Such a happy day it was, the rainy day they spent it. Raff said he was going to take a sabbatical from the Force (now called the Service), and he and Shelley and their little boy, Sam, then aged seven, were going to travel the coasts of Europe, learning how to surf.

It all went wrong. Mostly it was Raff's fault. He was invited to take his detective exams. This was the very thing he had always wanted; the reason he ever joined the Force. But then they told him he had to wait — too many others had applied. They put him off (he was young). They told him, not this year but next . . . so he postponed the great departure. His wife, meanwhile, was restless — and, always, tremendously flirtatious. Men adored her. Which, if Raff was honest, was one of the reasons he wanted to whisk her away in a motor-home in the first place. So he could have her to himself. Him and Sam. He used to feel jealous, the way his colleagues lit up when she came in the room. But he kept it buttoned up. Raff kept too much buttoned up.

He was right to have been jealous, in any case. Shelley was irresistible. And there was her husband, buttoning everything up, working so hard to get his detective exams. And there was the motor-home (with all her savings tied in) gathering rust outside the door. And there was Sam at big school already, and no sign of another baby on the way . . . The school advertised a vacancy for a classroom assistant but she didn't apply because she believed, at that point, that she was still waiting for the road trip. Raff kept saying — yes, yes, *very soon.* Let me just get these exams under my belt . . .

And then Shelley did what any restless, gorgeous, neglected wife would do: she had an affair. Even that might have been tolerable. The affair might have simply blown itself out. Raff might have pulled his finger out and taken the sabbatical. Problem was, the man she chose to have the affair with was an inspector at Raff's station. The wife of a fellow officer caught them spooning in a pub car park in Twickenham, and she told her husband, who felt duty-bound to inform every police officer in the Met. *Inspector Writhley was knobbing Raff Williams's wife. Poor old Raff.*

In many ways Shelley and the inspector were a much better match. Shelley liked dressing up, and the inspector (now a chief inspector, and very soon to be a superintendent) loved to go to fundraising balls, where he could ingratiate himself with his senior colleagues. If Shelley thought Raff was ambitious . . . Nevertheless, at least the chief inspector — he was called Stephen — at least Stephen's ambitions allowed Shelley to dress up and join in. Stephen and Shelley lived in a smart house in Surrey, with white carpets in the hall, and a conservatory at the back, and a cupboard full of golf clubs. Guests had to leave their shoes by the front door. And Shelley liked all that.

Raff emerged from the bust-up less successfully. He learned the truth about the affair just a couple of days before he was due to sit his detective exams. He failed them. And there is a moral in the story, about ambition and selfishness and the price of getting ahead, which was not lost on Raff; which he remembered at the end of every shift, when he unlocked the door to his motor-home.

Once the story broke, and it was official that the inspector wasn't simply knobbing Raff's wife, but nabbing her, there were heated discussions among senior officers as to which of the men should be transferred.

Inspector Writhley fell on his sword. They offered him chief inspector at New Malden and after *much* hand-wringing, he and Shelley agreed that he should take it. Raff kept his job and moved into the RV. Stephen left his wife and three teenage children, and set up house with Shelley and Sam. Shelley would have liked to have had more children, but it never happened. She drew solace, as far as she could, from shopping, and flirting, and being everybody's favourite gel . . . And though she was happy with Stephen, there was part of her which would always love Raff a little bit more . . . because in Raff's heart, at the core (though she wouldn't have put it like this), there was always the same note playing: pure, incorruptible, unbreakable. Shelley loved Raff. And Raff — well, after so many years pounding the streets, confronted each day by fresh dredges of humanity; the ugliest, the cruellest, the stupidest — Raff wasn't sure if he could love anyone any more. He didn't believe he had it in him. Except he loved Sam. Sam was what he lived for. Everything else pretty much passed in a blur.

Raff was on early turns this week. The day he met Dolly he'd been working since 7 a.m., so by the time he was called out to Tinderbox Lane it was almost the end of his shift. He and Ollie had spent a couple of hours on paperwork at the station. Now it was 6 p.m. and Raff was back at the RV — not so much his pride and joy any more, but his home. He could have afforded to upgrade into bricks and mortar by now — but what would be the point? The RV worked. And one day, he told himself, he might even take it on that road trip.

Sam was coming to dinner, as he did once a fortnight, every Thursday. Raff was cooking him the same dish he always cooked: because once, when Sam was about nine, he'd told his dad it was his favourite, and that was that. Neither Sam nor Raff ever thought to confirm whether it remained so. (Which it didn't, by the way.) Who cared? When Raff and Sam got together, they ate shepherd's pie. And afterwards, they went to the Sun Inn on Barnes Pond, found a quiet corner, far from the big-bellied bankers and their brassy blonde wives . . . and talked about football. So it is, so it was, and so it ever more would be. Or at any rate, until one of them got it together to find a girlfriend.

Sam was doing a PhD at King's College, London, in an aspect of astrophysical science, though Sam was incapable of explaining which. His father asked him often, and Sam tried the best he could, but the task was beyond him. Within a sentence or two, he would nose-dive into a world of assumed knowledge and scientific jargon which left no one any wiser, and everyone considerably more dispirited. It was a shame. Raff would have loved to understand what his son was working on, and Sam would have loved to be able to tell him. In the meantime, Raff's pride in his son's academic brilliance was something which, though he didn't bang on about it, got him out of bed each morning; fuelled him through all the agonies of a lonely middle age.

The RV smelled of burned onions. Raff had been cooking shepherd's pie all these years, but he still didn't do it well. He persevered. Burned onions . . . salt and pepper . . . Worcester sauce and mincemeat . . . sweet chilli, ketchup . . . bit of Branston . . . some Flora . . . *you could never go wrong with Flora* . . . Sam was sitting at the small, fold-out table behind him, drinking beer and reading the sports pages. A peaceful silence rested between them.

Raff's mind grazed over the day. It seemed that all his thoughts led back to Tinderbox Lane.

The elderly gentleman with the wounded face who had eventually come to the door was presumably the father of Ade Bousquet. A nasty piece of work. Ade

Bousquet had been "of interest" to the police since he was a teenager. He still was; but to different police now. He'd made money somewhere along the line, and he and his crimes had moved up the hierarchy. Beneath the old man's bruises, Raff thought he could see a resemblance between the two. Other than that, the incident was nothing remarkable: a domestic spat — with the victim (assuming he was the victim) unwilling to involve the police, and a busybody neighbour sticking her nose in. Except she *wasn't* a busybody. She was — Raff smiled into his frying pan . . . She was lovely.

"What are you smiling about?" Sam's voice interrupted him.

"Hm? Oh, nothing. You all right for beer? I thought we might nip out for a pint at the Sun Inn after. What do you think?"

"Sounds a bit radical."

Raff looked up from his cooking. Chuckled. "Actually, I was thinking about a lady I met this afternoon . . . Name of Dolly."

"Funny name."

"She was a Tarot reader, believe it or not."

"A Tarot reader?"

"Don't suppose a scientist like you would have much time for all that nonsense," he added. But the thing he kept thinking about, the reason his mind kept returning to Tinderbox Lane — it was the way she had reacted when she spied the old man's face. As if she had seen a ghost. But she hadn't seen a ghost. What exactly had she seen? "A lot of mumbo jumbo, of course," Raff muttered again. "Lovely girl though . . . lady. Woman. Whatever you're supposed to call her. I was hoping she might need to call us again."

"Her address'll be on your big brother computer, won't it? If you don't already know where she lives. You should call on her, Dad. Go on."

"Well, maybe," he said. ". . . How's your mum?"

"Buying a little apartment in Greece. Holiday let. Super cheap, apparently."

"Oh, yes."

"Should keep her busy for a bit."

"Hmm," he nodded, but he wasn't really listening. The Smash potato was ready. He plopped it on top of the meat and Flora mix, and flattened it down with a spoon, flat enough to fit beneath the mini grill. "You ready, then, Sam? Hope you're hungry."

"Actually," said Sam, "I meant to tell you. I've gone vegetarian."

"You *what?*"

They laughed.

Sam made the same feeble joke about being a vegetarian every time they sat down to eat. It was the closest they got to saying grace.

Raff and Sam weren't terribly interested in food — which, looking at the shepherd's pie Raff had just placed in front of them, was a fortunate thing.

CHAPTER
NINETEEN

Maurice and Dolly had been living side-by-side for seven peaceful years with never a sour word exchanged, and now they could barely speak. Maurice Bousquet, twiddling his thumbs that afternoon, alone at Number Three, discovered, to his surprise, that he minded. Their argument was obviously mostly Dolly's fault, but on reflection, Maurice began to suspect he might also have to accept a fraction of the blame. He had been rude to her once, when she came round to read his cards, and again, when she called the police.

She should not have called the police. People should never call the police to other people's houses. That was basic: a number one rule for getting along with the human race. *Never tell tales. Never involve the police.*

On the other hand, maybe Dolly didn't realise that, being white and middle class.

In any case he was fond of her. He missed their good-natured banter over the garden fence. And now he could hear her next door, shuffling around. She'd just switched on Radio 4, which meant she was on her own. It was a beautiful, mellow autumn day, and it had been a peculiar week. He *felt* peculiar: half terrified, half elated. No — He corrected himself. He felt *completely normal*. Except for the damned headache.

Actually, what he most felt like, on this mellow autumn day, was a trip to the pub, with Dolly.

Her back window was open. So was his. He shuffled out into his barren, mud-patch of a garden. "DOLLY! Hey, Dolly," he yelled over the fence, "what are you doing in there? It's a beautiful day. Want to come with me to the Bull's Head?"

He waited.

"Dolly?"

Dolly heard him all right. She was sitting at her broom cupboard table, mid-flow, scribbling notes for her talk. The date had been fixed and it was only a week away:

TAROT TALKS — AN INTRODUCTION TO
THE MAGICAL LANGUAGE OF THE TAROT,
BY DOLLY GREENE
... but most compelling are those cards that, when shuffling, jump unbidden out of the pack. The "jumpers", we call them. Or the "lively cards". Never ignore the "lively cards". These cards aren't simply talking to you, they're shouting ...

And so was Maurice. "DOLLY? Are you in there, darling?"

She smiled. Cheeky sod, calling her darling. He'd been so damned rude to her lately, she didn't feel inclined to reply ... Well, maybe she did. There were still so many unanswered questions ... and, really, she hated this new hostility between them. She waited. If he asked again, and *nicely*, she reckoned she'd probably accept the invitation.

"Dolly? *Come on!* Ha ha ha. I know you can hear me! I've got a £20 note burning a hole in my pocket. *I'm buying.* Are you coming or aren't you?"

"Funny time of day to be drinking, Maurice," she shouted, staying at her little table.

"What's that? Ha ha ha. My God, Dolly! First you call the police on me. Now you're telling me when I can and can't drink. Are you coming to the Bull or aren't you? I'm not asking again."

That annoyed her — enough to get her up from the table and speak to him directly. She poked her head out of the back door. "I called the police," she said, "because some poor sod was getting kicked to pieces in your house, and I heard it happening." She looked at Maurice, face all battered and bruised. She hadn't laid eyes on him since he'd slammed the door on her, two days earlier. And judging by those bruises, that poor sod was you. And by the way I like to think if *you* heard *me* getting beaten up in my own house, *you* might try to do something to stop it."

Maurice said, "Ha ha ha", but only because he couldn't think of anything else. She had a point. What was she meant to have done? Under similar circumstances, what would *he* have done?

He might have called Ade. Perhaps. He certainly wouldn't have called the police.

"Never," he said, "you *never* call the police on a black man, Dolly. You understand that. You *never call the police on a black man.*"

"Well," said Dolly. She felt foolish. Maybe he had a point. What did she know about being a black man in London, after all? "Well, I'm sorry. I am sorry, Maurice. If you think I was interfering. But I thought you were in danger."

He nodded. "Thank you," he said. "Thank you for apologising. And thank you — I suppose you didn't mean any harm. Just —" (he couldn't stop himself). "Just — *never do it again*."

"OK. All right."

They smiled at each other. It was nice. Really, it was lovely to be friends again.

"How are you anyway?" Dolly asked him. "You look a bit yellow. And that cut on your face — Did you clean it? You should, you know. Your face looks like a football, Maurice. A football with jaundice. Are you all right?"

"Ha ha ha." He shook his head. "I feel like shit, Dolly. Truth be told. I'd feel a lot better after a few drinks at the Bull. You want to come?"

Dolly didn't have any clients booked. "I'll get my bag. Wait there . . ."

"But none of your magic cards!" he shouted, as she disappeared back into the house. "And no nosey questions, all right? Just some nice, easy chit-chat."

Like hell, thought Dolly. But she kept it to herself.

CHAPTER
TWENTY

It was the pub where Pippa worked, three nights a week. This afternoon, however, it was fairly empty, not too noisy, softly lit: all very pleasant. Even so, for a while, Maurice and Dolly were on edge in each other's company, and they drank faster than their doctors would have recommended.

For a while, Dolly couldn't look at Maurice's smashed-up face without longing to ask so many questions . . . but each time she thought she was ready to broach one, she remembered how he had thrown her cards off the kitchen table. She remembered the resin burning into the Ace of Pentacles, and she lost her nerve.

They discussed their new neighbour, Rosie Buck. Neither had taken much of a liking to her, and once that had been safely established, what with the alcohol, and because it gave them something to bond over, they didn't hold back. Dolly told him the nicknames Pippa had given to Rosie and her husband . . . and Maurice laughed harder than Dolly had ever seen him laugh before. He wiped tears from his eyes.

"I tell you what, Dolly, you've cheered me up. I was feeling very low."

"I'm not surprised," said Dolly, carefully. "It's been a difficult few days."

"*Ha ha ha*," he said, laughing for real, for once, laughing so his shoulders shook. "*Heart Attack Hubby and Mrs Frosty-Fuck!* Your Pippa is quite a character, isn't she? I dread to think what name she has for me!"

"She's very naughty," said Dolly, with a pinch of pride. "She's young. So — you know — there's a toughness, isn't there, when you're young. You don't quite realise how difficult it is for everyone."

"You think it's difficult for Mrs Frosty-Fuck?" He started laughing again.

"I think it's difficult for everyone, Maurice." Her glass was empty. "Shall we have another? Is there any money left? Or have you spent it? I suppose it's my turn . . ."

Slowly Maurice pulled out another £20 and dropped it on to the table between them. He grimaced at her, the most melancholy of grins. "Let's just keep going, shall we . . .?"

"Good heavens," she said. "What's got into you, Maurice? Are you sure?"

He shuffled to the bar and returned with another round, spilling a little more of Dolly's cider with each step. "You say life is difficult for Mrs Frosty," he continued, "but her hubby creams it in, Dolly. And I know that because my boy has had a few business dealings with him. Ade says that man is as slippery as a nun's . . . and coming from Ade . . ." He took a slurp of his beer, creating a small puddle of lager on the table in the process . . . "Ha ha ha. Coming from *Adrian* . . ."

114

A pause.

Maurice replaced his glass, carefully, into the heart of the puddle. "*Ha ha ha,*" he said. He winked at Dolly. "Damn right he's my boy, Dolly Greene . . . Doesn't make me proud of him."

"I'm sure you're proud," she murmured, and waited. He wanted to talk. She could sense it.

"I'm quite certain I'm *not* proud. Thank you. That man only thinks about one thing. *Money.* Actually, two things. Money, and his prick . . . He's a nasty, *nasty* . . ." Maurice gazed over the top of his glass in morose silence. ". . . And as for that dreadful woman . . ."

"Which woman?"

Maurice looked at Dolly as if she was stupid. "Don't your cards tell you anything, Dolly?"

"Yes. No. I mean, yes of course they do — Do you mean Nikki?"

"He can't *stand* her! Ha ha ha. Any more than I can. But say what you will about Ade — and I do, Dolly. He looks out for the boy. Which is more than his mother does."

"You mean — which woman, Maurice? Do you mean Nikki? Yes. Of course you do. But — what boy? You're not telling me Nikki and Ade —"

"— Begat Toby. Ha ha ha."

"Begat *Toby*?" Dolly repeated slowly.

"Or so she says."

"Maurice! You're all family! You're telling me Nikki's *son* is your grandchild?"

115

He shrugged: looked a tiny bit uncomfortable. "If you believe anything that female has to say — which I do not, Dolly. And nor should you. She fobbed my son off with one of these DNA tests — and the idiot swallowed it hook, line and — whatever. Ha ha ha. *Hooker*, line and stinker, I should say. *The boy's white as a snowdrop*, Dolly. He looks more like Prince Harry than he looks like any grandson of mine . . . But if Ade wants to believe the boy's his — it's not my problem, is it?"

"But there was a DNA . . ."

Maurice shrugged. "Or so she says," he said again.

". . . And they all live together?" Dolly asked.

"*No!* God no . . . No. She does her own thing. Adrian does his own thing. They all do their own thing . . . The boy lives with Adrian, so far as I know. She's a *dreadful* woman, Dolly. Ha ha ha. Even her own son can't stand her." He fell silent. "But my goodness," he added. There was a gleam in his eye. "She likes it in the bedroom, Dolly. That's *her* problem. You see? Like those Hollywood stars, she's a sex-o-holic . . . Don't get many of those," he added after a moment's thought. "In the female form, do you?"

"So — Are you saying you and your son . . . *share* her?"

"No!" Maurice sounded shocked. "That's disgusting, Dolly."

"Well — all right then . . . I'm not sure I understand."

"Nobody *shares* Nikki. Or — that is — everybody shares her. She's a hooker, Dolly. More or less. Ha ha ha. Don't tell me you haven't worked *that* out?"

116

"Of course I'd worked that out —" Dolly said quickly, blushing scarlet, because of course she hadn't (despite Pippa having spotted it and pointed it out to her within five seconds of their meeting). "I'm just — a bit confused . . ."

"Adrian doesn't want her. He can't stand her. But she wants Adrian. All right? And in her teeny-tiny mind, she's somehow figured it that if she sleeps with me . . . ha ha ha . . . it'll get her back with Adrian. Or something like that. God, Dolly, *I* don't know. All I know is, she lets me . . ." No polite way of putting it sprang to mind, so he left it blank. "Y'know. From time to time. And she doesn't charge me for it, Dolly. So." He shrugged.

Dolly nodded. In seven years of Tarot reading, there wasn't much about human behaviour that shocked her any more. Even so. Maurice was hardly presenting himself — or any of his "family" — in a very flattering light. "It's a funny sort of relationship though," she said carefully. "Is it what Nikki wants?"

"What Nikki wants . . ." Maurice repeated, blandly. "Oh, she wants Adrian of course. I told you that. Ha ha ha. It's all about Ade, for Nikki — and in the meantime, she'll fuck *anything*, Dolly! Believe me. *Even better* if it's for cash! I don't pay her, mind. But that's because she thinks . . ." He waved the explanation away. ". . . Whatever the hell she thinks. And Ade won't touch her. Didn't she tell you about it? Didn't it come up in your —" he pointed dismissively at the lager-splattered table top, "Tarot cards?"

Dolly said: "A lot of men came up in her cards."

Maurice nodded. "Nikki's not important, anyway. It's about me and Ade, really ..." He nodded to himself and said it again. "It's about me and Ade ... I said to Ade, I said, '*If ever I win the lottery*, I'll take the old cow off you for good.' Ha ha ha. He went *apeshit*, Dolly! I'm not joking. Never saw that boy so mad ..." Maurice seemed to consider this, to be torn between confusion and laughter. "But he doesn't even *want* her! *Nobody* wants her, Dolly! I was just messing around."

"There's no love lost between you and Ade, then."

"Ha!"

"And all over Nikki?"

"No!" he said impatiently. "I told you! Nikki's just ..." He was going to say "a woman", but somehow, miraculously, he pulled back. "It's got nothing to do with Nikki. It's about me and Ade ... We've always been at each other's throats."

He fell silent, lost in unhappy memories. Finally, Dolly said: "Why are you telling me this, Maurice?"

Maurice was staring at the rim of his glass again. He heard Dolly's question, but he didn't feel like answering.

Dolly tried again. "First you told me Ade wasn't your son. Then you told me you didn't know anyone called Nikki. But you do know her. Very well indeed. So —"

"But I never recommended *you* to her. I have never mentioned you to Nikki. So someone else did."

"Oh, come on —"

"She could've just said she'd found you off the computer, couldn't she? Like everyone finds everything these days. So why didn't she say that?" He shook his head, defeated by Nikki's dimness. "She thought she was being clever, ha ha ha. Nikki, being *clever*! That'll be the day."

Dolly sighed: he was talking to himself, it seemed. It was quite annoying. "Maurice, if you're just going to talk in riddles then we'll be better off discussing the weather. Or they've got Scrabble behind the bar."

"I'll tell you who it was recommended you to the silly cow," he said, and started laughing. "What did Pippa call him again? That's who would've told her, I'll bet you. Because I certainly didn't. I told you I saw him down at the Flag a few weeks back."

Dolly laughed. "You didn't tell me anything of the kind."

"Didn't I?" He frowned. "Who did I tell, then? I've seen him in there a few times, Dolly."

Dolly had been inside the Flag only once. It was during her first year as a professional Tarot reader. She'd signed up with an events organiser, and been hired for the evening to sit in a corner and read cards, but — as she should have known they would — the punters blithely ignored her all night, preferring to stick their tongues into each other's mouths, throats, and, as the evening progressed, shirts, bras, flies . . . the pub had a sleazy reputation, to put it mildly. Normally, if there was an entertainer, it was a stripper, not a Tarot reader. Dolly would have refused to go back, if she'd ever been invited, but she never was.

"You mean the Flag Club, I presume . . ." Dolly laughed again. "What were you doing there, Maurice? Second thoughts, don't answer that."

"Ha ha ha. What was I doing? I'm a single man, Dolly. What was *Nikki* doing there? Well I think we can all work that out. Nikki's always there in any case. More to the point, you might ask yourself, what was Fraser Buck doing in there? With poor Mrs Frosty-Fuck, all on her lonesome back at Windy Ridge, climbing the walls for a bit of trouser action for herself *ha ha ha* . . ." He shook his head, started laughing again, his slim body rocking with pleasure. "Mrs Frosty-Fuck and Heart Attack Hubby . . . ha ha ha . . . '*Heart Attack Hubby*' had his head buried in somebody's beautiful breasts, that's what *he* was doing at the Flag Club a few weeks back. Oh my goodness . . . I only realised it was him when his bald head came up for air. All sweaty and shiny. Why do men like him shave their heads, Dolly? Do they think it makes them look younger?" Maurice shook his head in dismay. "Even at the Flag Club there are lines, Dolly. You've got to have *lines* . . ."

Dolly said: ". . . You're saying *Nikki* . . . and *Fraser Buck*?"

"No! I'm not saying it. In so many words. No — I'm saying, I wouldn't be surprised. Since she's in there half the time, and he's in there, and . . ." He laughed, a merrier laugh than usual, "I would have said they were a match made in heaven, Dolly. Wouldn't you?"

"Even so," said Dolly. "You're saying *you* and Nikki . . . and *Ade* and Nikki . . ."

"Ade won't go near her, Dolly. That's the problem. Her problem, I should say. Not anyone else's, clearly . . . Ha ha ha. Certainly not Ade's."

120

"My oh my," Dolly shook her head. "A busy lady!" *Lots of men in her life. And every one of them causing her strife.*

"All I'm saying is, it wasn't me who recommended you. Why would I? I'll be honest with you, until the other day I wasn't even sure exactly what it was you did. The quiet chap at the end of the lane — Terry — he said something about you being some sort of witch —"

"He did, did he?"

"Well — he didn't mean it badly. But as for me, recommending your Tarot reading services — I didn't have that information to recommend, Dolly. That information would have come direct from old Frosty Buck. Fuck. Mrs Frosty-Fuck . . . *ha ha ha* . . . The wife would've known. She's a nosey little thing. So. She would have informed her husband, wouldn't she? And he would have told Nikki. That's what I'm telling you."

"But you still haven't told me *why*, Maurice. Why are you telling me all this?"

He shrugged. "Why not?"

"That's not an answer."

"Well it's my answer."

But she had stopped listening. She sat back, feeling sick.

Before her eyes, Nikki's Death card shimmered. And, slowly, that bloated body they found down at Kew rolled over on to its back, eyes wide open . . . Dolly gasped.

"Maurice," she said. "Do you know where Nikki is now? Have you seen her? I've been looking for her . . ."

"I haven't seen her for weeks Dolly . . . Last I heard, she'd gone on one of her little walkabouts."

"Her walkabouts?"

Maurice shrugged.

"Does Ade know where she is?"

"Well I doubt it, unless he's killed her. Ha ha ha. In which case I'm not sure I blame him, Dolly. Frankly. The way she puts herself about." And then he paused, and he cracked up with laughter all over again. "I should think you're better off asking old Hubby Frosty-Fuck . . ."

But Dolly didn't see the funny side, not any more. She swallowed her drink and declared it was time she went home. Maurice tried, somewhat half-heartedly, to dissuade her; and when he failed, announced he would head on to the Flag by himself.

Back out on the street they paused to say their farewells. Maurice, if he was going to the Flag, would be heading in the opposite direction. But he was swaying pretty badly. He could barely stand. He seemed far drunker than he ought to have been after only four pints: three and a half, if you took in the spillage. "Well, good night then," Dolly said briskly. "Have a good evening. Good luck . . . And thanks for all the drinks. Maybe I'll see you at my Tarot Talk on Friday. You know where to come, don't you?"

"You bet," he said.

She might have turned at this point, but he looked so despondent. Also, as if he might be about to pass out. "Are you all right, Maurice?"

"You bet," he said again. And then: "Shall we walk back together Dolly? I don't think I can face it."

It was a twenty-minute trek back to Tinderbox Lane, along the same noisy road that Dolly walked to the shops. Neither she nor Maurice could muster the energy to say anything loud enough to be heard over the traffic, and so they trudged on, longing for their separate beds. The carefree mood was gone.

As they turned into Tinderbox Lane, Dolly caught the smell of tarnish once again — not from the house, but from Maurice: stronger than ever now — part rust, part rotting animal matter — a little sweet, a little metallic. She asked him: "Can you really not smell it?" But by then, he was lost to his own ruminations, and he didn't bother to reply.

They stopped outside his garden gate. It had started to rain. "That's odd," he said, sounding more alert. "Look, Dolly." The lights were on in his front room. "I never leave them on."

They stood together in silence, watching. It was true. Maurice would never have been so wasteful.

"*Maurice*, I think the curtain just moved," Dolly whispered. "Do you think someone is in there?"

"Probably a breeze. He probably left the back door open."

"He? *Who?*"

"Ade." He shook his head and chuckled, grim and gleeful, both at once. "He'll have ransacked the place I expect."

"*What?*"

"Well — good night Dolly. What a lovely afternoon."
He opened his gate and walked towards the front door
— a short walk, in a reasonably straight line: he had
sobered up on the journey home.

"Are you sure you don't want me to come in with
you?" Dolly asked.

He didn't reply.

She felt a chill pass through her, as if — what? She
didn't know. "Give me a shout, won't you, if you need
anything?"

He closed the door without replying.

CHAPTER
TWENTY-ONE

She waited in the rain, but Maurice didn't come out again. She heard him moving about, and then the light downstairs went off, and the light upstairs went on. It seemed everything was fine. She carried on home.

And then the following day she was busy: too busy to worry about Maurice and his lights. In the morning she had three clients, one after the other, and in the afternoon she was out. She didn't think about him. She got home about six, lit a couple of scented candles to blur the smell of the tarnish, which seemed to have grown stronger while she was away, and ate some bread and butter.

She was on the phone with Sandra when she heard a knock. She said a hurried goodbye to her friend —

. . . And there he was.

Strong and tall and reassuring and friendly — and handsome — on her doorstep. In his uniform.

"Well, there's a sight for sore eyes!" she said. And then blushed, because of the uniform. *It was too obvious*. But he did look handsome.

Raff grinned. "Is it the uniform?" he said.

"No."

A ridiculous pause. Like a couple of teenagers. She wondered why he had come. She hadn't called the police — *had she?* No. Perhaps Maurice had called them, as some sort of impractical, practical joke. Ha ha ha. Retaliation for the last time.

They both started talking at once. Dolly said: "What can I do for you?", which didn't come out in the way she had hoped it would. Raff said, "Sorry to barge in on you like this . . ."

"Has something happened?"

"No," he said. "Not at all. I just — I was coming off shift. Look —" he indicated his pocket. "No radio."

"Oh!" She wasn't sure how that was significant, but she smiled, and invited him in.

Raff removed his hat. He accepted her offer of a cup of tea, if she was making one. (She was now.) While the kettle boiled she fussed around, decluttering the breakfast bar to make space for the hat. He was taller than she remembered. Taller than Professor Filthy, and broader, too. And yet, Dolly noted, something about the way he moved (or something) meant he didn't make the room feel too small just by being in it, as the professor did. On the contrary, he made it feel . . . Well now, *he made it feel just right*. She offered him biscuits, and then remembered she specifically hadn't got any, because of the ongoing battle with buxomness. "Actually I haven't got any. Are you hungry?"

He said not.

Another silence. Dolly made the tea and they settled down, one opposite the other at the breakfast bar. Dolly

126

smiled. "Well? Are you ever going to tell me why you're here?"

But he wouldn't be rushed. He took a sip of the tea, replaced it neatly on the counter, cleared his throat. "I didn't want to upset you," he said.

"Oh!"

"I'm not even sure I should be telling you this . . . but I have to admit, I'm intrigued. The lady you were talking about — the drowned lady down at Kew . . . You remember?"

"Of course I remember. What have you found out?"

"You seemed to think there might be some connection between the drowned lady and the *fracas* next door . . . Do you remember? I assume everything's settled down with the gentleman now, has it?"

"Yes. Thank you." Dolly felt a flutter of anxiety, remembering the state she had left him in. "But what about the drowned lady. Have you found out who she is?"

He shook his head. "We still don't know. Nobody fitting her description has recently been reported missing. But we had a fast track put on the PM because it looks a bit —"

"PM?"

"Sorry. Post mortem. Normally these things will take weeks, but when you get a victim as young as she was, you tend to wonder if there's suspicious circumstances. Plus there were some nasty marks on the body — the neck. Am I being too graphic?"

"No! Of course not. I'm — listening."

"As I say, I shouldn't be telling you this . . . but the fact is — when you were talking about her the other day, we hadn't had any results back. We didn't know anything. We still don't, frankly." He leaned forward. "But what we do know now, what the PM showed up — *you already knew it*. You kept referring to the 'pregnant' woman. Do you remember?"

"Well, she was pregnant, wasn't she? I think they said it on the news."

"Sixteen weeks. But we didn't know it, Dolly. She was a big woman — nobody could have known it until they opened her up . . ."

"Well you must have known it," said Dolly, uncomfortably. "Otherwise . . ."

"No. That's why I'm intrigued. How did you know?"

She shook her head, bewildered, embarrassed, a little frightened. She wished Sandra could be here to do the talking. "I don't know. I guess I didn't know — I just — I'm a bit intuitive sometimes. We all are, really. It's just a thing — like a musical note . . . That is . . . the notes are always playing, it's just a matter of taking the earplugs out . . . If that makes any sense."

". . . I don't think so, no."

"It doesn't really matter though, does it?"

"I don't know if it matters," Raff replied. "It depends."

Dolly did not want this conversation. It was the last conversation she wanted to have with this handsome policeman/new friend/whatever he was/might yet become. She did not want to scare him away. On the other hand, if she thought she knew something about the drowned woman that might possibly help someone — however insane it sounded, then she had to speak. She had to.

"The point is . . ." Dolly breathed in. "I think I know who the woman is. That is —" The words tumbled out. "I think it may be the same woman who came to see me a few weeks ago. I read her cards. She was only a client. The point is . . . I knew she was pregnant and I knew she was in danger, because I read it in her cards."

Raff concentrated on keeping his expression bland. He was quite good at this. "Oh yes," he said.

"'*Oh yes*'." Dolly rolled her eyes. She knew what "oh yes" meant, from the lips of a solid-looking, sensible policeman (in a smart uniform). She pressed on regardless. "Soon after I read her cards, she called me in tears. That was a few weeks back now. She said she was on her way back to see me. But she never turned up. She never called again. Nothing. I've called her — I don't know, maybe ten times or more. More. But she never answers. No one answers. The thing is . . . I think she has something to do with Ade Bousquet . . . She's the mother of his child. According to Maurice next-door. And I actually think Ade has her mobile phone . . ." Dolly tailed off. It sounded convoluted enough, even to her ears. "I'm assuming she hasn't been reported missing?"

Raff shook his head, but he pulled out his notebook. "Do you have a name and address? I can run a check tomorrow if you like. Either way, I'll drop in on her tomorrow. Put your mind at rest. And mine," he added.

"I would be very grateful," Dolly said. "She's called Nikki . . ." A long pause. "But I don't know her surname. She's sort of half living with Ade Bousquet's son, so far as I can make out — and I have tried to track down *his* address but he's not listed. I can't find him. That's it. All I have. Wherever she lives, I understand her bills get paid by Ade Bousquet. Or they did. According to Maurice. But it's actually very hard to believe anything Maurice says . . . This all probably sounds completely insane —"

Pippa burst in then, saving Raff a response. Pippa was already in full broadcast as she pushed open the front door: "Oh my *God* Mum. I just spotted that idiot, Heart Attack Hubby, literally *yelling* into his —" She stopped short. "Is that a copper?"

"No Pippa, he's a strip-o-gram," replied Dolly.

Pippa looked ready to believe her, which rather killed the joke.

"This is Raff, Pippa," Dolly added hurriedly. "The police officer who came round when Maurice was having his fight — remember? I mentioned him. *Them.* I mentioned the two police officers."

Raff nodded at Pippa, sensing mild hostility. He wasn't certain if it was the uniform, or his male presence in her mother's house. "Hello there. You must be —"

"Dolly's little sister," smirked Pippa.

"*Very funny.*" Dolly smiled. "This is my daughter, Pippa. Raff came round to tell me something about that woman who washed up at Kew."

130

"Oh yes. The floater. Isn't that what you coppers call them? Mum's got a lot of theories on the floater, haven't you, Mum. Have you told him yet?"

Dolly winced. "Don't be like that, Pippa. Really. You met her. She wasn't 'a floater', she was a human being, just like you. Don't be a smarty-pants."

Pippa took a beat. She nodded. "You're right. Sorry . . . I think I was showing off. For the strip-o-gram."

Raff chuckled. Couldn't help himself.

"Mum seemed to think she knew her, didn't you Mum? But *from what I heard* she was just a sort of random prostitute," Pippa continued. "Poor thing. Is it true? — Like, one of these sex-slaves, without any ID or anything. Is that right?"

"How do you know that?" Dolly and Raff asked at once.

"I don't," she shrugged. "It's just what people are saying. Plus, I told you, Mum, Simon's dad had an allotment down there. Are you guys drinking tea or what? I brought a bottle of wine back, if you want some. I'm *definitely* not going out tonight. I'm knackered, excuse the pun ha ha . . ."

"Well, I'll have a glass of wine," said Raff. He didn't even drink wine, normally. But there was nothing he had to get back to this evening, except the RV, and the boa. And the boa (Dorothy) would still be sleeping off yesterday's supper. In fact she could probably survive another week without laying eyes on him . . . Which, it crossed his mind, pretty much summed up Raff's relationship with the world. He brushed that thought aside. In any case, he felt comfortable being here, in this small and friendly kitchen — despite any gently hostile vibes emanating from Little Miss Smarty-Pants. After almost thirty years in this uniform, hostile vibes were like water off a duck's back. He looked at Dolly. "That is, I'd love a glass of wine if I'm not overstaying?"

"Certainly not!" said Dolly, also more quickly than she would have liked. "What a lovely idea, Pippa. Thank you. I'd love a glass, too."

Pippa glanced at Raff. "Are you off duty then? I didn't think coppers were supposed to drink."

"I am off duty, yes. On my way home."

"In a police car? With the flashing lights? You definitely shouldn't be drinking."

"Not in a police car, no. But thank you," Raff winked, "for your interest and concern."

Pippa wasn't remotely interested or concerned. No matter. She brought out three wine glasses and settled herself at the breakfast bar, on the last remaining stool. It was a squash.

"I don't mean to be a gooseberry," she said.

"Oh don't be such a baby," snapped her mother, embarrassed.

Pippa turned to Raff: "Has she read your cards, yet?"
He laughed. "No."

"She will — won't you Mum? She'll have them out before the end of this bottle. Mark my words."

"Crikey, I don't think so," he said. "I hope not . . ."

CHAPTER
TWENTY-TWO

Pippa didn't stick around long enough to find out. Somebody messaged her and then all of a sudden she was going out tonight, after all. It left Dolly and Raff alone, with the rest of the wine. Dolly was itching to read his cards but, after what Pippa had said, she decided to hold back. There was no rush. She offered to cook him pasta instead.

"Thank you, Dolly, no." He reached for his hat and stood up. "I should get going. Leave you in peace. I'm on early turn again tomorrow."

"Oh, that's a shame."

He wondered if she meant it. "But I'll run a check on this Nikki character for you. Find out what I can. And I'll have a little word with CID first thing. Cross the Ts and so on . . ."

"All right," Dolly said. At that instant she was more concerned about Raff staying for dinner than the CID, or even, truth be told, the welfare of the unmissed and unloved Nikki. "You do whatever you feel is necessary."

"I'll let you know what I find out."

"Thank you." Dolly smiled. He smiled. And there was definitely a moment: a beat when something between them was acknowledged. The words slipped out before she had time to stop them: "Are you sure you won't stay, Raff? I'm a very good cook."

He laughed. "I bet you are," he said. And hesitated . . . *Why was he even hesitating?* "Hell, why not, Dolly!" He placed his hat back on the counter. "I would love to stay for your pasta. If you're sure. *Why not?*"

It was set to be such a lovely evening. They were up to speed on the short versions of each other's marriage breakdowns, and they had worked out that Pippa and Sam, four or five academic years apart, had attended the same secondary school: Dolly and Raff wondered if their children might even already know each other.

Raff told Dolly about his beloved boa constrictor, Dorothy, who slept in a large glass "boa-box" under a false floor beneath his bed.

Dolly, normally so good at coaxing information out of people, was more interested in learning about Raff's life as a copper than she was about the sleeping habits of his snake, but he seemed unwilling to go into details. "It's a love-hate thing," was all he would say about his job at first; and then, "I sometimes think there are people born to do it. Maybe. Or maybe not. There's certainly nothing *else* I would want to do . . . but it can get a little bit demoralising, sometimes." She let it rest after that. For the time being.

He was asking her about the cards, was on the point of asking her to read his, and *Dolly knew it*. They had finished the wine, and the pasta sauce was bubbling away, filling the little room with excellent smells.

134

Everything was perfect . . . And then who should trip-trip up the garden path but bloody Rosie Buck. And just half a minute after her, Derek West, aka Professor Filthy, who lived only two streets away.

"*I say*," Professor Filthy declared, edging his long, clumsy body through the front door. "Looks like quite a party you've got going here, Dolly! No Pippa? Did she mention I was popping in?"

Dolly looked a little blank.

"She forgot!" he cried, dismayed. "Oh she's naughty! I hope you don't mind. I can come back later if it's more convenient — but I shan't stay long." He turned to Raff. "I only live a couple of streets away! Dolly and I are collaborating, *n'est-ce pas*, neighbour? *Cooking up exciting plans to educate the city's great unwashed . . .* I wanted to chat over a few points."

"Oh," said Dolly, hopelessly. She was embarrassed. "Now's not ideal. Pippa didn't mention . . ."

"But you don't mind me barging in?"

What could she say? "Of course not, Derek! Come on in!"

"Shame Pippa's not here," he said, settling himself on the armchair (leaving Rosie the empty breakfast stool). "I suppose she thought she'd leave the wrinklies to it!"

"Speak for yourself," said Rosie Buck, forty-three years, "I'm not wrinkly *yet*!" She had come bearing a bottle of pink wine.

There was no way round it. Dolly pulled a face at Raff, and switched off the pasta sauce. She found a couple of extra glasses for the guests, and a tin of olives at the back of the cupboard.

"Crack 'em open!" cried Filthy.

The room felt terribly small, and Dolly felt as if her evening had been hijacked. Raff had barely spoken since the other two arrived. She could feel his discomfort.

"I must say I enjoyed our little din-dins the other night, Dolly," said the professor, winking at her. "I certainly hope you'll let me take you out again!"

Dolly turned to Raff. "Professor West is kindly helping me to organise a series of talks —"

"For goodness' sake," cried Filthy, "call me Derek."

"— on how to read the Tarot," Dolly continued. "Derek's a professor at my daughter's college. It's very exciting. I'm actually doing the first one on Friday, if you'd like to come along . . ."

Raff took a sip of his wine. "That sounds interesting."

"*Fascinating!*" said Rosie. "Can anyone come?"

"Absolutely!" said Filthy. "That's the whole point. And I've put myself in charge of all social media for the event — that's my area. So I can tell you now, it's going to be packed. Book up while you can! I shall let you know the wheres and wherefores in due course. Unless of course Dolly wants to give you the details herself?"

Rosie turned to Raff. "What about you? Maybe you and me can go together? Fly the flag and all!" *Like a cat on a hot tin roof*, thought Dolly, sourly.

Professor Filthy noticed it too. He didn't generally go for married ladies, but she seemed like a nice one. And

136

if she was up for it, and she certainly seemed to be, then maybe he could make an exception. Give it a go.

Rosie said: "I do think a man looks smart in a uniform."

"Hmmm," said Raff. "A lot of women do." He smiled. "Perk of the job."

"*I just bet!*" agreed Rosie. "I saw you wandering down the pathway just now . . ."

"Oh yes?" Raff replied.

"And I thought to myself, isn't that the same officer who came round the other day? With the unfortunate incident at the — at old Mr Maurice's house, next door?" She wrinkled her nose, as much as the Botox would allow. "He's a funny little man though, isn't he? I just can't seem to take him seriously."

"Take him seriously in what way?" asked Dolly.

But Rosie didn't think that question was interesting.

"I wasn't actually present for the 'fight', or what-have-you," she breezed on. "But I saw you jumping into your car, Mr Policeman. It *was* you, wasn't it? With a younger chap. Was that you?"

"It was," he said. "Please. Call me Raff."

"Well, Mr Policeman Raff," insisted Rosie. "*What was it all about?* Nothing about *me* I hope! Not that it would be."

Dolly said quickly. "It was all a bit of a storm in a teacup, really, wasn't it, Raff."

"That's right." Raff smiled at Rosie. "And no, he certainly didn't mention you. Actually he didn't mention anything at all. He told us to bugger off."

"My giddy aunt!" burst Filthy, from a cloud of confused silence. "D'you mean to say you're a real, live PC Plod? Of the real, live PC Plod variety? That's too extraordinary!"

Raff, Dolly and Rosie turned to look at him. Even Rosie was stumped.

"No, but seriously," he continued, "it's too funny! Remember that Plod I was telling you about, Dolly. Who kept the cobra in his caravan! I bet you know him, Raff! Do you? Is there a plod at your station who keeps a cobra under his bed? Watch out! I said to Dolly — didn't I, Dolly? There's a snake-loving plod on the loose!"

"That'll be me," Raff said. He finished his glass and stood up. He'd had enough. "Except it's a boa, Derek. Very different creature. But you're not to know . . . Dolly —"

"Oh don't leave!" she said.

"Early start tomorrow."

Dolly didn't want to beg. She waved him off, without mentioning pasta, though she noticed Raff casting the saucepan a wistful look on his way out. He said he'd be in touch "regarding the other business", and Rosie's head was up — *what business was that?* They pretended not to hear her.

There was a silence after Raff left. The professor looked a little crestfallen.

"That was rather awkward," he said. "How was I to know? There must be hundreds of policemen in this area, of that age . . . divorced or whatever. Looking for new partners. Using dating websites . . . At least a hundred, no? Or fifty? Twenty? It's the problem, isn't it? You think this city's so big but it's not, *really*, when you whittle it down — to a particular type. In a particular area. He and I are probably attempting to woo the same twenty or thirty women, you know, off exactly the same websites . . . *Oh dear*. Do you think I offended him?"

"No," said Dolly. She was hungry. She couldn't wait until he and Rosie left. On the other hand she could just swallow her irritation and be friendly. There was plenty of food, after all. "I'm making some pasta," she said, with an almost concealed sigh. "Does anyone want some?"

"*Carbs? In the evening?!*" cried Rosie. "You're a braver lady than me!"

"It's not that scary," snapped Dolly.

"I wouldn't do a poo for a week! Trust me. *Not* a pretty sight."

"The poo, or the carbs?" asked Filthy, cracking up. "Speaking for myself, Dolly, I would love some pasta. What's the sauce? Smells gorgeous!"

Rosie said she would forgo the carbs, thanks very much, but she'd stick around while they ate. She brought out her mobile to tell Fraser she'd be back shortly, tapped at it ineffectively for a moment or two and then sighed. The text wasn't going through. Never mind. The children knew where she was. And if he was worried, he could always call her.

She explained to Dolly (and Filthy) that the reason she'd dropped in was to discuss the school mums' Tarot and coffee morning. But there was a limit to how complicated even Rosie could make a plan which involved her neighbour walking fifty yards up the road with a pack of cards in her hand. In any case, the subject she kept returning to, which was clearly preoccupying her far more than any coffee morning, was Maurice Bousquet.

"I assume he's OK?" she asked. "He didn't *say* anything, did he? Did he mention I'd paid him a little visit? A week or two back?"

"Well — he mentioned something, I think," Dolly muttered.

"But it was only to say 'hello!' Because we hadn't really said '*hello*' up until that point. I took him a gateau. As a sort of 'hello neighbour!' type thing; like they do in America. And then he invited me in — and he was going on about the boiler being broken. So I said I'd have a look . . ."

"Have a look at his boiler?" repeated Dolly.

"I'm just wondering if he mentioned anything about *me*." Rosie laughed, "I notice his lights aren't on."

"He's very quiet tonight, isn't he," agreed Dolly. "Maybe he's feeling hungover. Or maybe he's nipped out to the . . ." She was going to say the Flag Club, but thought better of it. All things considered. "Pub."

"Only I don't want to sound paranoid," Rosie continued. "But I suppose we had what you might term a bit of a *funny exchange*. There was a misunderstanding. And I don't want to gossip. But he made a *teeny bit of a lunge*, Dolly. If you know what I mean. As I mentioned. I thought it was a little bit inappropriate,

140

and I suppose I may have said as much . . . and then I think *he* thought *I* . . ."

"Dirty bugger!" cried Filthy, with impressive chivalry. "Would you like me to have a word?"

"What? No! Only the thing is, Dolly, I was a bit offended and I sort of told him so, in no uncertain terms. And then the next thing I know, there's a gorgeous policeman at the door — so I just thought . . ."

. . . Dolly waited to discover what Rosie thought, or how the two could possibly be connected. But Rosie had ground to a halt.

She looked disproportionately concerned by the situation. She looked terrified. Dolly couldn't understand it, but she took pity nonetheless. "Maurice didn't mention any kind of disagreement, Rosie. Not to me," she lied, forcing out a smile. "He didn't say anything about that at all. So don't worry."

"He was a bit upset," Rosie said. "And I hate upsetting people. Although I think it was mostly because of his boiler being broken. I was only trying to help."

"Upset about his boiler?" Dolly was confused. "Well that's easy enough to fix."

"Depends what kind of warranty you're on," interjected Filthy. "I had to spend eighteen hundred quid on a new boiler last year. *Eighteen hundred quid!*"

"Well, you should have called my hubby," Rosie informed him. "Or *me*, come to that. It's what I said to Maurice. You need a boiler fixed — come to Windy

141

Ridge. PRC Plumbing and Heating — you know it? Of course you do! It's only the most successful plumbing and heating company in southwest London."

Dolly and Filthy nodded politely.

"It's only where Fraser and me met! A million moons ago now, of course. Mr Buck was one of their top-notch technicians . . . I was only a receptionist, mind. But there's not much you don't pick up, sitting in a plumbers' reception for three years!"

Filthy gave what he felt was a fittingly suggestive laugh. "You can say that again!"

They ignored him. "Anyway, I said to Maurice, if he wanted a hand he only needed to ask, but he got a bit tetchy. I so *hate* fighting with people . . . Is there any more of that scrumptious rosé, Dolly?" She was refilling her glass when there came yet another tap on Dolly's door. It made Rosie jump.

"Crikey!" grumbled Dolly. "It's like Piccadilly Circus round here." Maybe Raff had left something behind.

Sadly not. It was Heart Attack Hubby, on the warpath for his wife.

"Sorry to bother you, Debbie," he said, displaying his teeth, as per "smile" mode. He craned his shiny head around her body, and spotted Rosie by the breakfast bar, already on her feet; "*There you are!*" he said, gnashers glinting. "The kids are wondering where you got to. Nadya says she wants a snacky thing. I've no idea what she's on about. Are you coming home?"

Rosie looked terrified. Like a frightened rabbit, Dolly thought. She was slurping back the last of her wine, wobbling slightly on her little boots. "Sorry, babe. I did try to call you," she said.

"You certainly didn't succeed!" he said, grinning still.

"I don't know how I'm *supposed* to get hold of you really though . . . You insist on changing your number every other week. I can't keep up, babe!"

They continued to speak to each in chirrupy, tooth-glinting tones for a moment longer, but Dolly had stopped listening. She couldn't think straight. She could only think of Nikki and Fraser, Nikki and Fraser at the Flag Club . . . Had they ever met? Did he know her? *Had he seen her lately?* How could she find out?

". . . I'm ever so sorry, babe," Rosie was saying.

"Never mind 'sorry'. Are you coming or am I going to have to drag you home by the hair. Dearest?" Grin-smile-grin.

Eventually even Filthy picked up on the noxious vibes bouncing between husband and wife. He stepped up to defuse them.

"Don't you worry, Mr Somewhat-Grumpy-Husband!" he interrupted, trying his best. "Rosie's been delighting us with stories about plumbing. And poos!" He fell about laughing but nobody else did. Dolly wished they would all go home.

"I did try to call," Rosie said again, struggling into her jacket.

"You could've emailed," he said. "Or does your phone not have that capability?" He grinned again — at Dolly, at Filthy, at anyone but his wife. *Did he know where Nikki was?* "If not, it's time for an upgrade, dear. That device of yours must be something out the ark!"

"I didn't think of it," Rosie said.

"No. Of course you didn't, babe."

Rosie said her goodbyes, but her mind was elsewhere. She had a position to defend and a nasty husband to go home with. *It's not easy for anyone,* Dolly remembered saying to Maurice ... In her irritation with Rosie for ruining her evening, Dolly had forgotten. She felt sorry. And so, on the doorstep, partly because of the wine, partly to disconcert Heart Attack, Dolly wrapped Rosie in a warm hug. Rosie squealed with embarrassment, and tottered off up the lane, to continue the argument in the privacy of her luxury marital home.

Which left Dolly and Filthy, and a lot of pasta. It wasn't what Dolly would have planned.

CHAPTER
TWENTY-THREE

Up the road at Windy Ridge, the girl Nadya had lost interest in snacky things, and when her parents came thumping into the house, she didn't look up from her iPad. Fraser threw his house keys on to the hall table with such ill-humour that they skidded across the full length of the table's surface and plopped on to the floor at the other end. Rosie picked them up.

"You do realise," he said to his wife, "if social services had been calling at that moment in time, we would have found ourselves in a situation. It's *against the law* to leave our kids unattended. Do you not have any sense of responsibility?"

"But I didn't leave them unattended," she said. "You did. I was only down the road. And I was only going to be another half an hour. I don't know why you couldn't have waited."

"Because . . ." he said. "Because . . ." And she flinched.

Maybe it was the financial stresses of taking on the new house. And the school fees for India . . . whatever it was, lately his temper had grown even worse. He frightened her. The slightest disagreement between them seemed to send him to the edge.

She apologised. Grovelled, actually. Which was how their exchanges generally ended: with Rosie apologising, and Fraser nursing his rage: livid there was nowhere left for him to spew it.

She asked him if he wanted anything for dinner but he didn't reply, which usually meant he was going out. He left her standing in the hallway and disappeared into what he called his "manhole": a small room at the side of the house, with a desk and a fridge and a massive, reclining easy chair, which could be used as a bed; and a cinema-screen-style TV.

Rosie peered into the "media room", to check on the children.

India and Nadya, seven and five years old, were lying on their stomachs, below the household's second cinema-screen TV. (There was a third in the "master bedroom", and sundry smaller TVs scattered around the house.) The media room cinema screen was currently broadcasting something noisy involving racing cars, but both girls had earphones in and were glued to their individual iPads, oblivious.

"Kids? What do you want for tea?"

They didn't answer. Rosie asked again. And again. About the fifth time, India (seven years) said, from behind her screen: "Not hungry."

Rosie sighed. She should send them to bed. She would do it in a minute. First, she needed a drink.

Yes. She needed a drink. First things first. She sat down at her own breakfast bar and dropped her head in her hands. *What now? What next?* At once, she felt the slow, familiar crawl on her skin . . . just as she always did now, since whenever it happened. Whenever she was alone. She couldn't stand to be alone.

And the harder she tried to make things better, the worse they seemed to become.

What if Fraser found out? What would become of her then? He'd leap on it as a perfect excuse to get rid of her, that's what. He would cut her off without a penny. He'd be ruthless — and she'd get nothing. Probably not even the kids. Fraser would paint her as the adulterer, the sex maniac, and then that *other thing* would come up. Fraser would make sure of that. Rosie pictured herself, trudging through South London, one of the army of office cleaners who go to work before the city wakes ... Except of course all the bloody immigrants were still doing those jobs. There'd be no work for her! Nothing. She couldn't work in an office any more, with all the new computers. She wouldn't know where to start. She didn't even know how to switch on her own TVs. And all the mums at school would have nothing to do with her. At the school gate they'd be so embarrassed they'd probably pretend they never even knew her. She'd be a vagrant: a friendless, jobless, *nothing* person. She'd be one of those annoying people who stood outside the supermarket, selling the *Big Issue* ... and all because of one misjudgement. A single moment of desperation. Rosie could feel her face throbbing with mortification. Terror. She poured herself another glass of wine. *Was she really so repulsive to men? But* why? How? *What was she doing wrong? She took care of herself. Wore nice clothes, kept herself in trim ... She was ever so positive. Always chirpy and fun. She went to the bloody gym three times a week. She bet her life Dolly-bloody-fucking-Greene didn't do that. And Dolly's house was positively crawling with men . . .* Rosie felt like crying.

The front door slammed.

Was that Fraser, leaving?

She waited another ten minutes. The house was silent. As quietly as she could, she felt for her keys: still in her pocket, along with the mobile. She was a little drunk, yes. But that was OK. Dutch courage. She needed it.

Quietly, quietly, she tiptoed to the manhole. He'd left the door open and the light off.

". . . Fraser?" she whispered. No answer.

Quietly, quietly, she tiptoed out of the house.

Approximately an hour and a half later, Rosie was standing by the bins, out on the lane, when she bumped into Heart Attack Hubby, staggering back home again. It gave them both quite a scare.

Rosie said: "Hello Fraser! Where have you been?"

He shoved past her. "None of your fucking business. Where the hell have you been?"

Rosie was accustomed to this kind of exchange. She hardly noticed: "Nowhere, my love," she replied soothingly. "I was just putting the rubbish out."

He didn't reply. He pushed open the front door, leaving it ajar for her to follow, and before she had a chance to say anything more, he had slammed himself back into his manhole. Much to her relief.

They didn't lay eyes on each again until the following afternoon, when the situation had become a lot worse.

CHAPTER
TWENTY-FOUR

Dolly awoke in an empty bed. Pippa, she assumed, must have stayed over with a friend. But then she looked at the time. Almost ten o'clock! Her daughter had been and gone, while her mother slumbered on like a lazy lump. Not good. Not *at all*. If she carried on like this there would come a day when she simply slopped off the perch, and nobody would even notice. She needed to get busier. Make more money. Make herself useful again. If she couldn't get more private clients, or if these talks at the college didn't work out, she would sign up on the event circuit again: offer herself up as party entertainment for spoiled Chelsea teenagers and pasty-faced corporate drunks. Whatever it took. She would not allow herself to become useless. And with that thought, she bounded out of bed, threw back the curtains, and let the daylight in.

It was another beautiful autumn day. The rich scent of damp, English earth filled the air. This, she thought, was the magic of Tinderbox Lane: when the traffic wasn't backed up on Station Road, poisoning the atmosphere with petrol fumes, you could almost believe you were in the country . . . She breathed in again. Something was different. That sour, sweet, cloying, rotten metallic odour which had been stinging her nostrils these past weeks, forcing her to fill the house with joss sticks and scented candles, it was gone!

She thought of Maurice, whom she'd not laid eyes on since their trip to the Bull's Head two days before. *The smell has gone,* she thought. *The cloud has lifted. He must be feeling better.*

She leaned out the window, craned her neck to see if he had thrown open his windows, as she had, to let the new day in. They were shut tight. Black holes, at the front of the house. Empty black eyes. All his curtains were open.

She felt it then, the first flutters of doubt. Was he already up, she wondered? He was a late riser, normally. Then again, it was already late.

"He's probably in the garden," she said to herself. "Or maybe he's gone out."

So she took a shower, put on yesterday's skirt, boots, woolly shirt . . . Her hands were trembling as she did up the buttons. *He's feeling better,* she told herself. *That's all it is. The black cloud has lifted, along with the smell.* But it didn't stop her hands from shaking. She ran downstairs, pulled back the blind above the kitchen sink and peered out.

"Maurice?" He didn't answer.

Usually, if she stopped and listened, she could hear him shuffling about. Or she could hear the TV. Perhaps he'd picked up a woman at the Flag Club last night, and stayed over? Perhaps that was why the smell had lifted. He had taken his misery elsewhere.

But by then she knew why the smell had lifted. She ran out of the house and up the garden path and hammered on his door. She didn't wait for him to answer, *because she already knew*. She peered through his front window, but she already knew what she would see inside.

The light from the store cupboard window shone into the room, illuminating his silhouette. He was seated on the ground, his back propped up against the open cupboard doorframe, his legs across the threshold, and resting on his thighs, held loose in two hands, was what looked like a mud-smeared cricket bat. His head was slumped forward. And there was blood — it had to be blood: a dark brown stain across his chest, spreading from the neckline. He was wearing a pale blue sweater: the one she had admired in the Bull's Head.

"Maurice?" She hammered on the window. "MAURICE?"

He didn't move.

Maurice sometimes kept a spare key hidden under a stone by the front window. She scrabbled for it, but it wasn't there. Not today. And then she looked up and, somehow, standing beside her was Terry Whistle, her pastel-shaded neighbour. Out and about in broad daylight. The sight of him, so close and so pale, made her scream.

"Mrs Greene?" He held out a skinny arm and touched her. He smelled of warm milk. "What happened? What's up? Are you all right?"

152

She indicated the window. "He's not moving. I think he's dead. Call someone. Call the police."

Terry called the police, and the ambulance too, and while they were waiting, he gave the front door a little push. Maurice didn't move, and neither did the door.

"Try again," Dolly said.

"It's closed," he said.

So Dolly tried. She tried again.

"I told you," Terry said. "It's closed."

"Let's try it together then," she said. But Terry shook his head.

"What about the back door?" Dolly asked. "Maybe we could force the back door? Mine's very weak. His probably is, too."

"You know what," said Terry, "I think we should wait for the police."

"Why?" cried Dolly. "He needs help!"

"I don't think so. He looks dead to me."

"I know, but —"

"I don't think we should force an entry."

"What?"

"It's an offence . . ."

"It's an offence to leave a man dying and not try to help him," she shouted. "*What is the matter with you?*"

He shrugged, stubborn now. "Sorry Mrs Greene. But he's quite clearly already dead. And therefore, no, we are not forcing an entrance. The authorities will be here any minute."

She tried again to push open the door herself. She picked up a stone — the stone beneath which he used sometimes to hide his house key — and swung it back, intending to smash his window. But Terry's reactions, honed on computer games, were too quick for her. He snatched the stone away.

"Not on my watch," he said.

She gaped at him: bewildered by his bland, blank face, behind that silly beard. "It's not 'your watch', you idiot. It's my friend."

This, right here, he reflected, clinging tight to the stone, was the reason he preferred computers to people. He wished the police would come and take the situation into their trained and salaried hands. In the meantime, he was determined to hold the line. There would be no forced entry on Terry's watch. No matter how much Mrs Greene insulted him.

Dolly peered through the front window again. She could hear the sirens, now. Soon, this place would be swarming with strangers, and the peace on Tinderbox Lane would be gone. Professionals who didn't know Maurice and who didn't care; who had never heard his bullshit, his mirthful, mirthless, impossible laugh, they would be bending over his body, sniffing and scraping, trying to discover what had happened to him.

Because clearly *something* had: something terrible. There was the blood — was it blood on the cricket bat, too? And things had been smashed. The leather easy chair had been dragged across the floor, forcing the rug askew. It was rammed against the back door. *Poor Maurice.* Who had he been hiding from? What had he done to deserve an end like this?

Terry said, "Ah! Here they are!" He sounded relieved. The police had come.

154

"Hello, hello." It was Raff's voice. "Back again."

"Back *again*?" said Terry.

Dolly glanced up the pathway and smiled at the two men. ". . . *My goodness!* Don't they have any other officers at your station?"

"Not many, these days," Raff said. "Only five teams on today. So you had a one in five chance . . ."

"Oh really? Five?" *Five* . . . So what? . . . The Five of Swords, the Ace of Pentacles, tarnished. She pictured Nikki's Death card. And then Maurice's Death card. Why hadn't she paid more attention?

"Are you all right, Dolly?" It was Raff's voice, again.

"I'm all right. It's not me, it's Maurice. He's . . ."

She started crying. Quickly, awkwardly, spontaneously, Raff reached out and squeezed her shoulder.

His partner was already peering through the front window. "Oh dear, oh dear," said Ollie. "Looks like you were on to something when you called us last time, madam. I'm sorry it had to come to this."

"He may still be alive," Dolly said.

"Hardly," said Terry.

"You have to smash the door down," Dolly said. "I wanted to smash the window. But this silly boy —" she indicated Terry, who on closer inspection (in daylight) wasn't a boy at all, he only dressed like one, "this idiotic man wouldn't let me get to Maurice."

"I thought it was a job for the authorities," Terry said. "Since the gentleman was clearly dead."

"I presume you've shouted for him?" Raff asked them. "He's not responding?"

"He's *dead*," Terry said.

"Have you tried the back door?"

"I wanted to. If his door's anything like mine, it'll probably open with the smallest shove, but this silly, wicked boy . . ."

"Excuse me," said Terry. "It's an offence to break and enter, isn't it?" He looked at Raff for confirmation. "And I am as sorry as the next person about the old man. Of course I am. But no way I'm getting myself a criminal record for him. No way . . ."

Nobody was listening. Raff and Ollie were peering this way and that, trying to work out the best route through to the back of the house. Dolly said — "*Quickly*. Come through my house. You can get in the back door that way . . . except there's the chair. You'll have to move the chair."

"You want me to get the enforcer from the car, Raff?" Ollie asked.

Raff took a look at the front door. "Doesn't look like it needs it, does it? Let's give it a quick shoulder, shall we? Ready? . . . One, two, *three*!" The two officers moved together, ramming their weight against the front door and there — a little click, and the thing pushed open. No breakage, no splinters — nothing.

Just the smell. Dolly gagged. She'd never smelled it so strong. "Can't you smell it?" she gasped. "You must be able to smell it!"

Ollie sniffed. "Smell what?"

"I can't smell anything, Dolly," Raff agreed.

Through smarting eyes, she peered into the room. "Maurice?" she called out. He didn't move.

156

"Stay where you are, madam," Ollie said. "You too, sir."

Terry nodded obediently. Old people's houses horrified him at the best of times, even when the old people were quote-unquote "alive". He certainly wasn't going in.

Dolly slipped past them all, past Terry, past Ollie and Raff, past the space where the leather chair was meant to be, past the enormous television, and the objects that lay smashed on the floor.

Maurice's head was flopped forward, as if he was asleep; his eyes were closed, as if he was praying. There was dried blood, lots of it, from the old wound on his face, and the blood had spilled down his cheeks and neck, and spread across the front of his sweater.

She crouched over him, kneeled down and touched his hand: it rested on his lap, its fingers curling loosely over the cricket bat. His skin was cold and hard. She touched his shoulder: slim, hard, cold, like a shop mannequin, in that ruined sweater. *"What happened?"* she whispered.

And then she felt a hand on her own shoulder — a warm hand. It was Raff. Gently, he pulled her away. "You shouldn't be in here, Dolly," he said. "We're going to have to seal the place off. Are you all right?"

She stood up. "It's the smell," she said. "There's something wrong."

Raff looked down at the body. He couldn't smell anything. But she was right: nothing about the scene looked as it ought. It looked like a crime scene. And

Dolly should not be anywhere near it. "You need to get back outside, Dolly."

Ollie had followed them inside. He sniffed. "What smell?" He didn't wait for answer. He looked across at Raff. "Shall I get her out of here? Do you want to radio it in? I reckon we're looking at the full circus, here."

"You radio in. I'll take care of her. And the other one. Is he still out there? We need to seal the scene."

Raff led Dolly out into the autumn sunshine. Terry was still there, and looking more lively now. He had taken a picture of Maurice's forced front door, and was just then posting it on to Instagram with the caption, #modernpolicing.

"Are you all right, sir?" Raff asked him.

"Hm?" Terry took a moment to look up. "Fine. Thank you." He nodded at the house. "Has he passed away, then?"

"I'm afraid so."

"Suspicious circumstances? Seems a bit strange, him sitting there with a cricket bat."

"Someone killed him, Terry," said Dolly. "I should've realised. I should've known it was coming."

"You couldn't have known," Raff said soothingly. He needed to take Terry's name, and confirm his address. Above all, he needed to seal off the cottage. "Can I ask you both to stick around for the minute? We'll have CID here in a sec. And all the rest, too, I should think. The full circus, as Ollie says."

"What about the ambulance?" interrupted Dolly.

It was a stupid question.

"Ollie's informing them right now . . . I'm sorry," he added, seeing Dolly close to tears again. "You saw for yourself, Dolly . . . There's no call for an ambulance now."

"So. No ambulance. What happens next?" asked Terry. He sounded querulous, as if they were purposely keeping him in the dark. He had a right to know it, whatever it may be, and (it went without saying) a right to upload it, too: something from the front line of experience, that's what he wanted: something about an old, black guy being dead, and the authorities doing nothing to prevent it.

Raff muttered about waiting for Forensics. Raff and Ollie's task was to keep the scene as clean as possible for everyone's arrival. In the meantime, he wondered if Dolly was willing to make a formal identification.

"Don't you dare ask me," said Terry. "For all I know that guy could have been anyone. Literally. We've only ever spoken about three times."

Dolly said: "Yes, well, he hasn't asked you, has he? *Idiot.*"

"Good," Terry said. He glanced at his iPhone. Three likes on Instagram already. Oops, four . . . "I'm not doing your dirty work for you. Yeah?"

Ollie came back up the path, carrying police tape. Terry took a picture.

"What are you doing?" Raff asked.

"Nothing," said Terry.

"Is he taking pictures of me?" asked Ollie.

"Last I checked," Terry said, "that's not illegal."

"Not illegal," said Dolly. "Just bad manners. You shouldn't take pictures of people without asking."

"You mean take pictures of the police?"

Dolly didn't bother to answer. She looked at Raff. "Of course I can identify him. He's my neighbour, Maurice Bousquet. We've been neighbours for seven years."

Terry posted the shot of Ollie carrying police tape, and added the tag: #notillegal. Strictly speaking, it didn't make sense. But did anything, really, when you actually quote-unquote "got down" to it? Terry didn't know. #whoknows? He had eleven likes on #modernpolicing already. #Boom.

Dolly watched as Ollie stuck police tape across Maurice's door. She turned to Raff: "He's moved the chair — you realise that, don't you? That leather chair. He's rammed it up against the back door. Like he's trying to stop anyone coming in. It's normally in front of the telly."

Raff nodded politely. They would have worked it out. Even so, CID would want to talk to her — without a doubt.

"If it's all right with you," she said, "I might wait for them at home. I won't go anywhere. I just don't like standing out here." Her eyes slid over to Terry, tapping away at his iPhone.

"Sir," said Raff, following her gaze, "could you do me a favour and put the phone away. Please."

Terry said, "Why?"

"I'm just asking. As a favour. If you wouldn't mind putting the phone away. As a mark of respect, sir. For the deceased. He probably wouldn't appreciate pictures of the death scene all over social media. Maybe put the phone away until the deceased has been removed from the premises."

"I'm not taking pictures of the scene," Terry said. "I'm taking pictures of you lot. Making sure you do your job."

Dolly turned away from Terry. She'd not realised until now quite how disagreeable he was. "I'm going to make some tea," she said. "Anyone want some?"

CHAPTER
TWENTY-FIVE

Alone in her house, Dolly did what she always did in times of turmoil. She turned to her cards. She took them upstairs, away from the growing crowd, as far as possible from Maurice's cold body, and sat down on the edge of her bed, just as she had the day the death of her own marriage had shimmered. *Tell me*, she asked the cards, *what's been happening? What am I missing?* She pulled out ten cards, laid them face down on the duvet, and paused before turning them over.

Dolly had no memory for names, and no memory for numbers: not even much of a memory for faces. She dealt more in impressions than in facts. But there was one thing she never forgot, and that was the cards that people drew. No matter who they were or how unremarkable their problems: inert young women in search of marriage proposals; career-obsessed young men in search of drab-sounding new job titles, Dolly could remember their cards.

So she remembered Maurice's exactly.
Pentacles: 4, 5, 6, 10 and Ace
Swords: 5, 7 and 8
The Star (reversed),
And, of course, Death.

She could picture his cards as they lay briefly on the table between them, and she could picture them afterwards, when he had swiped them on to the floor. She remembered which had landed face up and which face down, and which had stayed on the table. Above all, she remembered the Ace of Pentacles, with the curl of smoke rising from its heart.

Dolly trusted her cards — of course she did. She believed in their wisdom: had come to accept their peculiar magic, without worrying too much about the how or the why. But sometimes they frightened her. Sometimes the cards spoke at such a volume they became, even to Dolly, just plain spooky. This was one of those times. She stared at the cards on the duvet cover and slowly, as if they were alive, stepped back from the bed.

Ten cards lay face up on the duvet cover. Out of a pack of seventy-eight, many times shuffled since she read for Maurice, she had pulled:

Pentacles: 4, 5, 6, 10 and Ace

Swords: 5, 7 and 8

The Star,

And Death.

It felt like a rebuke. She had missed something the first time. Now, they were telling her again. The only difference today, the Star was the right way up.

The right way up, the Star was the "Wish Card", indicating good health, and dreams fulfilled — but in reverse, as it had been for Maurice? It could represent the opposite: sickness; dissatisfaction; a wish that can never be answered, or a wish that comes true but brings only pain and disappointment.

Last time she'd seen this spread, she'd been slightly drunk. The cards had made her chuckle. But there was nothing funny about them now. They were horrible.

She found herself turning over one more card: why, she didn't know. She wanted more — a final word. She laid the card on to the Star, at the centre of the spread . . . And there: she heard herself chuckling again. In the midst of all this, it shimmered, just as the Death card had shimmered once: the sweetest card in the pack.

The Two of Cups: *True love. A meeting of minds. A perfect match.*

Not so horrible, after all. Just, one hundred per cent confusing.

And then Raff Williams was at the door, pocketbook in hand. In work mode. He needed to take a statement. Also, he was trying to contact a next-of-kin. There was no one in at the address they had recorded for Adrian Bousquet, and nor was Mr Bousquet answering his phone.

"I'm not surprised," Dolly said.

"Nor me, frankly," he said. "Even so. We would like to get hold of him. I was wondering if you had his lady friend's mobile number?"

"Didn't I give it you last night?"

"Of course you did," Raff said. He flicked awkwardly through his pocketbook. He knew exactly where to find it. "Tell you what, though," he smiled. "I'd love a cup of

164

tea. If only to get away from that chap and his damn Facebook, or whatever. He's driving me potty."

"Can't you book him for driving you potty?" Dolly asked. She was only half joking. Perhaps he really could?

Raff shook his head. There were times when he was tempted to do just that, and he had colleagues who sometimes even did. *But not Raff.* "Comes with the job," he said. "Some people can't be round the police without wanting to piss them off. One of those things. And I'm not saying there aren't officers who deserve it, but . . ." He left it there. There was nothing more to add.

"Well, I don't want to piss you off," she smiled at him. "Come in. I'll put the kettle on."

CHAPTER
TWENTY-SIX

It was almost five hours since Terry had first dialled emergency services, and Tinderbox Lane was still crawling with strangers. Raff and Ollie were gone, but there were uncountable teams of police personnel still roaming about: some in uniform, some in plain clothes, several in white plastic bodysuits. The Bucks were there, and Terry and Pippa; also a two-strong, unaffiliated camera crew, which had somehow appeared from nowhere — probably thanks to Terry's Instagram efforts.

It had been a long five hours for Dolly. And in the end, except for when she and Raff were having tea together, she had wound up spending most of it outside with the rest of the crowd.

There was no need for her to be there. She longed to disappear back into her house, and yet she couldn't quite bring herself to leave. Perhaps, if Raff had still been there, it might have felt different. She trusted Raff. In the meantime, for as long as Maurice remained in his house surrounded by so many strangers, Dolly felt duty bound to stand guard. Why, she couldn't say. She and Maurice had never been close friends, not in any conventional sense. And yet, it occurred to Dolly, there had been a peculiar kind of intimacy between them — more peaceful and more accepting than many marriages. They knew the sound of each other's lives as few people ever would: the television and radio shows they listened to, the snuffling and sneezing, the microwave pings and boiling kettles, the climbing of stairs and flushing of toilets . . . Conventionally or not, they were friends, or so Dolly felt that day. She couldn't bring herself to abandon him. So she watched and waited with the rest.

Rosie Buck was sporting a nasty cut below one eyebrow. Her hands were shaking and she would not — could not — shut up. She talked on a loop: about hearing police sirens while she was in the shower, knocking her head against the shower frame (hence, apparently, the cut), about heading out for a coffee-with-the-girls and then spotting the police vans and fearing the worst, about what time her children finished school today, and how she hoped the body would have been removed by then.

"I don't want the kids coming back to this," she said, again, and then again. "What if India comes home just as — *you know* . . . just as . . ." She glanced across at Heart Attack. He was standing beside her, sweating, tapping angrily into his device. The knuckles and palm of his right hand were wrapped in a bandage, leaving dirty fingernails and swollen sausage fingers exposed: "What do you think, babe?" said Rosie. "Do you think I should take the kids away for a day or two? Go to Euro Disney or something . . . They'd love that. Until things return to normal. I don't want to upset them."

167

Fraser Buck didn't answer.

But Pippa did. Suddenly she couldn't stand the sound of Rosie's voice any longer. "Sorry, Rosie. But what is 'normal' exactly?"

Rosie laughed uncertainly. She said, "Well, I suppose . . ."

"I suppose," snarled Pippa, "that according to you, everything will be *normal* once the mess has been cleared away, and we can all pretend it never happened. Is that right, Rosie? We can all pretend Maurice never existed."

"Well — I — *no* . . ." Rosie looked at her husband, as if he might offer her support.

No.

"Calm down, Pippa," said Dolly.

"I'm just saying —" Pippa began.

"— something rude and stupid," snapped Dolly. "Of course this isn't 'normal'. None of this is normal. It's horrible. And it's perfectly understandable for Rosie not to want her kids to witness it."

"Thank you," said Rosie, lips trembling.

"And you can shut up, too," said Dolly. "For one second. Just shut your mouth for a second, can you? Give us all a rest." Dolly was on the very point of bursting into tears. The moment was saved by the unaffiliated cameraman shoving past. He had noticed movement in the cottage.

A van was pulling up at the end of the lane. Somebody opened the front door. The camera crew jostled further forward . . . And there, between stretcher and covering sheet, flanked by strangers in

168

white, plastic bodysuits, was Maurice. Or, the Maurice remains.

"... *It's not quite the Exit I was hoping for, Dolly, ha ha ha*," he whispered to her. "*Thought you and me were going to St Lucia ...*"

"What the hell happened?" Dolly asked him.

But Maurice didn't reply. Rosie did. "We're all upset, Dolly," she said, patting Dolly on the shoulder. "He was such a lonely old man. I wouldn't be surprised if he did it to himself. That's what Fraser said. Didn't you, babe? Only yesterday. You said what a miserable, unhappy, lonely old man he was."

"I don't remember saying that," replied Fraser. "Must've been one of your boyfriends, Rosie dear." He cackled, looked up from his phone, and looked down again.

Pippa said: "Lonely people don't generally beat themselves up with their own cricket bats, Rosie."

"*We-ell*," said Rosie, patiently. "People can sometimes do the strangest things. Look at Isis ... So called 'Isis' ... and the suicide bombers and whatnot. And those girls who go offering themselves up as brides ... You'll discover that not everyone always acts in their own best interests. Unfortunately."

There wasn't much to be said to that. The trolley bearing Maurice's body had paused on the garden path and its empty presence imposed itself on them all. They fell silent.

The police pushed back the small crowd to clear a route out on to the lane: there was Terry, with iPhone aloft, taking pictures; and Pippa, Dolly, Mr and Mrs

Buck, and of course, at the front, the camera crew. They huddled together, subdued now, in the presence of death — and the body was rolled out on to the lane. The small crowd followed it: a motley little cortege. They walked silently up the lane and on to Station Road, where the police mortuary van was parked, its doors open and waiting, and the stretcher slid inside.

CHAPTER
TWENTY-SEVEN

Pippa left for college early the following morning, leaving Dolly alone in the house. There was a "community support officer" sitting outside Maurice's front door, guarding it, and Dolly had offered her a cup of tea in the hope of gleaning some new information. But the woman didn't appear to know anything at all: not how long she might be sitting out there; barely even what possible crime scene she was meant to be protecting.

Raff hadn't called. She'd not heard anything from him since he took her statement yesterday, and nor had anyone been in contact from CID. The stillness, and the absence of news, was driving her a little nuts. Raff had told her the CID would call, if they had any more questions.

Well maybe they don't, thought Dolly irritably. *But I certainly do.*

For the hundredth time since that body had washed up at Kew; for the twentieth time since yesterday, Dolly dialled Nikki's number. Nobody ever picked up, and yet the number was still working, which meant someone — Ade Bousquet? — must still be charging the battery. Why? She listened to it ring, her mind roaming. *There must be something she could do, beyond dialling this wretched number?*

It was a shock when someone answered.

"Fuuuuuuck, man," said a croaky, male voice. ". . . When're you going to leave me a-fucking-*lone*?"

Dolly said: "Is that you, Ade?" It didn't sound like Ade.

A pause, and quite a long one, followed by slow, sleepy laughter. "This is not Ade, madame. This is Toby, madame. May I have the courtesy of you asking who is this?" He was high. Fifteen years old and high. Clearly, she wasn't going to get much sense out of him. But fifteen and high was better than no one at all.

"Toby? Toby I am a friend of your mother's," Dolly said patiently. "Why have you got your mother's phone? Do you know where she is?"

More laughter. There were people with him, also laughing. "Is that Toby who?" he said, meaninglessly.

"I'm looking for your mother. Where is she? Where's Nikki?"

"Nikki?" As he spoke the laughter around him gained momentum: "Nikki-sicki-dikki? . . . Nikki-loves-a-dikki . . . Dikki-Dikki-Dikki-loves-a-quickie-Nikki . . ." until the words were liquidised by his own giggles.

"Where is she, Toby? When did you last see her? Please, you need to help me. I think she's in trouble. Have the police been in touch?"

At mention of police the laughter died instantly. "It was *you*." The boy — Toby — moved his mouth away from the headset and explained to his companions.

172

"She gave the police my fucking number. Can you *believe* that?"

Someone said, "Hang up! Why you even talking to her?"

"Toby," shouted Dolly. "*Where is your mother?* Why are you answering her phone?"

"Why?" He sounded incredibly self-righteous. "Because it's *my phone*. She gave it to me. For the seven millionth time. All right? ME. *Not anyone else.* ME. And if you don't stop . . . harassing me . . . I am calling the police!" Dolly heard whoops from his friends. Toby was laughing again.

She sighed. "Toby. Please. Just tell me where she is. Tell me she's OK and I'll leave you in peace."

But he was giggling too hard to answer.

"What about Ade? Have you seen Ade?"

"Ade?" Somebody was distracting him — blowing farts or smoke rings, doing moonies: and now his giggles were completely helpless: mindless, goofy, youthful — useless.

"Please, Toby. Try to concentrate. Tell me, *where is Ade?*"

Gurgles of wild laughter, and then: "I think he's in hospital . . . far as I know . . . *Aww you WANKER! You fucking FARTED . . . That is fucking disgusting!*"

"He's in hospital? Why? Where? Since when? What's wrong with him?"

"Skull damage."

"*Skull* damage? Can you be more specific?"

". . . Skull damage . . ."

"Where? *Where is he?* Which hospital?"

But he was really giggling now. Wrestling with someone in the room who'd done something *fucking GROSS man, you fucking FUCK Fuuuuuuccccck* . . .

"Which hospital, Toby?"

He didn't answer. There was the sound of more wrestling, hysterical laughter, a *bang* as the telephone dropped, and the line went dead.

Raff had given Dolly his mobile number. "Any problems . . ." he'd said. But she felt bashful about calling him, so she called the police station first, and had a long conversation with *someone*, whoever it was at the other end. She didn't take a name. Stupidly. And then she waited. But nobody called back. A day passed. The following morning, she called Raff and spewed everything on to his voicemail: about Toby the Stoner, Nikki the Unmissed, Ade and the damaged skull . . . And, above all, the urgent need to check the hospitals.

Raff texted her: "Thank you, Dolly. We're on it." And for a while, that was it.

CHAPTER
TWENTY-EIGHT

TAROT TALKS — AN INTRODUCTION TO
THE MAGICAL LANGUAGE OF THE TAROT
BY DOLLY GREENE

. . . Aces in all four suits represent beginnings: new projects, new journeys; new hopes; new loves; new chances; new ideas; new adventures. They represent a gift to you from the Universe, but it is always up to you, how you use the gift . . .

The Ace of Pentacles, (sometimes called the Ace of Coins), represents the start of something material: a new business venture, perhaps; an inheritance; a new source of income; a prize; a win on the horses. Pentacles can often simply represent money . . .

Dolly sat at her broom cupboard table, hard at work. In two days she was due to give the first of her talks at the college, and though she had, in fact, done more than enough preparation, it didn't stop her from being worried.

She glanced at her watch. If she hadn't heard from Raff by lunchtime she would call him. Definitely. She would speak to him directly.

175

. . . The Ace of Cups, meanwhile . . . is the card we would all be hoping to see at the beginning of a new love affair, or perhaps a new creative project . . .

Ten minutes later, Raff was knocking on the door, radio handset buzzing. His partner, Ollie, looking impatient, was standing a few yards behind.

"Raff!" That's what Dolly said. *Ace of Cups*, she thought. "I was just thinking about you. Well, you and — everything else. Come in! Would you like some tea?"

He indicated Ollie, and then the handset. "I can't come in, unfortunately. I'm on shift, Dolly. We were just passing. I wanted to check you were OK . . . Are you OK?"

"I'm *fine!*" she said. She would have been finer if he'd agreed to come in for tea.

"Has CID been in touch?"

"No. I thought they would."

"No?" He looked surprised. "Well. Maybe they felt they'd got enough from your statement. It was fairly thorough."

"Is there any news yet? Do they know what killed him? The knock on the head, I presume. All that blood."

He shook his head. "It'll be a few days before anything comes back, even if they put a rush on it. Which I imagine they will."

"How about Nikki? Any word?"

"Nope. Nothing. No sign of her. No reports of her missing . . . Sorry, Dolly."

"And Ade? Did someone check the hospitals?"

Raff shook his head. "Last I heard, still AWOL."

A pause. They looked at each other. He took a breath: "I was wondering . . ."

"We should get cracking, Raff," Ollie shouted behind him. "Zebra 13, top end of Castelnau. I think we should pick it up."

"I . . . was wondering," Raff said again, "if you weren't busy this evening. Maybe I could take you to dinner? To make up for the other night . . ."

"Raff. *Sir*. We should get going."

"Just a moment there, Ollie . . ."

"Oh!" said Dolly. It was the last thing she was expecting. She beamed. Couldn't help it. "Well — what a lovely thing, Raff. What a lovely idea. Yes *please*. I would love that." Maybe she sounded too keen? Too bad.

"You would?" He sounded quite surprised: as surprised as she felt. "Well that's great news! *Excellent* news. I'll come and get you about seven, shall I?"

"Sir . . ."

"Yes, I'm just coming, Ollie."

"There's a gentleman here says he wants a word with you . . ."

Dolly thought the word "gentleman" was a bit generous, after his behaviour. Nevertheless, they were neighbours; *and Raff had just asked her out to dinner*. She greeted Terry with a friendly smile.

He nodded. "You all right?" There was no eye contact, but it sounded polite.

"I'm all right, Terry," she said. "Thank you. What about you?"

He shrugged, and turned to Raff. "You got a moment?"

Raff said, "Of course . . ." and then to Dolly, sotto voce, "See you at seven!"

Dolly watched them disappearing into Terry's house. "What d'you think he's saying?" she said to Ollie, because he was standing there.

Ollie shrugged. "Probably nothing. People like him just want to feel involved."

But Dolly wasn't so sure. Or at any rate, she wasn't satisfied. There were times when her curiosity — and her Tarot cards — led her to do things that others might frown upon. She glanced at young Ollie, standing on her pathway, looking sulky and bored. "Excuse me," she said, and closed the door on him.

She and Terry lived as close to each other as she and Maurice had, but she felt none of the shared intimacy with him. Partly, this was due to the hours he kept, and his generally unsociable manner, but it was also due to the fact he existed almost entirely without making any sound. And this, of course, was because he existed mostly through his computer, and whatever noises it made were delivered, via soundproof earphones, directly into Terry's head.

She could never know, for example, what TV shows or "podcasts" he might be listening to; nor anything about his musical taste. Terry never had friends round, so far as Dolly knew, and never seemed to talk on the telephone, presumably because he preferred to send people emojis. Occasionally, she heard the kitchen tap turned on; every now and then she heard a toilet flush. And, in early spring, before he'd stocked up on antihistamines, she sometimes heard him sneezing. But he moved like a cat, if he moved at all; and if he ever slept, it must have been on the floor by his computer terminal, because she never heard his feet on the stairs.

The walls between their houses were thin. She could hear the buzz of Raff's handset, without even trying, but *Every Little Helps.* She'd done it often, as a child, the better to eavesdrop on her parents, and she knew it worked. She fetched a glass tumbler and placed it carefully between the wall and her ear.

She could hear Terry mumbling an apology, and then Raff, reassuring him: "*Not to worry, sir. Better late than never. What did you want to tell me?*"

. . . There came more muttering from Terry. What with the noise coming out of Raff's radio, Dolly wanted to yell at him through the wall to speak up.

Then it was Raff again: "*Well, if you can just tell me what you saw, I can pass your words on to CID. And if they believe the information is useful they will obviously be in touch . . .*"

"*I'm saying I don't know what time he died,*" Terry said.

"*No,*" Raff replied patiently. "*We're waiting for that information to come back from the lab.*"

"*I don't want to make trouble. It probably isn't anything.*"

"*If you just tell me what it is you think you saw . . .*"

"I don't know her name. The woman with kids and the baldy husband at the end of the road . . ."

"Mrs Buck."

"Mrs Buck, then. I'm just saying that on the night when the old man croaked —"

"Do you mean on the night before you and Mrs Greene discovered Mr Bousquet's body?"

"— I was out getting some air. I tend to walk out quite late at night. I don't think that's a crime . . . "

"Of course not."

"I was being sarcastic."

"All right."

"I'm just saying — on that night, when — Mr Bousquet — died, I saw Mrs Buck at his door. She was peering through the letterbox. There weren't any lights on in the house — and I didn't want to hang around. So. I don't know if he let her in, or what. Or maybe she let herself in. Or whatever. She had a bunch of keys, I think — there was something in her hand. I just carried on walking past. Fast as I could. She didn't see me. People usually don't. Anyway. That's all I wanted to say . . . I probably should have said something before. Only everything was freaking me out . . ."

An urgent rap on Dolly's window made her jump. Ollie was peering at her though the glass. She removed the tumbler from the wall and tucked it behind her back as casually as she could, and opened the front door.

"Sorry, Ollie," she said. "I didn't realise you were still there. Did you want something?"

180

He stared at the arm that held the hidden glass, but said nothing more about it. "I was wondering if I could use your toilet?" he said.

"Oh my goodness, the toilet!" cried Dolly. "Yes, *of course!*"

CHAPTER
TWENTY-NINE

First question: what to do with this new information?

What she ought to do, she supposed, was nothing. Wait for Raff to do his job, report his conversation with Terry to CID, and then wait for CID to do theirs. On the other hand ... Dolly searched for a justifiable excuse to do anything other than that. Didn't find one. Realised it made no difference. Wondered if she should ask the cards, and decided against, for fear they too, might discourage her. And proceeded.

She decided it was time to drop in on Rosie Buck. Rosie Buck, after all, never seemed to stop dropping in on her. It seemed fair that she should be allowed to return the favour.

Rosie had a cappuccino moustache and bloodshot eyes when she opened the door to Dolly. There was a thick layer of make-up around the cut beneath the eye, which only served to highlight it. Otherwise, she looked much the same. Fussy top and posh boots, jeans a half-size too small and every yellow hair on her head in perfect place.

"Oooh! Hello neighbour!" Rosie said. She seemed nervous, but not displeased to see Dolly. In need of company, perhaps. "I was just having a super-quick sit-down. Come on in!"

Dolly followed Rosie through the hallway: blanched wooden floorboards, oatmeal walls, a side table crammed with silver-framed photographs of the Buck wedding day; and on a slim glass stand in the centre of the room, a shiny metal sculpture of a naked woman's thighs and torso, legs asunder and directed somewhat aggressively at the front door. Perhaps, thought Dolly, in this tasteless, barren décor, the sculpture was meant to represent the Buck Eye for Art. As her hostess tottered, flushed and ladylike, past the sculpture, towards a half-eaten muffin, open copy of the *Daily Mail*, and clutter-free breakfast bar, it represented nothing, to Dolly, but a bullying husband. Poor Rosie. That's what it said to Dolly. *Poor Rosie.*

"Can I get you a coffee?" Rosie asked her. "I tell you what, Dolly, I'm happy for the company this morning. I've been a bit all over the place since — you know . . . Since it happened."

Dolly settled on to a stool at the slate breakfast bar — a breakfast bar, she noted, that was probably four times the size of her own. The Buck kitchen had been extended across all three cottages. There was a wall of glass at the back of the room, where it had also been extended into the garden. The place was vast: oatmeal, modern — a bit like a club-class airport lounge: a bit like every other kitchen in every luxury family house in the window of every estate agent in southwest London. Dolly had only ever seen photographs of places like this before. She looked around her, appalled by the blandness:

". . . lovely . . ." she said. She had to say something.

"Mmm. Yes, we like it," Rosie replied. "It really works for us. Which is nice. Fraser has his little *manhole* . . . and he's already talking about digging into the basement, can you believe?"

"I brought my cards," Dolly said. She hadn't come to talk about décor.

"Your *cards!*" cried Rosie. She was hard at work at the coffee machine, making the milk froth. She turned to Dolly, bloodshot eyes open wide. "What, you mean *playing* cards or *funny* cards? I call them your funny cards, Dolly! Do you mean your Tarot cards?" She looked terrified.

"I thought, as you were intending to hire me for your coffee morning, you might like to test out the service first. Would you like that?"

"I don't think so," Rosie said. She returned to the frothing machine. "Is that why you came?"

"No!" Dolly laughed. "Of course it wasn't. After everything that's been happening, I thought it would be nice to have a chat. It's such a shock, isn't it? For all of us."

"Oh it's dreadful. The kids are beside themselves. They can't get their heads round it."

"Did they know Maurice well?"

"Crikey, *no*," Rosie laughed. "Absolutely not, Dolly. No, I didn't even want the kids *talking* to him, to be honest with you. And now — well, it turns out I wasn't wrong, was I? Obviously he was mixed up in a lot of

184

funny business . . . But that's the problem with London, isn't it? You can buy a super family home like this one, and everything seems just right. But at the end of the day, you can never be quite sure who you're living next to . . ." She passed Dolly a coffee cup, fussed around with spoons and sugar and plates with added muffins and finally allowed herself to sit down. A silence fell. Rosie and Dolly slurped on their frothy milk. Wiped their moustaches away.

"What about you, Rosie?" Dolly asked, leaning towards the muffin plate. "What are they, blueberry?" She took one, and quickly asked the question again. "I know you mentioned there was a tiff, but were you and Maurice on friendly terms by the end?"

Rosie appeared to think about it. "I wouldn't say *friendly*. But 'friendly', yes. If you know what I mean."

Dolly nodded politely.

Rosie said: "Not *friendly*, friendly. Just sort of . . . Friendly."

Dolly took a bite of the muffin.

She didn't even like muffins. But it encouraged a naughty-but-niceness between the two women. Dolly knew it. After all those years winkling out confidences in her broom cupboard, she knew what she was doing. She said: "Maurice was a strange fellow, Rosie, much as I loved him. Seven years he and I were living next door to each other, and I only discovered last week he had a son! Did you know he had a son?"

"No."

Silence.

It was possible. Maurice had said that Ade Bousquet and Fraser Buck were in business together, but Rosie might not have known it. If it weren't for the colour of Rosie's ears, and the uncharacteristically succinct denial, Dolly might have considered believing her.

"He's called Ade," Dolly continued. "Maurice was *very* secretive."

". . . Yes, he was a dark horse, wasn't he? I mean — not *dark*, dark. Obviously. But dark . . ."

"You mentioned the other day that you and he had a little disagreement —"

"I may have said he made a bit of a lunge at me — but I'm not really sure he did, now. After everything that's happened, I feel a bit — I don't think he *did* make a lunge at me really, Dolly. I think I imagined it. I can be very sensitive . . ."

"Well, maybe he did and maybe he didn't." Dolly chuckled. "He was certainly lively. Sexually speaking. For an old man."

"I suppose so . . ." Rosie looked truly wretched.

"He told *me*," Dolly said, a teasing note in her voice, "that he'd taken quite a fancy to you!"

"He did?" Rosie looked at her suspiciously. "When was that then? I thought you said —"

"In the pub. Just before he died. I didn't want to mention it, with the professor there."

Rosie smiled: a secret, happy smile. She would have reached for a cigarette if she hadn't given up on her wedding day. She reached for another muffin instead. ". . . Did he really, though? Did he actually say that?"

"He went on and on about you," Dolly smiled. "But you must be used to that. Gorgeous woman like you!"

"*Hardly*. God. Not for a long time, Dolly."

. . . Not since she married that man, thought Dolly. He'd provided her with a slate-topped breakfast bar, and a wall of glass at the back of an oatmeal kitchen — and robbed her of any self-esteem she ever had; if she ever had any. Dolly pressed on. "Maurice thought you were *gorgeous*," she said again.

Rosie frowned. Her mood changed. She looked tearful, suddenly. "Well, it certainly wasn't the message he gave me . . ."

"He could be quite rude."

"I don't think he liked me very much. We got off to a bit of a funny start . . ."

"So you said . . . Well, but you obviously made up for it!"

"I'm not sure . . ."

"Otherwise he wouldn't have kept inviting you into his house, Rosie!"

Rosie looked confused. "He didn't 'keep' inviting me. He didn't invite me at all."

"You were in there a few weeks back, weren't you? Well, I know you were, because he told me! And the night before last, after you dropped in with me — didn't you drop in on him later? That's two visits already. In almost as many weeks."

Rosie stared at Dolly. "No," she said.

"No?"

"I didn't drop in on him. How could I have dropped in on him? He was dead."

"Well — obviously . . . I meant before he died . . ."

Rosie stood up. "D'you want another coffee?" It sounded cold. Angry, actually, Dolly thought. Rosie picked up their mugs without waiting for an answer, and turned back to the coffee-making machine.

Silence. Dolly watched her. Without thinking, she delved into her large bag and brought out the Tarot cards.

"Amazing these new-style coffee machines, aren't they?" Rosie said. It sounded normal again. The Rosie of old.

Dolly didn't reply. Quietly, she shuffled the cards. If Rosie didn't want her cards read, that was fair enough. Dolly just wanted to bring the cards out, to have them in the room with her, absorbing the atmosphere, helping her to see. She pulled three cards from the pack: just three. Face down. Laid them on to the counter.

Clankety-clank . . . The milk was getting frothed . . .

And then, suddenly, Rosie was crying. She kept her back to Dolly, but her shoulders were shaking.

"*Hey* . . ." Dolly stood up, leaving the cards on the counter. "*Hey, it's OK* . . ." She put an arm round Rosie's shoulders. "*It's all right* . . ." Dolly sounded so kind and Rosie was so unaccustomed to kindness, it only made her worse. She bent over the kitchen worktop, rested her head on the coffee machine and began to weep, until her entire body rocked.

She said: "Oh God, Dolly, what am I going to do?"

"It's OK," Dolly said, rubbing her back. "It's *OK*."

"Maurice and I got off to a rocky start, Dolly. And it doesn't even matter any more why, or anything. I don't even know how it happened — just — we had a silly squabble." She stopped, suddenly. "*You mustn't tell Fraser.* Promise me you won't tell Fraser."

"Of course I won't tell Fraser."

"I was so upset, Dolly. Nobody likes to be on bad terms with their neighbours, do they?"

"Not at all."

Rosie straightened herself up and turned around to face Dolly, eyes bloodshot and wild. "I wanted us to be friends. That's all it was. I wanted to make peace with him. But I didn't see Maurice, not — *not* on the night when he died. *I didn't see him.*"

". . . All right . . ."

"I didn't see him or speak to him."

"No. All right . . . I'm sorry Rosie. I absolutely — the last thing I wanted was to upset you. I just thought you might have exchanged a few words, and then we might have had a better idea what time he died, or maybe — you know — what kind of mood he was in that night."

Standing in Rosie's kitchen, Dolly was discovering a side to herself; a ruthlessness that disconcerted her. Here was Rosie, in terrible distress, and here was Dolly, not letting up, still pumping her for information. But something had happened to Maurice. The cards had forewarned her once, and she had not listened. They had told her again, the day he died. She had a duty to persevere, to find the truth: it's what the cards were telling her. A duty to get to the truth, no matter what. It was as simple as that.

"*I didn't see him, Dolly* . . ." Rosie was still saying, "I went round to make peace with him, and he wouldn't let me in. I should have said something to that policeman chappie, but how could I? And now I keep thinking to myself, maybe if I'd insisted or something . . . I thought he wouldn't let me in because he hated me. But now I realise he wouldn't let me in *because he was already dead.*"

A little later, when Rosie was calm, they returned to the breakfast bar together, coffee cups refreshed, and quietly, privately, Dolly turned over the cards: the Nine of Swords, the Five of Cups, the Seven of Swords.

Anxiety, Grief, Deceit.

So Rosie was lying. The questions remained, how much, why, and what about?

CHAPTER
THIRTY

Standing outside Windy Ridge, Dolly hesitated. She had an hour before her first client was due and she didn't want to go home yet. She turned the other way, out on to Station Road, and headed towards the river. There was a patch of grass and a bench, overlooking the water. If she walked quickly, she'd reach the bench in time to sit on it for a few minutes before having to turn back. She needed to think. She needed to get away from Tinderbox Lane.

Bad luck on Dolly. And bad luck on Fraser Buck. Escaping the tentacles of Tinderbox Lane wasn't destined to be so easy that morning. Because there he was, pacing that same patch of grass, in front of the same bench: a man with a lot on his mind. Dolly might have hurried on — except he spun around at exactly the wrong moment, and collided with her.

"Hello, Fraser."

It took him a moment to recognise her. "Oh. It's you," he said. "Hello, Diane."

"Good to see you, too."

"Hm?" His attention had returned to the mobile: *tap tap tap*.

Dolly might have come to the river in search of solitude but here was an opportunity she couldn't ignore. "Awful goings-on," she said to him cosily. "I hope the family isn't too upset?"

"Hmm," he nodded, tapping away. "Sure is."

A woman he didn't want to have sex with, who couldn't aid him in any immediate, material fashion, was nothing much to Fraser: honestly — though he wouldn't put it like this — she was barely there at all. It wasn't that he meant to insult her/it, Dolly reflected. He just couldn't focus: like some people just can't read novels, or understand maths. Dolly didn't mind. She didn't want to have sex with him, either.

"Too awful, isn't it, Fraser?" she tried again. "Poor Rosie. She's terribly upset."

"That's right," he said, without looking up.

Dolly said: "Fraser, have you got a moment? I'd love a quick chat."

"In a bit of a rush," he said. "Sorry."

"It won't take a second." She indicated the bench. Hesitated. *Did she really want his nasty backside polluting her favourite bench in London?* "Sit down," she ordered, and he did.

"I've been reading your wife's cards," she said.

"Reading Rosie's cards?" He stared at Dolly, beads of irritable sweat glistening on his forehead, beefy thighs splayed like he owned the bench. "I don't even know what that means, Diane. Deirdre. Whatever your name is. Frankly. Is that what you wanted to say to me?"

192

She said: "No. I just thought you might be interested."

"Not really." He smirked. Or smiled. She wondered if he had any idea how rude he sounded.

"No? Oh, well. Then I guess I'll keep all her amazing secrets to myself! Never mind! All's well that ends well in the wonderful world of wonderful Rosie!" She was talking nonsense. It didn't matter. She decided to risk it. "Have you seen Nikki lately?"

He looked at her, then. "— Pardon?"

"Nikki. Large lady — friend of Maurice. In the Flag Club a lot of nights . . ."

He shook his head, and laughed — still not sure if he'd heard right. "I have no idea who you're talking about."

But Dolly's nose was quivering (metaphorically speaking). He was lying. Dolly had not been alive and watchful all these years without being able to spot when a married man was lying about his sex life. And this lying man was even easier to read than most. She hadn't been certain before, but she was certain now. She said: "You know Nikki, Fraser! Big lady. Very curvy. Long, dark hair. Super sexy! She came for a reading with me a few weeks back. *Of course* you know her. She certainly knows you!" Dolly leaned across the bench and winked at him. "She knows all about you!"

He stopped laughing then. Dolly didn't flinch. He glared at her. She gazed right back. She was on a bench, in a public place, in broad daylight. He couldn't hurt her.

"*Have you seen her, Fraser? I can't find her anywhere.*"

Fraser stood up. His trousers had rucked up around his meaty thighs. He was built like a wrestler. "I have no idea what you're talking about, you nosey old hag. As I said . . . So why don't you keep your witchy little nose in your own business?"

"How did your wife really get that cut on her eye, Fraser? Do you know?"

He bent down until their faces were so close Dolly could feel the heat off his eyeballs: like a character out of a comic strip, she thought. Except terrifying. But she didn't back away. "Well now," he said, "why don't you ask her? I wouldn't mind knowing myself. And while you're at it, ask her what she was doing night before last, when she was supposed to be at home looking after our kids, and she was actually sneaking around Tinderbox Lane like the slag she is. Why don't you ask her what she was doing? Because I surely don't know . . ."

"But it's not what I was asking," Dolly said.

He stood back, eyes still locked on her face. Yes. He was seeing her now. "You should be more careful, lady," he said. She blinked. "And, by the way, next time you're looking for a place to shove your ugly nose, why don't you and your policeman boyfriend shove it in the direction of Adrian Bousquet? Because where the fuck is *he* in all this? Has anyone seen him?"

"We've been looking for Ade. I was going to ask you. Do you have a number for him, Fraser?"

194

He continued to glare at her, until she could feel the hairs rising on the back of her neck, but she didn't look away.

"You take care, Deirdre," he said.

She watched him leave, beefy thighs rubbing against each other, back and shoulders rigid with outrage. She wasn't sure which of them had come out of the conversation worse, but she could feel her whole body shaking. He was lying — that was clear. And she was prying. And she was out of her depth. Tonight, over dinner with Raff, she would unburden herself of everything she had learned; and then, perhaps, she would be free to grieve her unfathomable friend, Maurice, in peace.

CHAPTER
THIRTY-ONE

Raff called his son, Sam, for some tips on where to take Dolly for dinner, but it wasn't much help. Sam earned almost nothing, and spent what little spare cash he had on expensive biking gear and following his football team to matches around the country. He knew nothing about "fine dining", as he reminded his father. "Why don't you take her to the pub?"

"She's not that sort of woman," said Raff. Except she was, of course: it was one of the reasons he liked her. It was also one of the reasons he wanted to spoil her, and take her somewhere decent. It would be a treat for them both.

In the end he looked it up on TripAdvisor. He took her to a restaurant in Mortlake, overlooking the river. It was expensive, and the menu would be full of complicated dishes with incomprehensible ingredients. But he reckoned Dolly would be in her element. She may have been perfectly happy to spend an evening in the pub, but he knew she knew about food, because she'd told him so. It would give them something to talk about — just in case they ran out of conversation.

They didn't, though. Not from the moment he came to her door, and she opened it, and she was wearing a dress that made her buxomness look — well, if Raff had been less reticent, he would have said *goddess-like*.

"You look lovely, Dolly," he said instead. And Dolly knew he meant it: partly because of the heartfelt way he said it, and partly because she *felt* lovely. She hadn't felt so lovely in a long time. The dress was from H&M. It was her going-out-somewhere-smart dress, her date dress, her funeral dress. She must have worn it forty times, and what she knew and he didn't was that it was fraying at both shoulders: a single, sudden movement away from tearing . . . also, because dressing up often coincided with feeling nervous, that it was *very slightly discoloured under the arms* . . . Also, she'd sewn up the hem three times already. He didn't know that. And, what with her clean hair and high shoes and Chanel perfume, and what with the way he looked at her when she came to the door, she might not have known it either. She felt lovely.

Raff didn't have a car: he had the motor-home which, *in extremis*, could be made to motor. But he didn't want to introduce her to his motor-home just yet: nor to his beloved boa. Normally, he used a motorbike to get around town, but he arrived at Tinderbox Lane on foot.

They took a black cab to Mortlake. Dolly didn't say so, but as she settled back in the seat she felt like a child, on a birthday treat. Black cabs were for tourists, millionaires, and people on expenses — Dolly hadn't been inside one for a couple of years, at least.

She said: "They're lovely, aren't they?" And Raff, sitting beside her, knew what she was talking about.

The experience was quite novel to him, too. Raff, though he earned more than Dolly, was not a man who liked to spoil himself. He didn't much like money, and he gave a lot of it away — to distant cousins, or cancer charities, or homes for orphaned snakes. He put most of what he earned into a trust for Sam, so that one day (unlike his father), Sam might be able to buy himself a house. Sam didn't want a house, and often asked his father to stop — but Raff wouldn't. Couldn't. Didn't want to. He didn't like spending money on himself. But spending money on Dolly — that was a different matter.

"London won't be London without black cabs," he agreed. "They'll be extinct soon though, won't they? Better use them while we can!"

It was a good restaurant. As they handed their coats to the front desk, Raff felt quite proud of the choice: there were smiling waiters and linen tablecloths, there was soft lighting and posh-looking food, and a table (specially requested) by the window, by the river's edge. It was dark outside by the time they sat down, but the restaurant lights reflected on the water surface, and the full moon was out; and it was beautiful. They ordered a bottle of wine. Clinked glasses.

Raff said: "We got the results on the floater."

"On the . . .?"

"A prostitute, name of Melinda Stevens. Thirty-seven years of age. Reported missing seventeen years ago in — Dagenham, I believe it was. There were bruises all over her body. And she was pregnant, as you say . . . Possibly a suicide. But the bruises are suspicious . . . Anyway," he said. He smiled at Dolly. "Bad news for Melinda. Good news for your friend. Unless of course, which is possible, 'Nikki' *is* — or was — Melinda, and she changed her name . . ."

It took a moment for Dolly to absorb this somewhat brutal flood of information. Nikki was still missing. Maurice was still dead. The questions remained.

"Do you think she was murdered?" Dolly asked.

He shrugged. "We don't know. Possibly. It's hard to be sure of anything at this stage, because the body was so long in the water, and no one seems to know anything about her . . . Possibly because she is — was — living under an assumed name . . . The marks on the neck were consistent with mild strangulation — possibly sex related . . ."

"You think that's what killed her?"

"We don't know."

". . . Were there drugs involved? Can you tell?"

"Not really. Not without results from toxicology . . . But, I would have said yes. Probably. There usually are . . . Poor old thing. Nasty world." Raff leaned over the linen tablecloth. ". . . I know what you must be asking yourself," he said. "At least I think I do."

"Oh? What am I asking?"

"You're asking — Well . . . That is, *in your place*, I'd be asking . . . in any case it's the question I keep asking *myself* . . . how in heaven's name did you know the poor girl was pregnant?"

Dolly said: "It *is* rather odd, isn't it?"

"A weird coincidence."

"As my friend Sandra would say, *there's no such thing as a coincidence.*"

"Do you believe that?"

"Maybe." She smiled. "It wasn't what I was thinking, anyway. I was thinking, if that *wasn't* Nikki, then where is Nikki? And where is Ade? And why have they both disappeared at the same time that Maurice has been murdered?"

"We don't know he was murdered."

". . . blood all over the place, things smashed on the floor, back door jammed shut, cricket bat covered in blood . . . And Maurice, hale and hearty one day, lying in a pool of blood the next. What do *you* think?"

"But no sign of a forced entry."

"Because there didn't need to be! Ade has a key. And the spares are still missing. Plus the back door only needs the tiniest little shove, which is obviously why he put the chair there . . . Whoever it was, must have come at him, whacked him on the head with that cricket bat, dumped the cricket bat . . . And then left him to bleed to death . . ."

"But why would they do that, Dolly?"

"*I don't know.* But *someone* did *something*, didn't they? Because now he's dead."

The waiter arrived. Raff only wanted a steak, but Dolly (no matter the other subject) wanted to spend time examining the options. Raff waited patiently while Dolly wavered between the lambs' kidneys and the sweetmeats. She settled on the sweetmeats. "Or, no, wait a moment —" she buried her head in the menu yet again. "I haven't looked at the fish . . ."

200

After a while, Raff leaned across the table and, with a finger, lowered the menu, so he could see her face. "The question is," he said, in a lovely, soft voice that only she could hear: "why would anyone want to kill Maurice?"

"Exactly! That's *exactly* my question!"

The waiter said: "Have you chosen, madam?"

Raff leaned back, removing his finger from the corner of Dolly's menu, so it bounced back in place. "Go on," he said. "Hurry up!"

"One second," Dolly said.

Fifteen seconds later (he was a reasonably patient man), Raff leaned across the table again. "By the way," he said, "I've been doing a bit of investigating. Not officially." He winked. "Above my pay grade and all that. But I've gone into the database and discovered a few things about your neighbours that might surprise you."

Dolly turned to the waiter. Ordered the steak.

"You definitely don't want kidneys?" Raff chuckled. "What about the fish?"

"What? No. *Tell me!* What have you discovered?"

"Firstly: there's no sign of Ade Bousquet. Not anywhere. No one seems to know where he is."

"I could have guessed that."

"No one of that name has checked into a hospital in the UK. So much for your young stoner friend —"

"Not a friend."

"— If Ade Bousquet's got 'skull damage', he's either checked in somewhere under another name, which is possible, or he's taking care of it himself."

Dolly thought about it. "Fraser Buck's been looking for him, too. Maurice Bousquet told me Fraser and Ade were in business together. Did you know that?"

"That was the next thing I was going to tell you. Buck and Ade are — or were — in the middle of a purchase — it's a block of flats, just round the corner from here, actually. Ex-council . . . Upwards of a few million . . . And now the whole thing's in the air, due to Ade Bousquet having gone walkabout. From what I understand, Bousquet was putting up eighty per cent of the cash."

"*My goodness.* He's rich!"

"Well," said Raff — "(Shall we get another bottle?) Either he's rich or he isn't. Because the money isn't there, is it? Fraser Buck must be climbing the walls."

"I told you Maurice had a theory that Fraser and Nikki were up to no good together. He spotted them both at the Flag Club."

"Yes, you told me . . . But Fraser Buck was trying to buy the Flag Club. That's something else I discovered. Not with Ade, on his own. But it means he may well have been in there on business. So to speak. You said Maurice wasn't exactly reliable. Did you believe him?"

"Well . . ." Dolly hesitated. It was a good question. She hadn't really believed him, not at first. It seemed — well, it seemed too good to be true. But that was before she talked to Fraser. "I'm fairly certain that Nikki was someone who supplemented her income, so to speak . . . with her favourite pastime. And I can tell you she was *definitely* keen on sex . . ."

Raff laughed.

202

"That is to say . . ." Holy, bloody hell, was she *blushing*? What was she, sixteen years old? She'd told Pippa to stay away tonight, just in case. *Not that anything* . . . "What I mean, Raff, is that she was very, very, *very* keen. Like you'd need to be, to spend an evening in the Flag Club . . . with Fraser Buck." Dolly took a gulp of wine. Regrouped a bit. "And my goodness you should hear Pippa on the subject of Fraser Buck. Not that it's evidence. But Pippa's as sharp as anyone. Anyway, short answer: *yes*. I only half believed it when Maurice first told me. But I completely believed it after today. I asked Fraser if he'd seen Nikki lately."

Raff looked unhappy. "You did what, Dolly?"

"He is not a nice man, Raff. *Luckily*, we were in a public place . . ."

Dolly reached for a breadstick. Raff put his hand on hers and for a loopy moment, she thought he was reminding her of her diet, which he didn't know about.

"*What?*" she snapped, snatching her hand away.

"Fraser Buck," Raff said, "is a nasty piece of work."

"Well yes, I just said that."

"You don't want to go messing around with the likes of him. He's . . ." Raff paused. Tried again. "I told you I had a bit of a poke around at work. All right. Firstly, your friend, Mrs Buck —"

"Again. Not my friend —"

"— has a criminal record."

"No!"

"For shoplifting. Back in 1991. Which you may not think —"

203

"Hmmm." Dolly leaned back, disappointed. "I'm not sure teenage shoplifting really counts."

Raff said: "Maybe not. Except 1991 was only the first time . . . She's been cautioned *seven times* in the last three years, Dolly. She's actually been banned from the Sainsbury's on Barnes High Street. They won't let her in."

"No!"

"She's obviously got a problem — when somebody as well heeled as Mrs Frosty-Buck . . . feels the need to steal — the last time she got caught she was trying to make off with a lot of Tupperware . . ."

Dolly said: "Are you *smirking*?"

"I'm just observing . . ." he was smirking, "— that she's not quite like the mums you see in the Persil ads . . . that's basically what I'm saying. She's a nutter."

"Rosie Buck, a kleptomaniac! When you say it — I shouldn't be surprised."

". . . And then there's Fraser Buck. And by the way this, Dolly, I am not smirking about. This, I need you to listen to. There's an organisation, name of UglyMugs — it's a charity. A remarkable organisation, in actual fact. What it does, it allows sex workers to share information, so that those who sign up to it (and anyone else for that matter) are provided with a type of warning system . . . helping them to recognise and avoid punters with a violent or dangerous track record. It doesn't give out the full names, because it can't. There's nothing anyone can legally do about these characters until someone presses charges, and as you can imagine, victims often aren't that keen. But in the

204

meantime UglyMugs gives a description, maybe a first name, and when it's possible, that character's mobile number, with the last three digits removed . . . It's saved a lot of lives, Dolly."

"I'm sure."

"UglyMugs works with the police. All right? So although they can only release limited information via the network, they actually release *all* the information they have, to us. So we have it on our database. Names, mobile numbers and so on . . ."

". . . Fraser Buck?" Dolly muttered.

He nodded. "He's on the list. With three or four mobile numbers attached, which suggests he is a repeat offender . . . And yet, there's nothing on him. Nothing. He's spotless."

"Bloody hell," she said. "Can't you get him? Somehow?"

Raff said: "I wish we could. And we will, eventually." He looked at Dolly. There was something fearless about her — something foolhardy — and it made him afraid. "I want you to be careful," he said. "I don't want to come across all heavy handed and whatnot, Dolly. But he's dangerous. We'll get him eventually. I'm sure of it. In the meantime I strongly advise you not to tangle with him. If you can avoid having anything more to do with him you'll be doing yourself a favour."

"Do you think," asked Dolly, her mind racing: "do you think he had anything to do with Maurice's death? Do you?"

"Are you hearing me, Dolly?"

"Yes! Of course I am. But he lives two doors up from me, Raff. I can't exactly have *nothing* to do with him. Do you think he killed Maurice?"

"He may have done," Raff said. "If Fraser really was balling Nikki; and Maurice was shouting about it all over town. And now she's gone missing . . ."

. . . It happened to Raff every once in a while, more often recently — and especially right now. He would think of those flunked detective exams, all those years ago. And think, *maybe it's not too late to try again?*

"So Fraser Buck may have a motive, yes," he continued. "Rosie Buck has one, too. I suppose. If Maurice was gabbing off about her accosting him, he would have been putting not just her comfortable marriage at stake but, given the violent proclivities of her husband, her own physical safety, too. Add to that, Ade Bousquet's vanishing act, which clearly begs a few questions. Add to that the disappearance of the Bousquet Junior and Senior's on-off girlfriend, Nikki Surname-unknown, who seems to have been knobbing every man on Tinderbox Lane and beyond. Excluding the young Terry Whistle," he smiled, ". . . so *far as we know* . . . That's a lot of questions unanswered, Dolly. And we're still waiting on results from the PM for cause of death."

"You saw the scene," said Dolly. "Someone beat him to death."

"Maybe." Raff shrugged. "We don't know for sure. I'm not a detective, Dolly. And neither are you."

"Yes," she blurted, "but I bet you want to be!"

Raff faltered.

206

"Sorry. That was stupid. Stupid of me. I was getting carried away. I know you're not a detective — any more than I am. I just . . ." Dolly stopped.

"No worries, Dolly," he said, but he was blushing, ashamed she had so easily identified his sore spot. Was it that obvious? He looked out over the water and for a moment — only one moment — they both fell silent.

The river was always beautiful, but tonight, in the moonlight, it seemed especially so . . . Raff turned back to her and smiled: she was lovely. Everything was lovely. He was happy. "You're right, Dolly. Sometimes I do still wish I was a detective. But not right now . . . D'you fancy a pudding? Shall we get the menu back?"

CHAPTER
THIRTY-TWO

They didn't mention Maurice again. It wasn't hard. They had no shortage of things to talk about. Dolly tried, once more, to get Raff to describe an average day out on patrol, but he didn't like talking about it much. He said the most important thing was being able to switch off at the end of the shift. People who took their police-work home with them didn't last for long, he said. He was keener to talk about his beloved boa, also named Dorothy, sometimes "Dolly" for short. They were into their second bottle by then. Raff said: "That's two girls named Dorothy I'm destined to love." And then he realised what he'd said, and looked, for a moment, as if he might die from the embarrassment. Dolly felt for him, and felt her heart skip. Because he was destined to love her. And that's what that Two of Cups had been telling her. And the Ace of Cups before it. Should she play it cool and pretend she hadn't noticed? Should they both brush over it?

She burst out laughing. "I look forward to meeting the other one," she said. "That is, I *think* I do . . ."

It was a mile or so walk from the restaurant to Tinderbox Lane, and a slightly longer walk to Raff's motor-home. Dolly didn't want to say it, in case he got the wrong(ish) idea, but since she'd instructed Pippa to make herself scarce tonight, she knew they would have the house to themselves. She invited him home for a nightcap. "And then you can get a cab from mine," she said. *Just to be clear.*

He laughed. "Just to be clear," he said.

"That's right." It was a bit early in their friendship to be falling into bed, she supposed. No, she knew. She'd regret it in the morning. But even so, she hadn't spent an evening with a man she fancied quite so much in years. So maybe it wasn't too early. She would see. See how it went . . .

Forty-five minutes later they were strolling happily along Station Road — when who should pull up behind them, flashing his lights and waving like a madman, but Derek West, aka Professor Filthy.

"Bloody hell," muttered Raff. "Not again."

"Shhh!" giggled Dolly. "Poor guy. I think he's dreadfully lonely . . ."

"Hello neighbour!" cried Derek West, rolling down the window, leaning across the passenger seat. "What a lovely surprise! How *really lovely* to see you!"

"Hello Derek. You remember Raff, don't you?"

"Hullo, hullo, hullo," said Derek. "Of course I remember Raff! Well! Isn't this lovely? What a really lovely surprise," he said again.

"Evening Derek," said Raff, without any enthusiasm. "Good to see you again."

"Well I was just on my way back from a bloody long day at work and *feeling a bit blue*, to be frank with you — and *here you are*! What a turn-up! There's something about it, isn't there: *bumping into the neighbours.* I love it. Feels like home."

"It certainly does," said Dolly. *Poor guy,* she thought. *Mustn't be cruel, must be kind. He's lonely.* She smiled.

"Where are you two off to then?" the professor asked, feeling encouraged. "Dolly, are you ready for the big day? Got your talk ready? *I hope so!* Only a few days off now, isn't it? Aaaargh! Social media's going crazy for it! Can I offer you both a lift?"

Dolly didn't want a lift. Nor did Raff. Obviously. But sometimes, hopeless blunderers like Professor Filthy can be oddly effective at making things go their way. Professor Filthy was feeling lonely, and now, by chance, he appeared to have found a way through it: a couple of friends to spend the evening with. It was going to take an atomic bomb to put him off the scent. He aimed his conversation mostly at Dolly, whom he sensed instinctively was the least likely to send him packing; updating her on his Tarot Talk-related social-media triumphs, while intermittently referring to their dinner at the curry house, as if it had been the hottest date in living memory. Dolly could feel the professor's need for company and she felt sorry for him — and in her desperation to camouflage her desperation to be rid of him, overcompensated by laughing much too hard at his feeble jokes . . . As a result, both men misread the situation one hundred per cent. Dolly's kindness backfired on them all.

210

Raff listened to Dolly's encouraging laughter, took note of the warm smiles, couldn't miss the references to the hot date at the curry house . . . And because the other man had a flash yellow car, and a fancy title, and a job in academia, and because, in 1997, Raff had failed his detective exams, he came to the conclusion that Dolly wanted to be shot of him as soon as possible, so she could spend the rest of the evening with the more upmarket professor.

Filthy, meanwhile, basking in Dolly's encouraging laughter and warm smiles, thought it was amusing to insist on addressing Raff as "Inspector Plod"; and then to pepper his conversation, at random, with the words, "Hullo, Hullo, Hullo."

Finally Dolly said, "Don't be an idiot, Derek." But by then it was too late: he was overexcited. Dolly thought that if she kept on telling him not to be an idiot, she would only highlight his crassness, and make the situation worse. So she stopped telling him to stop, and so he continued.

"Well," said Dolly, desperately. "Nice to bump into you, Derek. I'll call you tomorrow, shall I? We can discuss everything then."

"Nonsense!" said Filthy. "I insist on giving you a lift somewhere. I'm not doing anything and the night is young! There's a lot to update you on. Shall we have a quick drink? Oops, *hullo, hullo, hullo* I see Inspector Plod there, reaching for his breathalyser! Not to worry, sir! I'll be imbibing an Appletiser! Can I buy you both a drink?"

"No thanks," said Dolly. She looked at Raff for support. He misconstrued it. Somehow he thought she *wanted* the bloody lift. He shrugged.

"But I insist," said Filthy.

It was feeble of Raff, actually; and feeble of Dolly. They should never have allowed him to sabotage their happy evening, and yet somehow, mostly because it was early days and they were diffident about imposing themselves too adamantly on one another, Professor Filthy won through. Raff returned to his motor-home alone. Dolly climbed into the professor's car, and he drove her back to Tinderbox Lane.

At the top of the lane, he pulled the car in to park it, but by then Dolly had realised quite how effectively the professor had winkled her away from her evening, and she was livid. Sympathy all gone. He said: "Can I come in for a bevvy, Dolly? Now the inspector's made tracks, I can probably allow myself something a bit wetter. If you know what I mean!"

"For your information, Raff is not an inspector," Dolly snapped, pointlessly. "And no you cannot come in for a drink. Either a wet one or a dry one. Whatever that means. I'm exhausted. Thank you for the lift. I will call you tomorrow."

"Wait!" he said.

But she couldn't stand to be in the same space with him for another second. She clambered out of his car, slammed the door, and strode into the darkness of Tinderbox Lane without looking back.

The lane was crowded with ghosts and shadows that night. But they didn't frighten her. She was too drunk, too disappointed, too angry. She let herself into her house, dumped her evening bag on the floor, threw off the high heels, dropped her tired body on to her tiny sofa, and allowed herself a moment of quiet defeat. She let the tears roll down her cheeks; and it felt wonderful — to be alone at last, and a little drunk, and free to grieve her old neighbour in peace.

CHAPTER
THIRTY-THREE

Her Tarot cards were on the table by the sofa. She reached for them automatically, and as she did so, a card fell out of the pack.

It landed face down, just out of her reach. Dolly stretched towards it uncomfortably. The waistband of her H&M dress was a whisper away from splitting: she had eaten too much tonight, dammit. As she reached to pick it up, praying the dress would hold, there came a noise; a deep rumble, growing steadily louder. It was coming, quite clearly, from the empty house next door. She paused, listened. The sound stopped.

And then the stench hit her, the one she hadn't smelled since Maurice left for the morgue: the one she had almost forgotten about — But yes, here it was again. She felt her skin tighten, and the temperature drop.

Next door, the low rumble returned, louder this time . . . It sounded like the boiler: Maurice's ancient boiler, growling back to life.

Was someone in there? But that was impossible. Wasn't there supposed to be a police officer, watching the house? It occurred to Dolly that actually — no: there'd been no police officer out there when she walked by a moment ago. She'd been too lost in her own thoughts to have taken note. So where had they gone? She waited and listened. But the house had fallen silent again; and the smell had vanished as quickly as it came.

She turned her attention back to the card, still lying on the floor. With a sullen heave, she stretched and picked it up.

The Ace of Pentacles, (sometimes called the Ace of Coins), represents the start of something material: a new business venture, perhaps; an inheritance; a new source of income stream; a prize; a win on the horses. Pentacles can often simply represent money . . .

She stared at the card, and the burn mark in its centre. The card was telling her something — but what? *Why was she being so damn slow?*

There came another noise from next door, this one more human. An object dropping on the floor, perhaps? And then Maurice's voice, clear as day:

Well, Dolly? Are you going to stay there, sitting on your backside, or you coming in?

"Dammit, Maurice," she grumbled. Slowly, she clambered to her feet.

First, she peered through the front window. She'd been right: there was no police officer out there, not any more. And no lights on in Maurice's house, either. *Dammit.* She was beginning to feel frightened.

Ha ha ha . . .

It wasn't funny. There came another thump from the other side of the wall, this one making her floor shake. She opened her mouth to call out — and thought better of it . . . The last thing she wanted was Terry and his Instagram turning up. Never again. She tiptoed to the back of the house, through the broom cupboard — and softly stepped out into her little garden.

Maurice's back door was ajar . . . and now the smell of tarnish was so strong she covered her nose and mouth to prevent herself from choking on it.

But she couldn't turn back, not with Maurice goading her on. He would never leave her alone. In any case it was not in her make-up to retreat. She wished it was.

The wooden fence between their back gardens had always been low and feeble. Since all the police activity earlier in the week it was in a worse state than ever: trampled and splintered and broken. She stepped over it into the barren patch that had been Maurice's garden —

This was a possible crime scene. It was an offence to be trespassing, or tampering with evidence — *but someone was already here.* She wasn't thinking straight. She wasn't thinking at all. Her feet carried her forward, one step at a time . . . Maurice's chair had been shunted aside. She slid through the back door, heard breathing, and spied a moving beam of light.

A large man, tall and brawny, was in the room with her. He was pulling books off the walls, opening them, shaking them, and tossing them aside. The floor was strewn with objects wherever his torch beam fell. He must, thought Dolly, have been in here, quietly ransacking the place, since before she got home. The man's silhouette reached for another book, and the torchlight shone eerily on to the surgical stitches that ran from his nostril, forked at his cheekbone and ended at two corners of the eye. It was Ade. He looked like Frankenstein's Monster.

He must have sensed her fear, because she had not made a sound, and yet he turned and stared, the whites of his eyes picked out in the torchlight. Like a wild animal, she thought. He was cornered.

The front door had been nailed shut since Ollie and Raff had forced their entry. Which meant Dolly was blocking his only way out. He would have to knock her aside to escape her. And that is what he did. Without a word, he charged at her, sent her flying across the little room. She landed on the ground, smacking her head against the far wall. By the time she sat up, he was gone — sprinting through her garden, through Terry's garden, and into the scrubland beyond.

Had he got what he came for? It seemed unlikely. Would he be back? Dolly didn't want to hang around to find out. She wanted to call the police. But then again — she hesitated. Ade was gone. Raff had told her it was an offence to trespass on a crime scene. What if they didn't believe her? What if they got the wrong idea and arrested her instead?

She wasn't thinking straight. All she knew for sure, was that she wanted to get out of there.

"*What, are you leaving already?*" Maurice said.

She ignored him. She clambered back over her broken garden gate, and locked herself into her own house.

She didn't go to bed. She was too afraid to go upstairs, so she lay on her sofa, wide awake for hours, heart beating like a hammer, alert to every movement, every creak and every breeze.

But she must have fallen asleep at some point, because she was woken at noon by the mobile on her lap. She was still on the sofa, still fully dressed, and too befuddled to check the caller's identity before picking up.

"Morning to you, Dolly." It was Raff. He sounded guarded.

"Raff . . . Hello Raff!" she cried, trying to regroup and sounding slightly manic. "Such a lovely, beautiful evening last night! I wish it hadn't ended how it did though! *Never mind!*" She did mind, very much. And yet, to Raff, it seemed that everything in her tone suggested the opposite.

He turned directly to business. "I thought you might be interested to know the results came in from the PM."

PM? . . . PM? . . . PM?

"Post mortem," he said.

"Yes! Of course! I knew that. Post mortem. Do you mean Maurice's post mortem or Nikki's, Raff?"

"I think," he said (he sounded embarrassed), "we've been getting ahead of ourselves."

"What's that?"

"Your neighbour wasn't murdered, Dolly. He died of carbon monoxide poisoning."

"Carbon monoxide? What?"

"You mentioned his boiler was broken."

"Carbon monoxide poisoning? That's ridiculous. How do you know?"

"I just told you, Dolly. PM results came through. He should have got his boiler fixed."

She shook her head. "It can't be as simple as that."

"Accidental death, Dolly. Results came in last night. Hence — you probably noticed — no police watch outside the door."

"I did notice that! Where the hell was she? I needed her!"

He wasn't listening. He wanted to get off the line. He felt a fool — on many counts. He felt a fool for letting the professor take his date away. He felt a fool for imagining Dolly might ever have wanted to spend the rest of the evening with him. He felt a fool for having been swept along by her, allowing himself to imagine intrigue — romantic and criminal — where it turned out now there was neither. "An old man with a broken boiler dies of carbon monoxide poisoning, Dolly. It's hardly a suspicious death. We don't tend to have officers available to guard every house in London where someone happens to have died."

"There's no need to be snide."

"I wasn't being snide . . ." But he was. ". . . Anyway, I'd better get on. I just thought you'd want to know. Thought you might be wondering where the police officer had gone. I'll catch you later, maybe."

"But Raff — what about the blood? And the smashed glasses? All the chaos?"

"We're assuming it was his blood. As you recall, he had quite a gash on his face previously, and when we found him — when you found him — you may remember — the wound had pulled open."

"I don't remember, no."

"Well. It had. As for the chaos — carbon monoxide poisoning sends the victim to sleep before it kills them, but for a while before that, extended low-level exposure can significantly affect their intellectual functions, too."

"Meaning?"

"Meaning, it can send them a bit deranged," he said. "Dizzy, confused, delirious, sometimes even psychotic . . . It would explain his hostile behaviour in the days and weeks before the death. If his boiler had a slow leak, which then deteriorated more rapidly on the evening he died. You mentioned he hadn't been himself."

"No, but . . ." Dolly fell silent. But what? She wanted to tell Raff about Ade, running at her in the darkness the previous night; the stitches on his face; the torchlight — and Maurice's voice, and the Ace of Pentacles . . . and the Star card, reversed. There was so much she didn't trust him enough to tell him — couldn't tell him — and yet, still, she wanted to keep him on the line. "I just wanted to say thank you for a lovely evening, Raff. And I really hope we can do it again. Maybe next time, without Professor West barging in and taking over."

A pause, long enough for Dolly to wonder if he was still there.

". . . I'll tell you something that might amuse you though," he said. He didn't want to hang up either, not any more. Because she was lovely, if a little insane: because he liked the sound of her voice. "They found a copy of Maurice Bousquet's last will and testament in his trouser pocket, if you can believe it — signed and dated a fortnight back. Which, in itself, is a little curious you might think. Except it turns out he used to change his will the whole time. According to his solicitor. You get elderly people like that, sometimes, don't you. Very sad. It's the only power they feel they can wield any more, so they go on wielding it until even their solicitor's sick of the sight of them."

"Not much power, poor old fellow," said Dolly. "He hadn't got two brass farthings, so far as I know."

"Maybe so. But he left them both, all the change down the back of his sofa, and everything else he owned — to a lady named Lucky Crystal . . ." He laughed. "She's the Tuesday-night stripper down at the Flag Club . . ." He was still laughing. ". . . Lucky old Crystal, eh? . . . *Two old chairs, and half a candle, One old jug without a handle . . .*"

"*These were all the worldly goods, Of the Yonghy-Bonghy-Bò . . .*"

"Ah! You know it!" He was delighted. "You see? I may not drive a yellow sports car. Or convene with the spirits and whatnot . . . not yet, anyway . . . But we *do* have things in common!"

CHAPTER
THIRTY-FOUR

Even so, they hung up without making a date. Dolly's secrecy about the incident with Frankenstein's Monster/Ade coloured her tone in a way she could not control. Raff heard it amplified in every word, and assumed the worst: that Dolly couldn't wait to get him off the telephone. Disaster. Dolly felt bereft. After the call, she didn't know quite what to do with herself.

Sandra had left a voicemail: a friendly message. She wanted to hear the dirt on Dolly's hot date with Raff. She wanted to share the dirt on her own hot date with — Sandra never seemed to have a shortage of dates. Also, after all the upset with her old neighbour, Sandra wanted to check that Dolly was all right.

"In fact [she said] there are literally *thousands* of things I want to discuss with you. So please call me at once. And I've got tomorrow night written in, carved in stone, so I hope you're not feeling too nervous. You're going to be *great*. The Greatest Tarot Talker in the history of Tarot Talking, right? I'll be bringing along my new hot date, hope-you-don't-mind, name of 'Chas' — *how posh is that?* — Actually, no, scratch that, darling. Scratch the name. Because I might *not* bring posh Chas. I might bring someone else, and I don't want you putting your great hoof in it, calling someone Chas, who's actually called . . . oh, bollocks, I'm jabbering. Call me, Dolly. Soon as you can."

Dolly called there and then, but she had missed the moment. According to her assistant, Sandra was already en route to the Mission-Critical New Media Usability conference out in Hendon. Lucky thing.

So Dolly tried Pippa. But Pippa never picked up. In any case, Dolly preferred not to bother her. It was hard enough for the poor girl, having to share a bed with her own mother: the least Dolly could do, was to leave her in peace during the day. With an effort, Dolly refrained from sending Pippa a text. Instead, she paced the room, worried —

And then called Raff. At that same moment he'd been pulling out his mobile to call her again. He sounded absurdly happy to hear from her.

"Dolly!" he said. Beside him, sitting in the passenger seat, Ollie smirked. "I was just about to call you — I can't believe we hung up without making another date."

"No! Yes! *I know*," she said. "Aren't we ridiculous? — Raff, I'm so sorry to bother you again. But there was something I didn't tell you. And I can't tell you over the phone . . . I think I did something illegal. No. I *did* do something illegal — It's Ade, Raff. I broke into the —"

"Careful now," he said. "Shh-shh. *Careful*. No need to tell me here and now. No need for that." He glanced at Ollie. "I can meet you later, if you like. Or I can meet you now for a quick half-hour . . . Ollie? You all right with that? If I take a quick break?"

They arranged to meet at noon (assuming no police crisis) on the towpath just up from Barnes Bridge. It was a midway point between the police station and Tinderbox Lane, and on a weekday the only other people down there were joggers with earphones in. Nobody would overhear them.

Raff arrived half an hour late. "We had a situation," he said vaguely. "A situation," he expanded, when Dolly pushed, involving an individual locking himself into his motorcar and a wife launching empty beer bottles at the windscreen. "Which in itself would have been containable. I would have got to you on time." But then a piece of broken bottle had bounced off the windscreen and cut the arm of the driver of a passing van. "Mayhem after that, Dolly," he said. "We had to close the road . . . Twenty-odd years in this job, and I swear, it still astonishes me, quite how stupid full-grown adults can be."

"You must get to see a lot of crazies in your line of business," Dolly said, with a certain amount of relish.

"I should imagine," replied Raff, "that you get to know quite a few of them in yours."

She didn't contradict him, and they walked together in silence for a while.

CHAPTER
THIRTY-FIVE

". . . Sometimes," Dolly said, as they walked along, looking over the water, "when I'm feeling really miserable and lost — which by the way isn't often — I come down here to this footpath, and stare at the river flowing by, and it actually speaks to me: it offers up the answers."

"Is that right, Dolly?" said Raff, politely. "I love this river, too."

He came down here himself sometimes, just for the peace and quiet. Some days, all you could hear was the splash of the rowing boats, and the echo of church bells from St Nicholas across the water. He would have liked to bring the boa along for some mud play. She would have loved it. But then people would spot her and they would be bound to freak out. ". . . So what's up, Dolly?" he asked her at last. "What have you done? Robbed a bank?"

Leaving out any mention of ghostly voices, Tarot cards, and ancient boilers returning to life, Dolly told Raff what had happened. That is, she told him about Ade.

Raff said: "You should never have gone into the house alone."

"I didn't want to. But your police guard had wandered off. What was I supposed to do?"

"Call the police."

She thought about it. "Well, I didn't, did I? I called you."

"Dolly. This isn't funny. You said yourself, you believed Ade Bousquet was capable of killing someone."

"I do believe that."

"So what were you thinking?"

"I wasn't. All right? I wasn't thinking. I just acted. It was instinctive. Plus I had no idea it was Ade until a second before he ran me down . . . And now, here I am. Asking for help, Raff. Please, don't lecture me."

He bit his tongue, and they walked in silence again. The tide was very low. The riverbed looked like a vast, muddy beach. Automatically, Raff scoured its surface, as he always did. Because *you never knew* what secrets the Thames might wash up: a dead body, a long-lost treasure chest . . .

"Would you be willing to make a statement?" he asked her finally.

"Bloody hell, *of course not* Raff. I shouldn't have been in there in the first place. I don't want to incriminate myself."

"You shouldn't have been in there," he said. "On the other hand, in the circumstances, the law might take a lenient approach. Added to which, now I think about it, Maurice's house is no longer being considered the scene of a crime, so you'd only be done for common trespass, which isn't even a criminal offence."

226

"It *is* the scene of a crime," Dolly said stubbornly. "I don't care what the post mortem says. If everything was above board — then what do you think Ade was looking for? In the pitch black, in the middle of the night. And by the way, did I mention he was looking like bloody Frankenstein's Monster?"

"I have no idea what he was looking for, Dolly. Perhaps he was looking for his birth certificate. Or perhaps he wanted to borrow a pair of his dad's braces . . ."

Dolly turned on him. "Are you laughing at me, Raff?"

"Of course not. I'm just saying — if you're unwilling to make a statement about what you saw last night, there's really not a great deal we can do. Ade Bousquet broke into his dad's house. He actually has a key, though, doesn't he?"

"*Exactly!*"

"So, strictly speaking, he didn't even break in."

"Except, as you say, the house now belongs to Tallulah the Stripper . . . What was her name?"

"Lucky Crystal."

"— So he *was* breaking in. Plus the house is still in probate, presumably. So he's got no business to be in there."

"But if you won't make a statement, Dolly . . ."

They fell silent yet again. It was unsatisfactory. Everything about the situation was unsatisfactory, except the beauty of the river path and their pleasure in each other's company. She asked him if there was any news on Nikki. He told her they weren't even looking for her currently, due to the fact that nobody had actually reported her missing.

"Do you think I'm crazy, Raff? Do you think I'm imagining all this?"

He laughed. "I think you're barking, Dolly. But then again, who isn't? And no . . ." He chose his next words carefully, "No, I don't think you're imagining all this. I just think there may be less mischief afoot, than you — errr — well, than you *possibly think*."

She smiled. "I'm not crazy," she said.

Just ahead of them, sticking out of the mud, was a large white object: not a treasure chest, but a fridge or an oven. It was a blot on their lovely landscape.

"*Who does that?*" tutted Dolly. "What is it? A fridge?"

"Cowboy builders — tip all their crap into the river when everyone's asleep . . . Not much we can really do about it, except clear up after them."

But Dolly wasn't listening. A dazzling new idea had just struck her:

"*Raff!*" she burst out. "The BOILER! We forgot about the *Bucks* . . ."

"Forgot what about the Bucks, Dolly?"

"What if the Bucks, and Ade — and maybe even Nikki — *what if they're all in it together?*"

"In *what* together? Dolly there isn't a 'what'. There's the death of a man you were fond of — and I'm sorry. I'm sorry, because I can see you were fond of him, but . . ." He sighed. "I've got to go. I've got to get back to work —"

228

"RAFF! They're both trained plumbers. Heating engineers. Whatever they call themselves these days. People who work with boilers. That is, *Fraser* is a trained boiler man! And *Rosie* said something like: 'There's nothing much I don't know about boilers!' Remember? Don't you remember? Raff — I think they killed him! That is — I think *Fraser* did. But the fact is either one of them could have got into house, tampered with his boiler . . . He probably caught them red handed — and that's why he died, with his stupid cricket bat in his hand. He was guarding his stupid bloody boiler . . . Little did he know it was too late . . .''

"It doesn't sound terribly —"

"No, it doesn't, does it? It sounds ridiculous. I agree with you. But so does the alternative: an old man dies, covered in blood, in a house that's been smashed up. And meanwhile all the people with reasons to want him dead have either gone missing or they're acting very weirdly indeed . . . and yet, on the basis of a single, little 'post mortem', your precious police force comes to the conclusion that Nothing Suspicious has taken place . . .''

He laughed. "Not that little. Quite a big post mortem result. Quite a decisive one, Dolly."

"Don't. Patronise. Me. *Please*. You know what I mean . . . POSSIBILITY ONE:" she began, "Maurice was blabbing about Fraser 'balling' Nikki (your expression, Raff . . .) who has since gone missing. Rosie Buck happens to tell Fraser Buck about Maurice's boiler being on the blink. He spots his chance, inveigles his way into Maurice's house, offers to mend the boiler. Creates the leak. *BAM*. Maurice is dead. No more gossip connecting him and Nikki. Convenient for Fraser on so many levels."

"Doesn't explain how the house got smashed up," interrupted Raff.

"I'll come back to that. POSSIBILITY NUMBER TWO: Rosie Buck. She had a bloody great cut on her face the other day — did she ever tell you how she came by it? No. She told me it was getting out of the shower. But I don't believe it for a minute. Add to that, Terry says he saw her going into Maurice's cottage that night . . ."

Raff laughed. "Terry says that, does he?"

"I put a glass to the wall. Didn't Ollie tell you?"

"He did mention it."

"She could have killed him, Raff. Same method. Maurice was blabbing about her lunging at him, humiliating her, threatening her marriage. She must have been mortified. If word reached her husband, what would he do? We don't know. What's certain is she's frightened of him. And with good reason."

"Hm."

POSSIBILITY NUMBER THREE: Ade. Has a nasty, long-running spat going with his dad, we don't know what it is, culminating when he knocks him on the head with the cricket bat and leaves him to die . . . little knowing the carbon monoxide 'situation' might have saved him the trouble . . ." Dolly fell silent. Nothing sounded quite satisfactory. She knew it. "In any case," she said. "I think we should talk to Fraser first."

"Who said anything about us talking to any of them?"

"I meant, me. Not us. Sorry. I didn't mean to make assumptions. I know you need to get back to work, Raff. But I can't do nothing. I can't. I cannot let my neighbour just — die — and not at least try to find out what happened . . ." She thought of Maurice's cards, coming back to haunt her; and of Maurice's voice last night, urging her into the cottage. There was no question of her walking away. ". . . Not to mention, you know — not that I really care about her, but she's still human, and it really doesn't look like anyone else seems to care much — What about Nikki? She's completely disappeared. And quite honestly, I wouldn't be surprised if Fraser had something to do with that, too."

"Fraser is a nasty piece of work," Raff agreed. "But to suggest he's somehow involved in murder —"

"He's got an office in Putney," she interrupted. "I'm going to pay him a visit."

"No you're not, Dolly. You're not going anywhere near him."

"At risk of sounding like my delightful neighbour, Terry . . . and for all your fancy uniform and manacles and foldaway truncheons and Taser guns and whatnot . . ."

"I'm not carrying a Taser."

"You are carrying manacles then?"

"Handcuffs. I'm carrying handcuffs, Dolly."

She let it hang there a moment: they both chortled.

"You can't stop me from going, Raff. You can't."

"I can't stop you — but I can ask you. As a friend. He's dangerous. He's a dangerous man."

"Well if this situation is so damn dangerous, why aren't your colleagues looking into it?"

Raff sighed. How many times did he have to explain it? As far as the police were concerned, there was no crime to investigate: no murder, no missing person, no forced entry — not even a case of trespass. There was nothing. A lonely old man with an ancient, broken boiler had died of carbon monoxide poisoning. He said: "I get off at four this afternoon, Dolly. It's only in a few hours. Can you wait until then? I'll come with you — as a friend, mind, Dolly. *Not* with my work hat on."

"But you look lovely in your work hat," Dolly said. He scowled, irritated. "*Sorry,*" she added. "That was feeble. What I mean is, thank you. And yes, of course I can wait. And maybe afterwards, assuming we survive —"

"Facetious. Again," Raff said. "This isn't a game, Dolly."

"Patronising. Again. I'm not stupid."

"I realise."

"I was going to say, maybe afterwards you might let me cook you dinner, to say thank you?"

Raff said: "I can't tonight —"

"Oh . . . No." *Of course not.* Crash landing. What an idiot she was.

"I would have loved it," he said. "But I have my son, Sam, tonight. Every other Thursday . . . Never changes. Not since the divorce . . . But maybe, one day, if you're not busy, you might be able to come over and join us?"

232

CHAPTER
THIRTY-SIX

He watched her putting the door key under a stone by the bins. He tried not to say anything. He knew it would irritate — but he'd lost count of the number of house robberies he'd responded to over the years: the number of houses that had been broken into, simply because very stupid people hid their keys in very stupid places. The question was, which was worse: to irritate Dolly in the millisecond it took to make the comment; or to sit back and wait for her house to be robbed? He wouldn't be able to forgive himself.

"Just out of curiosity, Dolly, how many people d'you think know about that hiding place? Or — if they don't know about it, how many people do you think might perhaps be able to make a pretty good guess?"

"It's OK Raff," she said. "I've been doing it for years . . . Don't you worry, I can look after myself."

He made a mental note. It was not the end of the matter.

By then it was 5p.m. Raff had gone home and changed out of his work hat, and Dolly had texted him that she'd spotted the Buck Range Rover parked up on

Station Road, which meant Fraser Buck was already home.

They walked together up the lane to Windy Ridge. Not a long walk, by any stretch, but long enough for Dolly to wonder what the hell she was doing. By the time they reached the Bucks' front door her heart was beating so hard she thought it might burst through her throat.

"You sure you want to do this?" Raff murmured.

"Absolutely," she replied. It sounded calmer than she felt. "I'll start it, shall I? I'll start the talking. Get us past Rosie, and into the house."

". . . Ooooh!" said Rosie, panic registering on her still-bruised face. "Hello there neighbour! Have you come to see me? I was just cooking the kids' tea."

"I was looking for Fraser, actually, Rosie. Hope you don't mind. I wanted to ask him something — quickly. You've met Raff before, haven't you? We were walking by, and I was telling Raff how much Fraser loved to play golf."

"Does he?" said Rosie. "Well! If you say so!" She rattled out a laugh. "The stuff I don't know about my husband! Well, come on in! I'll give him a shout. He's in the media room with the kids. I think they're watching rugby."

"Raff wanted to ask his advice about golf memberships. Didn't you, Raff? He's looking for a club not too far out, this side of town — that sort of thing . . ."

"Not too expensive," added Raff.

"And I said to Raff — we were literally passing by the door — I said to Raff, *I know just the man to ask!*"

Rosie wasn't listening. She was only relieved they — or the policeman — hadn't come to talk to her. She led them across the hallway to the media room, and popped her head in: "Babe, you've got visitors! Dolly and Raff want to ask you about golf clubs! The joining sort, I think. Have you got a mo?"

He was stretched out on the leather sofa with his younger daughter, remote in one hand, stroking the girl's forehead with the other — and it was such an unexpectedly tender scene, it put the two visitors at a moment's disadvantage. There they were, all revved up to confront a monster: they found a man on a sofa, watching rugby, with his arm around his five-year-old child.

The sight of Dolly and Raff soon wiped the tender look off his face. He stood up, and sent both children out of the room.

It left the three of them alone, with the rugby in the background. And all Dolly could think was, *Thank God Raff came with me.* She said: "Are you a rugby player, Fraser?"

"How dare you come in here?"

Raff said: "Dolly's got a few questions she wants to ask you, Mr Buck. I'm here to help out. So if you wouldn't mind —"

"Well why don't you fuck right off and help out somewhere else?" said Fraser. Which didn't make sense, if you broke it down. But the general message was clear.

"I don't think you understand," said Raff, patiently. "I'm here *for Dolly*. And *she* has one or two questions she wants to ask. We'll be leaving together. And by the way, if you want my advice —"

"Did you hear me asking for it?"

"— I would get your coat, and come out for a little walk with us," Raff dropped his voice. "I'm assuming you don't want your wife and kids knowing why you've been blacklisted by prostitutes in the local area."

"I haven't the faintest idea what you're talking about."

"Yes, you have," said Raff.

Fraser's eyes bulged. "Are you here on official business, fuckwit? Because if you aren't, I swear to God you are in fucking hot fucking water, standing in my house, divulging a lot of shit you have no business to fucking divulge . . . Aside from the fact," he added belatedly, "I don't even know what you're talking about."

"It's in the public domain, Mr Buck."

"That information is *not* in the public domain."

"Enough of it is in the public domain," interrupted Dolly, "for me to know exactly what kind of a man you are, neighbour. Why don't you log on to UglyMugs and look yourself up? Knock yourself out, Fraser."

Fraser Buck watched her lips moving. It was the longest stretch of words, uttered by a female, he had ever before attended to; and as she continued, he became aware of two things: firstly, that she wasn't as one hundred per cent dumb as he had initially assumed, inasmuch as he had bothered to assume anything about her at all, except that she stank of joss sticks; and secondly, that he really, really wanted to punch her. If the off-duty policeman-twat hadn't been standing there, right beside her, he might even have done it. Instead, he fetched his coat.

Outside, they headed for Station Road: Fraser walked between them, Dolly on one side, Raff on the other. Dolly said: "What were you doing, Fraser, the day of the fight, when I saw you running up the lane away from Maurice Bousquet's house? Why were you there?"

Fraser laughed — a bark of surprise. "None of your fucking business."

"Maybe not," said Raff. "But I think you should satisfy her curiosity. Unless of course you want us to direct Rosie and your kids to the UglyMugs website. And I presume you wouldn't want us to do that."

Fraser stopped to face them. His eyes darted, rat-like, from one to the other, as he calculated his options.

Raff said: "Let's just get this over and done with, shall we? And then we can all get on with our evenings. Why don't you tell Dolly what you were doing the day the fight broke out at Mr Bousquet's place?"

"Ha!" said Fraser, shaking his head. "Fucking hilarious . . ."

"And then," continued Raff, "you can get back to your rugby."

"Doesn't it depend on what he actually tells us?" Dolly interrupted.

Raff shot her a glance. She shut up.

Fraser said, slowly: "And what about Ade? Have you even *spoken* to Ade Bousquet yet? Instead of harassing me. I haven't done anything, *nothing*. Meanwhile his dad drops dead and he's fucked off the face of the planet . . ."

"So. What were you doing there? At Maurice's house?" Dolly asked again.

There was a long pause and for a moment Fraser looked quite human: as bewildered and unloved and isolated as he felt, every moment of every day of his stupid, brutal life. ". . . I was just going to *talk* to him," Fraser said, shaking his shiny head. "Jesus — I don't know what happened to him, any more than you do. I wanted to talk to him because — Dolly, you know why. Everything was too close to home. That's all. I had only just found out — the stupid slut bothered to inform me — that my new neighbour, Maurice Bousquet, as well as being yet another of Nikki's innumerable fuck-buddies, was also my business partner's *father* . . . I mean. Christ allbloodymighty. And not only that, she and my business partner have got a bloody kid. I mean — of all the luck . . . So I went round to — have a little chat, I suppose. Make sure he kept quiet. We'd never spoke before. I thought maybe I could soften him up with — cash. Yeah? OK, so I was going there to offer him cash. Butter him up. I went to the front door, heard the kerfuffle — just like you did, Dolly. Diane. Whatever . . . I heard the fight, had a quick look-see through the letterbox — and fuck me, there was Ade! And fuck me, there was old-man-Maurice coming at him from behind with a bloody cricket bat! All right?

. . . And then *you* shouted through about calling the police, remember? And we *all* fucking stopped, didn't we? And that's when I ran away. And that is the last time I saw either of those bastards, alive or dead. So. There. That's it." He looked at Raff, gauging his response. "Can I go now?" he said.

"When was the last time you saw Nikki?" asked Dolly.

A beat. Fraser stared back at her. "Nikki?"

"When was the last time —"

"— I dropped her off at a 'termination' clinic somewhere in St John's Wood, a week ago on Friday. If you must know. With enough money to pay for the — procedure, and two thousand quid in so-called *recuperation* money. Silly cow. No proof it was mine, of course. She probably wasn't even pregnant. And the last time I saw her was the night Maurice died, three nights ago. She called me from a hotel in town — where she's spent the last week watching TV and eating ice cream, so far as I could tell. On my money, thank you very much. She asked me to come over and fuck her." He shrugged. "So I did."

"Which hotel?" Raff asked.

". . . Does it matter?"

"Do you think she might still be there?"

"She'll be there until the money runs out, I imagine. And then she'll wander back to the Flag, with her fanny out . . . It's not the first time she's pulled a stunt like this . . . I know that much . . . All right?" he said. And then he laughed suddenly. A big, belly laugh of joy — as if there were some joke that they weren't in on, but he was. He looked happier than Dolly had ever seen him. "If I tell you the hotel," he asked them, "will you fuck off and leave me in peace?"

CHAPTER
THIRTY-SEVEN

"Now what?" said Dolly. "Did you believe him?"

"I did, yes," said Raff. "You did too, I think."

Dolly nodded. "Don't know what he looked so happy about though, at the end, did you?"

"He looked relieved, didn't he? I suppose he realised we weren't going to say anything to his wife."

"— Revolting man . . ." Dolly was Googling the hotel address as they walked. "It's in Piccadilly," she said. "Quite close to the tube, Raff."

"We won't need the tube. I've brought the RV." He chuckled. "Thought we might need a quick getaway."

Dolly stared at him: "You brought the snake?"

"Of course! Unfortunately she's asleep though, so you won't be able to meet her properly."

"Oh," said Dolly. "What a shame."

So much for a quick getaway. The RV didn't want to start. While Raff buried his nose under its bonnet, Dolly surveyed the living space. It was remarkably tidy. There was a photograph fastened to the wall of a young man, pale and smiling, with a generous face and sharp blue eyes. Sam, presumably. And above the sofa (brown, corduroy — Dolly assumed, correctly, that it also functioned as a bed), she found a bookshelf crammed with novels, mostly thrillers. There were also several books about snakes and snake-care, well thumbed . . . and tucked at the end, to her delight, a thick, new book, its spine, admittedly, not yet broken: *Tarot for Beginners*. She was touched, amazed — and a little wrong footed. Perhaps she should borrow a book about boa constrictors from the library?

Aside from the books and the photograph, there weren't many clues to Raff's character lying about. Dorothy (the snake) was still asleep in her boa-box under the sofa bed. Thankfully.

Dolly opened the fridge. There weren't many clues to the man in there, either: a vacuum-sealed pack of lamb mince, a half-pack of instant mash potato — she thought they'd stopped making it in the seventies — and a tub of Flora . . . With all the demands she had been making on his time, Dolly worried Raff had forgotten to buy dinner for his son. She put her head out the window.

"Your fridge is a bit empty, Raff. What are you cooking for Sam tonight?"

"Shepherd's pie. Same as always, Dolly. He loves it."

Dolly turned back to the fridge. ". . . Are you sure?"

There was a shop four minutes' walk away — not a good one. She generally avoided it. But anything was better than Raff's food cupboard. She told him she'd be back shortly, and hurried off before he could stop her. By the time she returned, carrying onions, herbs, olive oil, some limp-looking green vegetables and some actual potatoes, Raff was already at the wheel, engine running.

242

"How about you drive," she said. "I'll cook your son dinner."

Raff didn't like that idea. He said cooking in an RV was illegal while it was in motion. But after a little probing, it turned out this wasn't his chief concern. Sam was accustomed to his father's shepherd's pie. They'd been eating it every other Thursday night since 1997. Raff worried that Sam might be disappointed.

"I doubt it," muttered Dolly. "You won't have time to cook it, anyway. What time is Sam coming round?"

And so it was decided.

They had caught the early end of the rush hour, and progress was slow. On Park Lane, Dolly came to join Raff in the front passenger seat. The windows were open and the food was cooked. And the RV was stuck in an almighty traffic jam.

After ten minutes of absolute non-movement, Dolly voiced the obvious question: "What shall we do?"

Raff didn't have an answer, so he didn't reply.

"You're going to be late for Sam," Dolly said. "And it's just occurred to me that we are never going to be able to park this thing. Had you thought of that?"

He had. As yet, he'd not come up with a solution, which was why he hadn't mentioned it.

"There must have been an accident," he said. "It's not usually as bad as this."

Another minute ticked by and still they didn't move. "Of course," he muttered sheepishly, ". . . You could always just pick up the phone and call hotel reception. Ask them to put you through."

Dolly took a moment to digest this, most obvious of proposals. "Why didn't we think of it before?"

"Well, *I* did," Raff said. "But I wanted to show you my RV."

"You wanted me to cook your son's supper!"

"Ha! Believe me, that was a bonus . . . Bloody hell, and I tell you, Dolly, it smells so good, I've been struggling not to climb back there and eat it."

CHAPTER
THIRTY-EIGHT

Nikki lay on her hotel bed, eating toffee popcorn and wondering whether to complain to management about the sluggishness of her TV handset. There was nothing on the telly, and the porn channels were useless. She was bored. Really bored. Tomorrow, she realised, or possibly the next day, she would check out of this dump and head home.

It was fortunate timing for Dolly because it was at this moment, as Nikki's ennui was really cresting, that her bedside telephone began to ring. Normally she wouldn't have troubled herself to answer it. Nobody knew where she was, so it would obviously either be housekeeping (boring) or a wrong number (very boring) . . . Unless of course it was Fraser, wanting sex. Nikki snatched it up.

"That you, Fraser?"

Dolly said: "Nikki! Is that *you*?"

"What? Who's that?"

"It's Dolly Greene — the Tarot reader. You came to me for a reading. Do you remember?"

". . . Dolly . . . Dolly . . ." It took her a moment to place the name. And then: "*Wooah!* . . . How d'you . . . Are you *haunting* me?"

"No, no, I'm not haunting you! I got your number from . . . one of your friends."

"Really?"

"I've been worried about you!"

"Really?" Nikki said again. She sounded unconvinced. "Why's that then?"

"Why didn't you answer my calls?"

"What calls?"

"I called you. Hundreds of times."

"When? Oh. You mean on the mobile. If you mean on the mobile, I lost it. Or Toby nicked it, most likely . . . Or his dad. His dad's done it before. He can't have enough numbers, can he? Stupid sod. So what's up? You sound funny."

"I sound *funny*?" Dolly didn't know quite what to say. All this time, she'd been imagining Nikki's river-bloated body, dead in the morgue.

"The last time we spoke you were in a state . . . You called me in a terrible state, don't you remember?"

"Hormones, Dolly." She chortled. "You remember that DEATH card, don't you?" Bloody terrified me. But it wasn't what I thought it was, thank God. It was something else. Just the termination. That's all it was! You didn't tell me I was pregnant, did you. Fat lot of use you were."

". . . So . . . you're all right?"

"I'm recuperating, Dolly. What do you want?"

"I just wanted to be sure . . . everything was all right." Dolly hesitated. She wondered if Nikki knew about Maurice. "Have you spoken to anyone lately? Anyone in your family?"

246

"Hardly," said Nikki. "*No thanks!*"

"How about Fraser? Have you seen him?"

"Pardon?" she said. "Fraser who?" Nikki was not a great actress.

"Oh, come on. Have you seen him?"

"I don't know any 'Fraser'."

"How do you think I found you Nikki? No one else knows where you are." *Or seems to care*, she didn't add.

". . . If you must know, he dropped in for an hour or two Monday night. But don't say I said so, for God's sake."

"Why not?"

"It'll upset him."

Dolly said: "You're providing him with an alibi, Nikki. I don't suppose it'll upset him unduly. And by the way, if he's coerced you into falsifying . . . anything . . . realise there'll be CCTV at the desk. The police will find out."

"Say what?" Nikki pulled the telephone from her ear and looked at it briefly, in disgust. "There you go, talking fucking Russian again. What are you talking about 'alibi' for anyway? If you can't talk in normal words, I'm hanging up, Dolly. I've got better things to do."

"I'm sorry. I should have said . . . I thought perhaps you already knew. Maurice Bousquet died on Monday night, Nikki. I'm sorry. Sorry to tell you the bad news."

". . . Maurice Bousquet? As in Maurice, Maurice? That's a shame. *He was old though*, wasn't he? What did he die of?"

247

"*That*, Nikki, is the million-dollar question . . ."

But she wasn't interested. Something else, apparently more urgent, had occurred to her. "Dolly," she said. "Dolly — you remember when I called? When I was crying and that?"

"Of course I do. It's why I've been trying to find you all this time. I was worried."

"It wasn't just hormones. And the Death card. Hormones and the Death. I kept telling myself — the Death was just the baby — but I *knew* it wasn't the baby." She stopped. "I was so frightened. That's why I called. And now it's all right, isn't it? I suppose it must have been Maurice all along!"

The traffic on Park Lane had started edging forward again. Dolly couldn't hear her properly. "What did you say, Nikki? What must have been Maurice?"

"Because when I saw on the news about the body down at Kew . . ."

"The body at Kew?" Dolly glanced at Raff, to be sure he was listening.

"I thought it was my friend."

"Nikki — it was a pregnant woman. I thought it was you."

She wasn't listening. "But thank God it was only Maurice! I got this bad feeling about my friend from the moment she didn't come round. When she said she would. And there was no answer on her mobile, and then with the Death card, Dolly . . . I felt sure they should've been looking for her, but who was going to report her gone? *Not me.* And then when they found that girl's body . . . But anyway, thank God it was only

Maurice! All this time, I've been carrying around this bad feeling."

"About your friend?" asked Dolly.

Nikki didn't answer.

"Nikki? Are you still there? Nikki, *who* should they have been looking for? Do you think you know the woman — at Kew?"

But Nikki couldn't speak. It sounded as though she was weeping.

"Nikki — are you there? If you think you know her, you *have to* make a report. Can you do that? Apparently — Nikki, listen to me — apparently the dead woman was called Melinda. Was your friend called Melinda?"

"Oh — oh Dolly . . . No. No she wasn't. Not Melinda." Nikki was really sobbing now. "Not since she was just a little thing. Not since before I knew her."

"Do you have an address for her?"

"Are they saying it was Melinda? Oh holy . . . oh, holy Mary, mother of . . . She had the baby coming, and it was going to be like a new start for her, Dolly. With the baby coming . . . She didn't call herself Melinda any more. She was Casey. I was going to tell her to pay you a visit but I never got a chance because I never saw her after. We were friends, Dolly. She was my friend."

Nikki said she would not make a statement to the police: "not over anyone's dead body". She refused to speak to Raff, and forbade either of them from coming to visit her at the hotel. So they parked up in a taxi rank on Mount Street, just off Park Lane, and Dolly took down what details Nikki had to give. The two women lived in the same block of flats, Nikki said. They worked in the same business. Nikki knew very little about the woman's past, or indeed, her present. But she knew that her friend was pregnant and she knew that lately, her friend had tried very hard to clean up. "Casey was like a changed person," Nikki said, over and again. "It can't be her. It's probably not her. I'm sure it's not her . . ." But she gave Dolly the woman's address. Dolly gave it Raff, and Raff immediately called the information in to CID.

They drove back through London, mostly in silence.

"Poor woman," Dolly muttered.

"Which one?" replied Raff.

It was far quicker getting back through the city on the way home, and less than hour later, Raff dropped Dolly at the top of Tinderbox Lane, in good time to be back at his regular spot on Barnes Common, and ready to receive Sam.

"He's not going to know what's hit him when he tries your shepherd's pie," Raff said, engine still running, blocking the traffic behind him. "Thank you, Dolly."

"It's me who should be thanking you." She opened the passenger door. "I wouldn't have wanted to do any of that on my own . . . I'll see you tomorrow — will I . . .? You're coming to the talk?"

"I'll be there," he said. ". . . Hey, Dolly . . ."

"Hm?" She turned back to him — and he surprised her: kissed her long enough for the cars behind to start honking angrily, and then kept kissing her.

"Hmmm," said Dolly, pulling away at last. ". . . Gosh . . . Well —" she smiled at him. "That was . . . even better than I thought it would be. I mean, really . . ." she almost cackled with pleasure — stopped in time, and beamed at him instead. She hadn't been kissed like that for years. ". . . Wow, Raff . . . My lucky day."

"Wow," he murmured. "Wow, indeed . . . See you tomorrow, Dolly."

CHAPTER
THIRTY-NINE

Back at Tinderbox Lane, Dolly discovered that her own fridge wasn't in much better shape than Raff's. Pippa was out, but she had obviously been on a feeding rampage before she left. There was nothing in there.

Dolly was too tired to go out again: too tired to eat, probably. She would make some tea (without milk, since Pippa had polished it off), take her Tarot Talk notes upstairs, have a long bath, think about Raff, and go to bed.

Rosie must have been lurking in wait for Dolly to get home, because Dolly had barely put the kettle on before she was at the front door, in tears, again. She wanted a reading. Dolly said she was tired. But Rosie wouldn't leave. She had money, she said. She could pay. "I've got £200 in cash in my wallet. Is it enough? I can get more."

"More?" Dolly blinked. Pippa was always telling her to raise her prices: maybe Pippa was right. "People *like* paying for things," Pippa always said. "The more you charge, the more the punters want to believe you must be worth it. It's the first law of marketing: people are idiots." Maybe. But at least some of them remembered to leave milk in the fridge.

"I generally charge £50," she said. "Come on in."

Since Pippa was out, they were doing the reading at
the kitchen breakfast bar. Dolly looked at Rosie's cards.
A lot of wands.

*... The meaning of each card depends on many fac-
tors: where the cards fall, for example, and what other
cards fall with them; who has pulled them, in what
number, when and how ... A good Tarot reader will
look at all the cards and be able to see patterns emerg-
ing ... Often it's the patterns and combinations that
will offer the most information ...*

And the pattern that Dolly saw was of abuse, misery,
guilt, fear, deception: and a serious shortage of sex.
   "Things have unravelled a bit, haven't they?" Dolly
said. "Time to take back some control . . ."
   "I have tried!" cried Rosie. "Look at me! I'm trying!
I've come here, haven't I? Fraser's left me, Dolly. I
hope he never comes back." She was drunk. "He thinks
I won't be able to cope without him. But I do, I hope
he never comes back." She looked down at the cards.

253

"So what do they say? Do they say I'm going to spend the rest of my life in prison? Because if they do — . . . I only wanted to help him. I didn't do anything wrong."

Dolly said: "Calm down, Rosie. The cards don't say anything about prison. Nothing at all. If you hang on and let me look properly, I'll tell you what they do say . . .

. . . In a traditional Tarot pack . . . the suit of wands, which are sometimes referred to as "batons" or "rods," generally represent action. Travel. Adventure . . . SEX —

And occasionally, for example in this instance, they represent cricket bats.

"Maurice was alive, was he? When you went round to call. Is that how you got the cut on your face?"

". . . I don't think so. No . . ."

"*Rosie,*" said Dolly. She waited. The longer the silence lasted, the more certain she felt. Sure enough:

"I didn't do anything, Dolly. I just hated us not being friends. We were neighbours. We should have been friends."

"I'm sure that's true . . . Or more than friends, possibly . . . It looks like things are — very bitter at home. Am I right? I think possibly you were hoping that Maurice could be more than a friend — and who can blame you? Maybe you dropped in on Maurice because you thought he might help you feel less lonely . . . Am I right? You went round for a little adult solace."

"I don't know what you —"

"*Sex,* I mean —"

254

Having said it, Dolly didn't want to look up. She could hear Rosie breathing . . . *Let her breathe.* Things were becoming clear . . .

"He hit you, didn't he — with that damn cricket bat. Like he hit Ade. So what happened? What went wrong?"

"The cards can't tell you that?"

Dolly looked up, "No, but you can. They're looking for a match on the blood on that cricket bat. Will it be yours?"

"But I *didn't do anything.*"

"Stop saying that. You obviously did do something, Rosie. Or you wouldn't be sitting here, now, scared to death. What did you do to him?"

Rosie began to cry again. It wasn't, she said, what she did to him so much as what *he* did to *her.* She was a bit drunk — she'd just been round at Dolly's, drinking wine with Dolly and her gorgeous policeman — and when she walked back past Maurice's house, with Fraser yelling at her, she felt him — Maurice — watching her. From his window. And she thought — she felt he was waiting for her, just waiting for her to take the initiative . . . And then Fraser went out, and the kids were in front of the TV . . . So she snuck out. Back to Maurice's front door. The lights were out, but she knew he was in there. She took the spare key from under the stone — "It was poking out, Dolly. Like an invitation. Like he'd placed it there on purpose." She took the key and let herself in. She opened the door, whispered his name — and *Whack!* Maurice and his cricket bat.

"He was like a madman, waving it this way and that, yelling at me to leave him alone. Maybe he thought I was someone else. Because he was *crazy*. So *angry* . . . And that's it. I got out. Fast as I could, Dolly. And then the next thing it was morning, and there were sirens and police . . . and Maurice was dead. And I am so frightened. They're going to find my blood on his cricket bat . . . I didn't hurt him. I didn't *touch* him. I didn't get beyond the front door."

Dolly's gaze moved to Rosie's face. ". . . What did you do with the key, afterwards? It's been missing."

Rosie fished into her too-tight jeans pocket, and slapped it on to the breakfast bar, jolting the cards. "I've been clinging on to it. God knows why . . . but I didn't hurt him. Why would I? I just wanted us to be friends. I just wanted —"

— *a good, old-fashioned frosty-fuck*, thought Dolly, *and what the hell's wrong with that? Everyone else is at it. Why not you?*

Rosie continued: "— for us to be friends . . . Do you believe me, Dolly?"

A long pause. Finally, Dolly nodded. "Yes, I believe you. Absolutely, I believe you. Maurice had a nasty temper."

It was as if Dolly had waved a magic wand: at her words, Rosie seemed to lighten and expand. She beamed. Dolly said, briskly: "In any case, looking at these cards, I would have thought Maurice Bousquet was the least of your problems . . . And Rosie, I would love to discuss all this in more detail — of course I would — but maybe not now. We can maybe make a time for a good, long reading tomorrow or the day after? Would that be all right? Only it's so late, and I'm so tired . . ."

Rosie snapped to attention. "Of course," she said, jumping up. "I barged in here, didn't I. And you've got your talk tomorrow. I'm so sorry."

"It's what neighbours are for," said Dolly, gathering up the cards. "And by the way, I meant to say — with regard to your other problem . . ." Dolly hesitated. She wanted to put it as delicately as she could. "If your lawyer's in need of any, shall we call it *evidential fodder*, yes? In your marriage dispute . . . just let me know. I can point him in the right direction."

Rosie looked a little blank. "Pardon?"

"I mean —" Dolly cleared her throat. "If it comes to divorce —"

"Oh, you mean *Fraser*!"

"*Yes*, I mean Fraser."

Rosie laughed. "Sod Fraser."

Dolly stared at her. "What did you say?"

"I hope he never comes back. I never thought he'd leave but now he has — it feels like . . ." She paused to find the words, didn't find them. Shrugged. "I'm getting the locks changed first thing tomorrow."

"Good idea."

"If he tries to break in, I'm calling the police."

Dolly looked at her weakly. Who was this new woman? ". . . Well! Good for you!"

"No." Rosie shook her head. "Good for *you*, Dolly. And thank you." She leaned forward, and gave Dolly a quick, embarrassed peck on the cheek. "See you tomorrow. Good night."

There was a voicemail from Raff awaiting Dolly when she woke, left at 6.30 a.m., by which time he was already a half-hour into his shift.

"Morning there, Dolly. I thought you might be interested to know that we've got one Adrian Bousquet in the cells this morning. Arrested late last night at a private address in East Sheen, for assaulting his late father's solicitor. And by the way, your shepherd's pie was out of this world. Sam —" he chortled. "My son, Sam, can't wait to meet you. Good luck tonight, Dolly. Don't get too nervous. You faced down Fraser Buck, yesterday. I should think you can handle a few students without too much difficulty. I'll see you there at seven."

It had taken them one whole, long day to act on Raff's information. But here they were, at last, standing outside a silent flat on the fourteenth floor of Esmee House, shouting through a locked door for Melinda, or Casey — or anyone: and getting no response. They had used the fire key to get themselves into the building and now, it seemed, the entire block was deserted: as if residents had sniffed the coming of the Law through the open passageways, and scurried back to their burrows to wait it out.

After several minutes standing outside on the abandoned landing, the detectives decided there was only one option. They returned to their car to fetch the tools, and smashed their way in.

The flat they broke into was clean and worn and very small — just a bedroom, a squeezed hallway, a kitchen and a shower room. It took barely more than a second to confirm the place was empty.

There was a two-month-old issue of *Closer* magazine lying on a scrubbed Formica table in the kitchen; some clean plates stacked neatly by the sink, and a calendar pinned to the wall with a picture of a kitten wearing a woolly hat. In the fridge were the dried-up remains of an Indian takeaway and some milk, six weeks past its sell-by date. And that was it. The room smelled of nothing but its own, long emptiness.

Casey's bedroom might have been in a different flat: carpeted wall to wall in shiny shagpile, the room was almost all bed, which bed, excepting the assortment of sex aids attached to its headboard, had been stripped bare, to a heavily stained mattress. There was a tatty Chinese silk embroidery nailed ineptly to the window, and Sellotaped on to the lilac painted walls — for the avoidance of any lingering doubt — there was a poster of two naked women entwined, glistening, depilated, collared and bound.

In the corner of the hallway, hidden under a sheet, the detectives found a cot. And inside the cot, a new Moses basket; and inside that, a little pile of babygrows, still in their wrappers.

And under the cot, they found Casey's metal cashbox, unlocked, with over £2,000 inside.

And hidden under the cash, an out-of-date passport belonging to Melinda Stevens, DOB 12 March 1978;

an application form — blank — for an adult literacy course and a small, pink vibrator.

And hidden under all of that, tucked away at the bottom of the box, they found a small black and white picture: an ultrasound of a foetus, dated three months back.

The detectives left without finding the most important piece of evidence. But it was OK, because they would be back again tomorrow, "with the full circus" — the entire murder team. And someone in Forensics would spot it, covered in dust, tucked in behind the toilet base . . .

A single gold and diamond cufflink, with two letters intertwined: *FB*. It had been an anniversary present from his dear wife, and when Forensics find it, which they will, they will notice a small spatter of blood caught between the diamonds, and they will match the blood to the bloated body in the Thames, and the cufflink to the bloated body normally living at Windy Ridge, Tinderbox Lane.

And Fraser Buck will be the most wanted man in SW13.

But it will be too late, of course. Because Fraser spoke to Nikki yesterday, after she'd spoken to Dolly; and she told him all about their conversation, and about how the police, thanks to her, now believed that the body down at Kew might turn out to be her missing friend, Casey . . . And all this time it had been eating away at him — *that fucking cufflink*. He had known all along that there was only one place he might have left it.

His wife could change the locks at Windy Ridge as often as she fancied. It was unlikely he would notice. Heart Attack Hubby was already halfway to Panama.

CHAPTER
FORTY

Pippa and her friends had put out thirty-five chairs. Sandra had arrived bearing a tray of sandwiches and four bottles of Prosecco. And here they all were, in Room 88 of the Environmental Science Department of Merton and South Kingston College: Pippa, and her two best friends, Sandra and her posh date Chas, Raff, Professor Filthy, Rosie — and Dolly. They were hardly able to stand for the wretched chairs. It was 7.15, and Dolly had to accept that no one else was likely to be coming.

Professor Filthy sidled up, suggesting they "get cracking", and asking if she wanted him to introduce her. She said probably not, since everyone present, except Chas, already knew her fairly well. "And I think he'll be able to put two and two together . . . I'll just go on up there and start talking . . . I suppose . . ."

"Good for you!" Filthy gave her the thumbs-up. "Go get 'em, girl! Plus you never know, maybe a few more people might turn up yet! *Never say Never*, not when there's London traffic involved!" He whacked her on the back: too hard, really. It made her cough. But he meant it well.

She walked through the jungle of empty chairs to her table at the front, where she'd already laid out her notes, a glass of water, and a pack of extra-large Tarot cards which she had bought especially, so that the audience at the back would be able to see.

As she waited for her eight-strong crowd to sit, she calculated that her outlay for the event (including large cards, bus ride and a new lipstick) had exceeded her takings by a ratio of 4:1. This was partly because Pippa, Pippa's two best friends and the professor had all come in for free.

She smiled at the faces, gazing up at her politely. "Hello everyone. All of you. And *thank you* very much for coming here tonight . . ."

"Shame there aren't more of us!" bellowed the professor. "Never mind, old girl! Let the show begin!"

She cleared her throat.

TAROT TALKS — AN INTRODUCTION TO
THE MAGICAL LANGUAGE OF THE TAROT
BY DOLLY GREENE
    I would like to begin by setting straight a few
misconceptions . . .

Her voice was wobbling. And in front of her, in a short, neat row, eight polite people sat silently, wondering how long this thing was going to take . . . And Dolly knew it. Everyone who had come tonight had come out of kindness, no other reason. She took a deep breath. It would get better.

. . . Tarot cards do not explicitly predict the future. They
will not tell you when or how you are going to die. They

won't tell you who's going to win the 4.45 at Epsom on
Saturday . . . And, believe me, if they could tell me next
week's lottery numbers, I would not be standing here
now, I'd be living it up in the Caribbean . . .

[She paused: cue for laughter.]
"*St Lucia*," she said.
". . . *I'd be living it up in St Lucia*." She frowned.
She hadn't written St Lucia. ". . . *I'd be living it up in
St Lucia*." Why was she saying it again? "*Excuse me. If
Tarot Cards could tell me next week's lottery numbers,
trust me, I wouldn't be standing here now, I'd be living
it up in . . . St Lucia*."
"We got it!" cried Filthy. "You'd be living it up in St
Lucia. Carry on!"
Dolly cleared her throat and tried again.

. . . Tarot cards do not predict the future, they reflect the
present, and in doing that, they can reveal the direction
in which our lives are likely to be heading . . . And by
the way, I don't need to look up from my paper — I can
see you all, quietly rolling your eyes. Because how could
a pack of cards do any such thing? How can a simple
pack of cards tell us anything? Is the Tarot magic? It
depends on what you understand by "magic" . . .

She glanced up at Raff. He'd come straight from
work and he was still in uniform. His arms were folded
across his in the script, "*A gift from the Universe can
be tarnished by human folly!* Nor was that in the script.
Dolly pictured the card. The Ace of Pentacles showed a

264

giant hand descending from the sky, holding out a large, golden orb. In Dolly's pack, the card had been burned, of course, and the golden orb was black at the heart." *Oh my goodness!* She stopped.

The audience waited; Professor Filthy, for less long than the rest.

"Keep going!" he shouted.

... The Ace of Pentacles, (sometimes called the Me of Coins), represents the start of something material: a new business venture, perhaps; an inheritance; a new source of income; a prize; a win on the horses.

Dolly read on, but her mind was far away now, back at Tinderbox Lane. She was in Maurice's kitchen again, on the night she read his cards. It was late, and they were both a little drunk, and there was a hint of flirtation between them ... She was looking at Maurice's cards, and Maurice was sitting back, his legs apart, still thinking he was in with a chance. The cards were laid out on his little kitchen table, and Dolly was laughing, and it irritated him:

"*So? What can you see?*" he asked her.

"*Money. That's what I see. It's everywhere, Maurice ... Down the back of the sofa, in the cracks in the walls ... It's like this entire house is lined with gold! Walls of gold, Maurice! ... Looks to me like you've come into a fortune.*" She remembered chest and he looked too big for his chair. He had no one sitting on either side of him, and he stuck out like a sore thumb, thought Dolly. He looked tired, too. But he was listening. He winked at her. She smiled back.

Dolly remembered being made to sit through church sermons as a child, staring at the sheets of paper in the priest's hand, trying to gauge how many sheets he was holding, how close the words were typed, how long she would be made to remain there, finding new ways not to listen. *Was Raff doing that?*

"— By the way, just so you know — there are six sheets of paper here, each one's got about three hundred words on — and I'll be breaking off to show you some of the cards . . . It's going to be about sixty minutes in all. OK? Maybe a little less. I'll try to speed up if I can."

She read on, and the words, so carefully written and constructed, piled up behind her. She was doing all right, though she didn't know it. People were listening.

. . . Aces in all four suits represent beginnings: new projects, new journeys, new hopes, new loves, new chances, new ideas, new adventures. They represent a gift to you from the Universe, and though they augur well, they guarantee nothing. Good omens can turn bad, when corrupted by human folly. And that, in my opinion, is what the Tarot is there for: it's why we need it — to warn us against our own folly . . .

She paused.

"Good omens can turn bad when corrupted by human folly," she said again. ". . . Or *tarnished*," she said. It wasn't his mood darkening. ". . . *Don't tell me you finally won the lottery?*

266

He'd never answered.

Maurice had bet on the same six numbers every week, "since numbers and lotteries were invented". His birth date, perhaps? When was Maurice's birthday? It didn't matter. Ade knew Maurice's numbers, and *he knew Maurice had won*. Which explained why he had started calling on his long-lost father; and why Maurice was so angry — so emotional — when Dolly mentioned Ade's name. Maurice had thrown Ade out of his house. He'd smashed him over the head with a cricket bat! He'd smashed Rosie's head with a cricket bat, too . . .

Dolly read on — she didn't need to concentrate: it was all there on the page, everything she needed to say. She pictured the ten cards in Maurice's spread.

Pentacles: *4 – meanness, excessive conservatism, fear*
             of the unknown
         5 – sickness
         6 – a windfall
         10 – family wealth

. . . and the Ace of Pentacles, with its tarnished heart

Swords: *5 – a Pyrrhic victory*
         7 – deceit
         8 – self-sabotage

The Star (reversed) *For a wish that turns sour. (Be careful what you wish for . . .)*
And, finally, Death.

CHAPTER
FORTY-ONE

". . . And that," said Dolly, looking up from the bottom of her sixth and final sheet, "pretty much completes my talk for today. Thank you all for coming. Thank you. I hope it was interesting. And I really hope —" She looked around her at the faces. They all looked rather dazed. "Oh dear, I'm sorry. I think I read it all too fast. But there's so much to say and I feel as if I've barely started — and I was so conscious of you all being here out of the kindness of your hearts. Next week, I'll do it much better! I promise you."

"Next week," said Pippa, glaring at the professor, "we might actually get the time and place correct in all the literature. I just switched on my phone . . . About a hundred messages coming in, Mum — I *knew* people wanted to come. They've been sitting in Room 55 for the last hour, wondering where the hell we are."

"It's *not* true!" cried Filthy, outraged. "Aren't people *stupid!* I ask you! We're only a few floors up."

"Yes, but they didn't know that, did they?" said Pippa.

"*Idiots*," he said, and turned back to Dolly. "Dolly, if I may say, that was *terrific!* I, for one, thoroughly enjoyed myself and I look forward to learning more next week . . . I feel you've only touched the tip of the Tarot iceberg and I can't wait for instalment number two! Although now I think about it, you may want to start from scratch next week, with said idiotic students actually *in situ*? In which case I'll probably give it a miss. Hoorah for Dolly Greene! Shall we jolly well have a round of applause? Yes, we jolly well shall!" He clapped his hands with great enthusiasm, and the others joined in. "I officially declare your speech 'a triumph', Dolly. And now it's drinks time. Drinkipoos everyone!"

Dolly glanced at Raff. He raised an eyebrow, as if to ask: *is this lunatic really a friend of yours?* She grinned, and nodded. Indeed he was.

Sandra came up from behind and threw her arms around Dolly's neck. "I knew you'd be brilliant!" She said. "I knew it, I knew it!"

"Oh gosh, I wasn't brilliant," Dolly said. "But I'll get better. Definitely. And thank you for coming — and thank you —"

"*Chas.*"

"Chas. Thank you."

"Absolute pleasure," said Chas. ". . . Fascinating stuff . . ."

Sandra said: "I like the look of your policeman, Dolly, I really do. And I'm longing to meet him properly — but can it be next time? I'm really, really sorry — I don't want to be rude . . . you were so brilliant. But Chas and I have to leave."

"What, right away?"

"— It's the madness of the internet!" She laughed. "You wind up doing the maddest things. Chas and I had a few drinks last night . . . and then, somehow, the next thing we knew, we'd booked ourselves on the Eurostar for a weekend in bloody Brussels." She looked quite put out.

"Brussels? *Wow*," said Dolly. "Well, that's wonderful."

"Yes, but *why Brussels?*" Sandra winked. "Because it was cheaper than Paris, that's why!" She leaned into Dolly's ear. "Can't work out if he's broke, or just a posh cheapskate. But in any case —"

"I'm not actually very posh," muttered Chas.

"In any case," Sandra said. "It's going to be wonderful. Fingers crossed!"

Dolly looked around the room. It wasn't going to be that hard to peel away, after all. Pippa had already left: she'd snagged two bottles of Prosecco and gone off with her friends. And now the professor, slipping the last bottle into his briefcase, announced he was taking Rosie out for a curry.

"I can pay," piped up Rosie.

"*Nonsense!*" declared Filthy. He turned to Dolly and Raff. "I'd ask you two love birds to come with," he said. "But I think we'd all have more fun, sticking to our couples. Don't you agree?"

He was probably right. It left Dolly and Raff, alone in Room 88, with thirty-five empty chairs to clear away, and a tray of curling sandwiches.

"We could find a different curry house," suggested Raff.

"We could," said Dolly. "I'd love that. Only before that, I need to go back to Tinderbox Lane. I'm so sorry. But the whole thing came to me in a flash in the middle of speaking: what Maurice's cards have been trying to tell me all this time. *He won the lottery, Raff!* And I think he won something really big."

Raff sighed. He'd heard enough about Tarot cards for one evening. He'd heard enough about Maurice Bousquet for a lifetime. He was hungry. He wanted to sit in a nice, warm room, and eat and drink and flirt with Dolly. Dolly chose not to notice this.

"Raff!" she said. "Did you hear what I said?"

"Of course I did," he said. There was a hint of irritation.

"OK — so. Listen. There was this very definite *moment* when Maurice changed. His personality *changed* — from being his normal grumpy self to being totally and absolutely miserable. And that, by the way, was *exactly* when the smell began . . . the smell-that-nobody-else-can-smell-except-me. Raff, are you listening? It was also at that same time that Raffs son, Ade, first made his appearance in our lane. OK? So he must have known his father had won. And you know how? Well, obviously, because *Maurice told me* that he'd been *using the same lottery numbers* every week since the lottery began. Ade knew that. He knew what those numbers were: and *that* was why he kept coming back to Tinderbox Lane. He wanted the winnings."

"If you're trying to say he murdered his father," Raff interrupted her, "I can stop you right there. Turns out he was in A&E at the Charing Cross Hospital all day on the Monday Maurice died, and there's CCTV to prove it. Monday night and Tuesday night he was checked into the actual hospital, and he didn't check out of hospital, according to their records, until after his father had been checked into the morgue . . ."

"— How do you know? I thought you said . . ."

"He used an alias."

"An alias? — *Why*?"

"I don't know, Dolly. Presumably because you weren't the only person in the UK who was looking for him." Raff smirked. "So. Tell me. What else did your Tarot cards say?"

". . . I see . . ." muttered Dolly, trying to ignore his tone. He'd just sat through an hour of her, talking about her precious Tarot. Had he been listening with his tongue in his cheek all that time? ". . . I see . . ." she said again. But then she couldn't stop herself. "Raff, if you think it's all crap, if you think everything I do and believe is nothing but a load of crap — then why don't you come out and say it? Then at least we both know where we are."

Raff laughed. "Come on, Dolly, I was teasing. I'm not saying I don't believe it. I wouldn't say that. I'm just saying — maybe, you know — you take it a bit far . . ."

"Maybe I do, Raff . . . Maybe. And in the meantime, I suppose you've got it all worked out, have you? All the magic and the wonder of the universe? I suppose you

272

have it all neatly formatted on to an Excel spread sheet — with profits in one column and losses in another column and . . . bloody . . . optimal operational targets in the other?" She wasn't making any sense at all, and she knew it. "Damn it, Raff. I'm just so . . . *Goddamn it, Raff . . .*"

She fell silent. Raff stood there, seemingly implacable. She felt a fool. So did he, though she couldn't see it. He was mortified. But she didn't give him a chance to make things better. She spun towards the exit, leaving behind the empty chairs and the curling sandwiches and the handsome man in a smart uniform she'd stupidly allowed herself to imagine was destined to be the love of her life . . .

And she caught the Number 49 back to Station Road.

CHAPTER
FORTY-TWO

Maurice's back door still hadn't been fixed, and now that the house was no longer a crime scene, it seemed there was no urgency for anyone to do anything about it. She stepped over the splintered fence in her own back garden, gave his old back door the gentlest of shoves. And she was in.

The house was dark and cold. She sniffed. This evening, the house did not smell of tarnish. It smelled of cold air, and Caribbean chicken curry. It smelled of Maurice. She looked around her. *Where to begin?* There was light coming in through the garden, from the light in her own broom cupboard next door. It left the space beyond Maurice's kitchen table still cloaked in darkness, but as her eyes grew accustomed, she could more or less make out the shape of things here at the back of the house.

She took a step into the empty room and felt a crunch underfoot. Broken glass. The mess of the death scene and then of Ade's midnight rampage had yet to be cleared away, and the crunch of her footsteps filled the dark room.

Where to begin?

Not with the books. Ade had already checked them. The kitchen cupboards, maybe? Under the saucepans?

She wondered — would it be reckless to switch on the light? Ade was in custody. Raff had said so. He'd said it was unlikely (though not impossible) that Ade would get bail. Even so . . . there was still Terry. If Terry was passing and he saw the lights on, he'd call the police. And there was still Fraser, *somewhere at large*, if he ever returned to Tinderbox Lane. She certainly didn't want to encounter him.

Where to begin?

"Down the back of the sofa, in the cracks in the walls — it's like this entire house is lined with gold! Walls of gold, Maurice! . . . Looks to me like you've come into a fortune."

She was standing at the threshold of the store cupboard, on the spot where Maurice would have died. It was the spot where he was sitting when she found him: her feet, where his bony arse had been. Her left hand was where his head must have rested before it finally slumped forward, and he allowed himself to sleep. She could feel his presence here now, smell his curry cooking, see his comedy apron . . . and there on the mantelpiece, above the single bar heater, his photograph of the beach and the Piton Mountains: the place he always said was home.

She was hit by a wave of tremendous sadness. It surprised her — weakened her. Slowly, she slid to the floor and sat down: sat on the floor, just as he had. Her legs stretched out this way, her back against the doorframe, just as she had found him. This was his resting place. This, the last place his eyes ever rested . . .

"*Down the back of the sofa, in the cracks in the walls — it's like this entire house is lined with gold! Walls of gold, Maurice! . . . Looks to me like you've come into a fortune.*"

. . . Oh, but it wasn't a crack in the wall — it was a crack in the floorboards, and it was directly beneath her left hand! She could see it: a corner of pinkish paper, peeking out between the planks.

She laughed aloud. "*Maurice, you sly old dog!*"

But he didn't reply. The house stayed silent and cold.

Her nails were too short. She couldn't reach it — or she could: she had it for a second — and then she dropped it again. She kept trying: kneeled up and bent closer, the better for her fingers to pincer —

"— *Yes!*" She held the paper aloft. Her cards had been right! Just as they always were!

She felt a shadow in the room.

There was somebody with her. Standing behind her. She could feel the warmth of his body. Hear his breath.

She dared not move.

"All right, Dolly?"

". . . *RAFF!*"

He laughed.

"Holy Christ, Raff! I've never been so frightened in my life! How did you get in here?"

"Same way as you did," he said. "Found your spare keys in the same place eighty per cent of householders tend to leave their spare keys, and I let myself in your front door. And then I came through your back garden. And by the way, I've just been told that Adrian Bousquet's been bailed. Unfortunately. I thought I should warn you." He glanced at the ticket in her hand. "Ah," he said. "Is that what I think it is, Dolly?"

"She nodded. "I think so . . . How long have we got before he gets here?"

"Well. It'll take a while for the paperwork. But I reckon he'll be over here tonight." Raff pulled out his phone. "Go on. What date's on the ticket? . . . Read me the numbers then. I can look them up."

Dolly squinted at the ticket. It was hard to see in this light, without her reading glasses. "He was sixty-one years old, Raff. What year does that mean he was born?

"1955? . . . No, 1954? Depends when his birthday was, doesn't it?"

"Ha! . . . You see? He's got 19, 5, 4, 22, 12, 11 . . . December the twenty-second 1954 maybe? I don't know what the other 11 is — maybe the month he got married? Maybe the month of Ade's birthday?"

"Maybe . . . but it doesn't really matter, does it?" Raff interrupted. "The fact is . . . he's got all six of them, Dolly. All six numbers . . . There were four jackpot winners . . . And one of them is still unclaimed."

Raff looked up from his mobile, at Dolly, staring back at him, still crouching on the floor.

Raff said, "Why wouldn't he have claimed it?"

"Because he was a nutter."

"Well, yes."

"Or maybe not a nutter. Just an old man, stuck in his ways. He'd been doing the stupid lottery every week since it began. It gave him something to dream about, something impossible to aim for. *But he didn't really want to win it.*"

"Ah!" said Raff. "Be careful what you wish for."

"Exactly." Dolly nodded. (*THE STAR, REVERSED.*) "I think he was terrified, Raff. He'd wished for something all his life, and then he went and got it." She held up the ticket. "It changed everything, didn't it? His entire life, turned upside down." (*4 of PENTACLES: EXCESSIVE CONSERVATISM, MEANNESS, FEAR OF CHANGE.*) "And he couldn't keep it secret, because *Ade knew*. His son had already guessed he'd won the big prize." (*10 of PENTACLES: FAMILY WEALTH*). "And that meant, not only would he be expected to share it with a son who, until that moment, hadn't bothered to contact him for years; worse than that, it meant he would have to follow through on his big dream. Maurice spent his life worrying about money, feeling bitter about not having his fair share, feeling exploited by everyone and everything in his adopted country. And then what happens? He wins the bloody lottery! His *raison d'être*: his entire modus for relating to the world comes up and whacks him on the backside." (*5 of SWORDS: THE END OF A LONG AND BITTER FIGHT; A PYRRHIC VICTORY.*) "So what does he do? He lies about it. He lies to himself, and he lies to everyone else. When I ask him if he's won the lottery, rather than admit the truth, he loses his temper and throws me out of the house. He hides the ticket." (*7 of SWORDS: DECEIT.*) "He used to tell everyone — including himself — he'd be happier back 'home' in St Lucia. But he didn't really want to go back to St Lucia. Of course he didn't. *This* was his home. He wanted to stay put, like most old people do:

278

he wanted to while away his remaining years, moaning about the weather, and feeling sorry for himself." (*8 of SWORDS: MARTYRDOM*). "He was just whingeing, because that's what Maurice did. He liked to whinge."

They looked at the ticket in silence. Such a small bit of paper. And yet it had the power to change lives. Wreck lives, in this case. "So," Dolly said at last, "what do we do with this? I suppose we hand it to Maurice's Tuesday-night stripper, do we?"

"Lucky Crystal, indeed."

Silence.

"Just out of interest," Dolly said, "just *idle* interest . . . what's the actual value of this thing? This teeny-tiny piece of paper that nobody else knows about, which I happen to be holding in my hand?"

"Not sure I want to know," Raff answered.

Silence.

". . . On the other hand . . ." he said, "we could just keep it."

She couldn't be sure, in the half light, but she hoped — she thought she hoped — she *half hoped* that he was joking.

Raff cleared his throat. *Of course he was joking.* "I think we should get out of here, Dolly," he said. "Pronto. Hand this bloody ticket in before — we change our minds. And before Ade Bousquet comes and kills us for it."

But Dolly didn't move. Something still wasn't right. Something didn't make sense. She looked around the room.

A movement. They both heard it. And then a sound — half mechanical, half human. It sounded like an old man, groaning. Dolly had heard it before. She'd heard it on the night Ade broke in. There could be no doubt where it was coming from. Maurice's old boiler was juddering back to life again.

"But it's been disconnected, hasn't it?" Dolly said. "It must have been."

"Of course it has," Raff checked. No lights. Nothing. Someone had been round and cut off the gas. It was safe, dead — and groaning.

"*I told you*," she said. "I'm not insane . . . unless we both are." She stood up. Sniffed. It was back. "*Now*," she said, "Now, can you smell it?"

Raff sniffed. And yes — this time, he could smell it. A horrible smell. He recoiled. "What the hell is it?"

She was standing in front of him, close, in that small dark room: in a perfect position for a kiss. She handed him the ticket. "Tarnish," she said. "Something's here, Raff. Something isn't finished."

Again, the boiler groaned. It sounded even more human this time; like the groan of a dying man.

"Fuck this," Raff said. He didn't often swear. He wasn't easily spooked, but this — He switched on the light.

"Not the light!" whispered Dolly. "What if —"

"Never mind *what if*, Dolly — what already *is*? I'm not scared of meeting Ade Bousquet tonight. I just — I seriously do not want to meet his dead dad. What the hell . . ."

The boiler juddered. It was a little lopsided, she noticed. There were scratch marks on the wall behind it, as if something or someone had pulled it loose. She peered closer — it was easier to see now, with the light on.

A loose brick. A crack in the wall.

Down the back of the sofa, in the cracks in the walls — it's like this entire house is lined with gold! Walls of gold, Maurice! . . . Looks to me like you've come into a fortune . . .

Dolly felt for the brick, its outer edges, and pulled it out.

" . . . *Et voilà!*" she said. " . . . Maurice Bousquet died, guarding a broken boiler. Nobody killed him! *The boiler* killed him, because he had lodged it out of place, and he was too damn mean to get it fixed."

Behind the brick, Maurice had dug out a shallow hole. Dolly delved inside it, and fished out . . . a wad of scratch cards. There must have been at least thirty of them, maybe more. She handed them to Raff.

"Holy cow . . ." muttered Raff. " . . . They're all winners, Dolly! Every one of them! . . . A thousand pounds . . . five hundred pounds . . . two hundred . . . ten thousand . . . ten thousand! What was he doing? Why didn't he cash them in . . .?"

" . . . Oh, Maurice . . ." sighed Dolly. "Oh, Maurice, you stupid, *stupid* . . . "

"I've got a nasty feeling," Raff said, flicking quickly through the stash, "we're going to find that every one of them is out of date."

The thought had already occurred to her. But then
— stuck to the back of the brick in her hand — she
spotted another card. It looked new.

"How about this one?"

The two of them examined it. £5,000.

Raff said: "It's still good, Dolly."

Dolly said nothing. She turned back to the hole and
peered in, one more time. Just in case. Half hidden in
the dust, there was one last card, larger and thicker
than the others. It was lying face down and the pattern
on its back was as familiar to Dolly as the back of her
own hand. An old friend. And yet she'd never noticed it
was missing. She pulled it out from beneath the dust.

*In a traditional Tarot pack, wands tend to resemble
long wooden sticks. The suit of wands, which are
sometimes referred to as "batons" or "rods" generally
represent action. Travel . . . Adventure . . . Sex.*

It was the Ace of Wands.

Ha Ha Ha.

Dolly smiled at the sound of her old friend's voice
and looked at Raff. But he hadn't heard.

Well get on with it, darling, go on! Maurice said. *It's
my treat. ASK HIM!*

So she did.

"What do you reckon, Raff? You think £5,000 might
get us a couple of weeks in St Lucia?"

Acknowledgements

Thank you to my teachers at the College of Psychic Studies, Avril Price and Geoffrey Beitz. Thanks too, to readers and teachers Tiffany Crosara and Deborah Winterbourne, who first introduced me to the Tarot.

Thank you to everyone at Notting Hill Police Station for letting me hang around asking earnest questions while they worked. Special thanks to Inspector Paul Blanchflower and Officers Luke Fraser and Celso Abreu; also to Detective Constable Phil McElhone of the Durham Constabulary Major Crime Team, Inspector Michael MacKenzie, and Penny Chalkley. Sometimes truth gets in the way of a good story. (Sometimes it's hard for an author to remember which is which.) Any inaccuracies or sillinesses in regard to police activity, protocol, etc. are, obviously, of my own invention, and bear no relation to the professionalism, patience and the remarkable kindness which I witnessed around the station, and out on patrol with Luke and Celso.

Thank you Sheila Crowley, Krystyna Green, Penny Isaac and Tash Galloway.

And finally, thank you, Zebedee, Bashie, Peter and Panda . . . I can never thank you enough.

Other titles published by Ulverscroft:

THE PYRAMID OF MUD

Andrea Camilleri

It's been raining for days in Vigàta, and the persistent downpours have led to violent floods overtaking Inspector Montalbano's beloved hometown. It is on one of these endless grey days that a man, a Mr Giugiu Nicotra, is found dead, his body discovered in a large water main with a bullet in his back. The investigation is slow and slippery to start with, but when the inspector realises that every clue he uncovers and every person he interviews is leading to the same place — the world of public spending, and with it, the Mafia — the case begins to pick up pace. But there's one question that keeps playing on Montalbano's mind: in his strange and untimely death, was Giugiu Nicotra trying to tell him something?

THE KILLING OF POLLY CARTER

Robert Thorogood

Supermodel Polly Carter was famed for her looks and party-girl lifestyle. Now she's dead, apparently having thrown herself from the clifftop near her home on the island of Saint-Marie. Those who knew her say Polly would never have killed herself; and when he is called to investigate, DI Richard Poole is inclined to agree there is more to Polly's death than meets the eye. Already fighting a losing battle against the intense summer heat of the Caribbean, Richard now faces fresh adversaries: a stream of alibis; a host of conflicting motives; and, worst of all, a visit from his mother — a frenzy that would surely allow a murderer to slip away unnoticed. Yet Richard is certain that the guilty party is still on the island . . .

THE SECRETS OF WISHTIDE

Kate Saunders

Mrs Laetitia Rodd is the impoverished widow of an archdeacon, living modestly in Hampstead with her landlady Mrs Bentley. She is also a private detective of the utmost discretion. In winter 1850, her brother Frederick, a criminal barrister, introduces her to Sir James Calderstone, a wealthy and powerful industrialist who asks her to investigate the background of an "unsuitable" woman his son intends to marry — a match he is determined to prevent. In the guise of governess, Mrs Rodd travels to the family seat, Wishtide, deep within the frozen Lincolnshire countryside, where she soon discovers that the Calderstones have more to hide than most. And when a man is found dead outside a tavern, Mrs Rodd's keen eyes and astute wits are taxed as never before . . .

THE HOUSE OF UNEXPECTED SISTERS

Alexander McCall Smith

At Botswana's No. 1 Ladies' Detective Agency, Precious Ramotswe and Grace Makutsi are intrigued by the troubling dismissal of an employee at a thriving local business. The ladies proceed with investigations as they are inclined to do, with Mma Makutsi's customary vigour, and Mma Ramotswe's rather more subtle caution. While Mma Makutsi's focus, as self-appointed Principal Investigating Officer, is firmly on the case, Mma Ramotswe's attention is diverted by personal matters. Not only has her disgraced ex-husband reappeared in town, but she has stumbled on an unsettling family secret of her own — one that might threaten what she holds closest to her heart. As Precious contemplates this painful possibility, she must draw on all her strength and compassion . . .